Fly Away Home

Fly Away Home

By

Rachel Heffington

Ruby Elixir Press

United States of America

ISBN-13: 978-0615948010

Cover by Rossano Designs

First Printing

Ladybird, Ladybird fly away home:
Your house is on fire, your children all gone.
All but one and her name is Anne
And she crept under the puddin' pan.

-Mother Goose

To all girls like Callie who crave glamor and glitz; may you learn to love Truth best. And to my family, without whose wisdom and patience I should be horribly adrift.

Chapter 1

Callie:

"Blast you, Bronkowski."

That was the best I could do at swearing today in this kind of heat. I leaned back in my chair, forgetting for a moment how much I hated it when my cotton blouse stuck to my skin. Elegance would have to go out the window if I was to find a rhyme for 'Bronkowski' and finish this stupid obituary in time for it to go to press.

I sprawled in the chair and wiped lipstick off the tip of my pencil from where I'd pinched it between my lips a moment before.

Bronkowski...cow-ski...mouse-ski? Clever, Cal. Real clever.

I groaned. Why did Mr. Shores always give me these half-penny jobs—especially the ones that rhymed? Why couldn't he give me a real break for once? He could have sent me to Helsinki to cover the '52 summer Olympics.

I'd have gone willingly.

I'd have frozen my tail-bone off.

I'd have lost all my fingers to frost-bite. Was Finland cold in the summer? Much I cared. I was stuck in this office writing obituaries while the rest of the world did pleasant things with pleasant people. One thing I could guarantee: whatever they were doing, the other kids weren't pasted to the backs of their chairs like soggy advertisements on a corporate telephone pole.

The whole death-dirge business kinda put a damper on the spiel I had long waited to give a celebrity:

"Callie Harper—St. Evan's Post, New York; journalism, short-hand...and the occasional obituary."

Yep—pretty grim way to earn your bread. But then, someone had to do it so why not me?

Why *not* me?

Certainly this rather decrepit form of journalism was necessary to the success of a girl who had determined on fame and fortune as her career of choice?

It was a day of fry-an-egg-on-the-sidewalk temperatures and I cranked the windows of the tiny ninth-floor office open as far as they'd go despite Jules' complaint that the flies would come in. Flies. He was always worried about flies as if they were Luftwaffe-bombers rather than mere insects. 1952 and *The St. Evan's Post* hadn't bought a single window air-conditioning unit. If Mr. Shores would just listen to me and install one then I wouldn't have to open the windows and sweat like a racehorse and Jules wouldn't have to dodge flies as if he was the lone survivor of an air-raid. I stretched my arms above my head, hardly bothering to feel embarrassment over the dark sweat-damp spots under my arms. No one ever paid me attention anyhow.

I kicked my pumps off and crossed my legs, resting my heels on the baize-covered desktop. My nylons itched like the dickens in this heat. If only I could take them off; a faint breeze ruffled my skirt—I longed to feel that air against me. Good idea. Not that I would have to think about it if Mr. Bad News would just give us an electric fan. Or a paper fan. Or any sort of anything to get the air moving. I peered over the top of my yellow legal-pad to see if Jules was watching me—No, of course not. He was hard at work in the opposite corner, hammering away on his battered type-writer, a pencil behind one ear. A corner of my mouth slid upward. Looked like the air-raid was over.

A drop of sweat trickled between my shoulder blades and slid down into the small of my back, congregating with the rest of the puddle. *Bet Lana and Frank and the other kids in Helsinki aren't sweating.*

That was it. I wriggled off my chair and huddled under the desk-top. It was hotter down here, if possible. I peeled my nylons off, stashed the damp wad in the mesh wastebasket, and hopped back into my chair. It squealed in protest like a professional gossip.

Jules whipped about in that insinuating way he had and cast an eyeball at me. "What the devil are you doing, Cal?"

My face burned. "Nothing."

"Listen, if you aren't finished with that obit by three, I'll have to tell Shores, and you know he hates it when you're late with your pieces."

I cracked my pencil in half and glared back at him. "You're not burning much rubber yourself, hub-cap."

"Just get to work so I don't catch the flak." Jules popped his knuckles, gave me one of his patronizing smiles, and returned to his typing.

I sulked in my chair then threw the halves of my pencil across the room. One hit the corner of Jules' desk, but he was used to my tantrums. He didn't even flinch. I wished for the Egyptian plague of flies to descend on the office and terrify Jules. I was working as hard as I could! It wasn't my fault the blasted fellow had been named Bronkowski.

"Complain to his parents," I mumbled.

"What's that?" Jules' eyebrows cranked upward at sharp angles. I'd miffed him for sure this time.

"Nothing." A fitful breeze came through the window and this time brushed my bare calves with blissful softness. Faintly consoled, I turned to my scribbled-over legal-pad. Blast it. Where was that pencil? Oh yes. I'd broken it and pitched it at Mr. Charmer's head. I pulled another from the drawer and frowned at its blunt tip. I hated dull pencils, but I'd have to stand behind Jules to sharpen it and he was the last person on earth I felt like talking to. Jules the motivated, Jules the dedicated, Jules the amazing. Frankly, I was tired of hearing his praises sung to the heavens. Just because you look like Cary Grant does not guarantee you're automatically the best guy in the universe, despite what Doris and Bette and some of the other gals in the office seemed to think. Weaklings. I wasn't moved by handsome men—not often, at least.

I grabbed a handful of my hair and squeezed it. How was my perm holding up? Drat. Split-ends. Time for a trim again. It cost far too much to go to the beauty parlor twice a week for a hair-styling session. I just couldn't afford it—people died often enough, but obituaries don't pay that well. I looked like Elizabeth Taylor sopping wet and run through a wringer—dark, wavy hair and all. Oh well. I never saw anyone of importance—Shores never let me leave the office. It'd been three weeks to the day since I'd even been sent on a show-review job—I was keeping tally on a sheet of paper taped to the underside of my desk.

I fluffed my curls off my neck and my fingernail snagged on my hair. Wretched home-manicures—they never worked either. I opened the drawer of the desk and fished around among the paper-clips and pencil nubs for a nail-file—all perfectly normal procedure. Nothing could have been more ordinary than this office, I swore daily.

"Aren't you s'posed to be writing, Miss Harper?" The cold, bluff New York accent startled me so I dropped the nail-file and legal-pad both.

"Mr. Shores!" My voice sounded queer—trembly as my fingers. I hated being surprised, especially in my rare moments of vanity. "I was…I was just finishing the obit you assigned me." I put on my sweetest smile—the one with the evasive little dimple that seemed to work wonders to get me out of scrapes.

Mr. Shores, however, did not appear to be effected by dimples, evasive or otherwise. "Miss Harper, when you came to work here, you told me you were dedicated to your craft."

I straightened, noticing the tall man standing behind Mr. Shores. I couldn't see his face, as he was looking the opposite direction; only the top of a brown fedora, a strong profile and the elbows of his coat. They were shiny, as if rubbed and worn to death. What sort of man was this, and why had Mr. Shores brought him in? No one made it past Doris and Bette, up to the ninth-floor office. A faint, fluttering panic shot through my heart —maybe he was related to that Bronkowski-stiff and he'd come to see that his brother or cousin or such had a proper obituary. And me, not even three words into the job.

I wished I'd not taken off my nylons—I felt exposed and embarrassed, caught like this. I picked up my pencil and retraced some of that dreadful name—Bronkowski—over again. The scratching of the lead against the paper instilled a measure of courage in me. Nevertheless, I kept my eyes on my handwriting. "I am dedicated to my craft," I said. It needled me to hear the petulance in my tone but all the same, I pushed my lips forward into a glamorous pout.

"So I see," Shores replied in an oyster-cracker tone.

I cast my eyes toward the far side of the room. Jules was enjoying this, shoulders hitched up as if to suppress laughter. The rake.

Well, the waters of my situation with Mr. Shores were already simmering—perhaps another degree or two wouldn't matter. I cleared my throat for good measure. "Mr. Shores, I am a dedicated journalist—truly. But I never get a chance to show it because you give every good assignment to Jules." I was whining. I heard my pathetic tone and despised myself. Whining. Rubbish. But at least I'd said it.

The grim lines around Mr. Shores' mouth deepened. He motioned for that man behind him to take the only empty chair in the office then perched himself on the edge of my desk like a foreboding crow. I couldn't help thinking of Poe's raven and its ominous "Nevermore." Nevermore—it was perfect for me. I was sacked and I knew it.

"Miss Harper, I have noticed you aren't happy here," Mr. Shores said. His words took me aback... Of course I wasn't happy, but those words didn't sound like my thoughts and my sentiments when he said them in that pompous way.

If course I wasn't happy but who made it his beef to tell the whole office so?

"You look....stifled." His cool blue eyes scanned the room and I knew he saw everything—from the dusty, open windows to the bitter coffee sediments at the bottom of my paper cup.

He saw the barely-started obituary and—I had no doubt of this man's cynacism—he saw that I had violated all the rules of professional society and was bare-legged. I scooted my chair closer to the desk and hid my lap and legs under it. There. That was a scrap better.

Mr. Shores' gaze came back and settled on the half of me tucked under the desk as if he could see through the wood. "Yes. Y'seem a little stifled. I have a plan, Miss Harper, and I need you t'agree with it." He slid off the edge of the desk and motioned to the man in the chair—the man I'd tried to ignore since noticing his presence. "This is Mr. Wade Barnett."

At the words, my eyes flew open—stomach trading places with heart—and I struggled to keep my mouth from dropping open. Mr. Wade Barnett. *The* Mr. Wade Barnett. America's most famous journalist. The idol of every kid coming out of school. Equal, in my opinion, to the successful bombshell Maralie Barrymore. And here I was sitting in his presence with a limp dress and a half-drowned perm, not even wearing stockings. Somebody must have a sense of humor. I snapped to attention and thrashed around this fog of thoughts for a proper reply.

Mr. Shores threw me a temporary life-line by way of a short laugh and slapped his hand against Mr. Barnett's shoulder. "See? Miss Harper is overcome with admiration for your talents—she's always toutin' you as her idol, you know."

It enraged me to hear my own thoughts thrown back in this way. If I wasn't counting on Shores for my weekly paycheck, I'd have scratched his smirking face then and there—the more chipped my fingernails the better. I studied my white knuckles and wished I was anywhere but in this room with these people. I couldn't bear to look at the famous man sitting opposite me, but he loomed in my thoughts all the same. Of course I knew what he looked like—didn't every young journalist? Dark hair, brown eyes, thin. Not wildly handsome but more than respectable. Lots more.

"Oh, I wouldn't put that much stock in me, Miss Harper." The kind, reassuring voice startled me. I was expecting something throaty and soft—perhaps even silken—like a gentleman's smoking-jacket. But there was nothing more prosaic than the voice I heard.

It gave me enough pluck to lift my chin. "I don't make an idol of you, Mr. Barnett. I don't put that much stock in your talents." Then, seeing a flick of amusement in his eyes, I hastened to correct my white lie: "What I mean to say is, gee, you're a fabulous writer and I love to read your work but I don't idolize you."

He lifted his hand and smiled. His eyes were lighter than in the pictures—almost a chestnut color. "Don't worry about it. I'd rather you didn't—makes it so inconvenient, having a conversation with a star-struck woman."

"Mmm." I gave a small smile, and felt like a cricket on a hotplate, leaping away from the awkward moment toward questions about Wade Barnett coming here in this manner. What did it all mean? I was thoroughly puzzled, and through the haze I saw that Jules shared my confusion. He had wandered to the window and stood there now, frowning. I crossed my arms, compelled to look at this paper-culture idol, yet unwilling to recognize the friendly inquiry on his face. So now I'd officially been embarrassed in a celebrity's presence by the father of all fatheads. Temper raised to the scaling point, I pulled my gaze from its idiotic clasp on Mr. Barnett and glared at Shores.

"Well I know we reporters are supposed to be able to make up what we aren't told, but I'm stumped. What's the game?" I bit my lip then released it with a hasty caveat: "And don't answer me with a question. You know I hate that kind of jazz."

Mr. Shores made a show of benevolence—I knew it was a show because his natural smile was more of a propped up frown. He gave me his Interview Smile—the one he tried to dope all the actresses with to get them to tell him all he wanted to hear. "Miss Harper—you are one lucky dame."

"Oh?" Cold. Mature. Stately. That was the Calida Harper I'd show to Wade Barnett. He needn't know I hadn't fortitude enough to keep my nylons on. I blushed like a loony and dug the claws of my glare into Shores' eyes. "I'm a lucky dame?"

He hopped onto the edge of my desk again and put his palms on his knees. The top button of his collar was undone against the heat, ringed with sweat-stains. "Yeah, hon. You see, we've been thinking for some time about expandin'. Starting up a magazine."

I am a clever woman, but my wits deserted me now. "What are you talking about Shores?"

"You're getting a job, dope!" Jules' voice startled us all.

Mr. Shores glared at him. "Leave the explaining for me to do, Mr. Cameron. Miss Harper, *The Post* has been thinking of starting a magazine for the families of America—incidentals. Stories. Heart-warming news and kitsch for the mommies and daddies and kiddos of the States. It'll be a huge hit—mark my words. Mr. Barnett has agreed to start it up. With his name at the top of each issue it'll shoot the moon in no time flat. But listen, Toots: he needs an assistant."

My mind was a blank, happy void. A new project—Mr. Wade Barnett—American families—Assistant—it was everything I could have wished for and more. But then a brilliant, red strike-though shot across the blank and ruined it.

"What's the snag?" I asked.

Mr. Shores drew back. "The snag, Miss Harper?"

"The snag, Mr. Shores. The hook—the catch. Why me?"

Mr. Barnett looked at me with interest and a little surprise. Oh well. Let him be surprised. I flicked a few pencil-shavings from my skirt and raised an eyebrow, challenging Mr. Shores.

He smiled again. "Why not you? You told me yourself you're dedicated. I know you can type like a woodpecker. Besides—Bette and Doris didn't want to leave Romeo there." He rolled his eyes and waved at Jules who turned red and stalked back to his desk. "The others are too valuable where they are. It's a win-win situation, baby-doll. I can get another girl to write the show-pieces and obits and things and you'll get a chance to make it big as the assistant of Mr. Wade Barnett. So?"

He grinned now—a real grin that brushed away the last of my reserve. I still didn't know how I'd got so lucky. I still hardly believed it was happening to me. I still didn't know if I could think, let alone *breathe* while working in the same office as *the* Mr. Wade Barnett. But I knew this. A diamond-deal comes once in a girl's life and this was my day.

I stood and shrugged, trying to act careless. "So?" I said. "Why not give it a whirl?"

The collected letters of Wade Barnett:

July 20th, 1952

My dear Maralie and Tobias,

Today, I met her.

I have performed the duty laid in my path, and found it not quite as unpleasant as I'd anticipated. The uprooting of old prejudices pinches and pulls, but I sense it is a good discomfort, like pulling weeds. But "details!"—thus clamors the world ever and anon, and I suppose you join them. Chief among the trials of being a man of repute: one has so much on one's proverbial plate, it pays to keep a journal and write letters as memory-joggers on the occasion the press conveniently remembers something you have "forgotten". We shan't give them a chance, shall we? Well then, the report:

In seeking out the Harpers, I have done right. Of that I am sure.

The first thing to be done, of course, was to speak to those who might have known the family in more recent days. I started in the War Office, remembering that poor fellow, Tristan, would likely have been called upon to serve his country in the last decade. The War Office was very helpful—if not cheering—in informing me that Tristan Harper had died in France not three months after enlisting. *C'est la vie.* I was sorry to hear that for the girl's sake, but I had already done more in searching out Tristan Harper than other men in my position would have done. I thought, perhaps, I could lay the matter aside as finished. Ah, but the Lord seemed to consider my job only begun. I extracted from the War Office—never mind how; Maralie knows my methods—the name and address of the girl I remembered. How did I remember the girl? I am not certain how—or why, rather—but I did, and found her to be one Calida Harper, age twenty-seven, living at Tarleton Apartments, New York City.

Last week—Friday, I believe—I sought her out after having settled my nerves with a good lunch at Annamaria's. I had been hard at work in that new office, putting up wallpaper, and wasn't in the best form. Annamaria hadn't cared, but I wasn't certain Calida Harper would feel the same way—something about that name inspires respect, doesn't it? Perhaps I had better not request an interview looking, as I did, like a dustman.

These premonitions coming strong upon me by the time I reached Tarleton Apartments, I thought it behooved me to stick to the basics and only ascertain that a Miss Harper did, indeed, live here. I walked into the lobby and was pleased to find that—though certainly nothing compared to my current "digs"—it was blessed with cleanliness and a friendly desk clerk. This man—an apparent Brit by the name of Jerry Atwood—was more than pleased to speak of our mutual "friend".

'She is a perfect lady,' he informed me, devotion beaming from his eye. 'Never a day goes by but I think to myself, 'Ah. There's a one what would never have escaped the guillotine in the French Revolution.'" A curious method of comfort, but it satisfied me on two points: one, Mr. Atwood is a well-informed man in matters of history; two, Miss Harper is not a gutter-snipe.

With these assurances in my back pocket, I asked about Miss Harper's health, her happiness, and what she did for a living. I wondered, too, if she had any family—husband, children? But to that, Mr. Atwood only polished his bell—a large, bright thing of brass—and turned red. I take it Mr. Atwood is pleased she doesn't have a husband and is rather in hopes of filling that vacancy at the soonest opportunity. After meeting Calida today, I wonder what she would think of that proposition. Something tells me she would take about as kindly to that as she would to being told who I really am. Jerry Atwood is the direct descendent of an obscure member of Bloody Mary's household—a gardener or such—but despite these charms, I doubt Miss Harper would see the merit in the alliance. She seems very pleased with herself.

Poor fellow.

I gathered from Jerry that Miss Harper is working as a journalist for *The St. Evan's Post.* I know the establishment well—Mr. Shores and his lackeys belong to the sort that I deny any association with. Yes, call me posh and stuck-up—call me archaic, even, for a man in this marvelous age of the 1950's—but please don't try to side-line all journalists as members of that breed. Tobias, I am surprised you stayed with our set long enough to fall in love with Maralie.

I confess to feeling helpless. How on earth could I, Wade Barnett, give Miss Harper a lift without getting the world on my case? Our association—or rather lack of—is a thing that must be handled carefully. How to burst into the ranks of petty journalism without betraying myself or Miss Harper? A complexity indeed. I gave you a call and when Maralie answered, told her what I could. Namely, that it was imperative I take an active interest in this Calida Harper, but circumstances beyond my control demand secrecy. Maralie is accustomed to my quirks, of course, from years on the job—she only laughed and told me that you two would be praying for me. A comfort, yes, but practicality requested something stronger to stomach.

"Maralie," I said, "How I can I avoid betrayal without looking like a criminal? If I can't think of something I'll have to resort to creeping around the city, dogging her footsteps."

"For heaven's sake, Wade, you sound as if it involved capes and daggers and poisons. Take out one of your dreams and dust it off and send to Miss Harper to work on. Goodness knows you have enough of them lurking in that awful brain of yours." With that, Maralie hung up and I was left with the sprout of a plan sunning in my mind.

That was yesterday, as you know. I mused on your words all afternoon then rang Mr. Shores of *The St. Evan's Post* in the evening. If the poor fellow smokes—and I believe all of them do—I'm afraid he swallowed his cigar whole when I announced who I was, and my purpose for calling. It was a one-sided conversation due—I fear—to the swallowed cigar. I politely informed him that I had an interest in beginning a small magazine for the families of America, and wondered if his firm would consider supplying an assistant for me. I had every intention of suggesting Miss Harper for the job, but when it came down to it, I couldn't think of a plausible reason for knowing the girl. It seems she's an obscurity I ought to know nothing about. Reminds me of a kitchen drudge in the bowels of those great English houses.

By some blessed event, Mr. Shores agreed to my plan. He shares the desire of all his type to 'not be taken in', by which I understand them to mean they won't allow themselves to believe in anything, lest it prove untrue. This trait added the complications of him doubting my seriousness, doubting I could get the thing together and doubting—above all—that he could spare anyone to help me.

"Haven't you any…dispensables?" I asked. "Anyone just taking up space in the office?"

"Why are you so hot to get someone from this office, Mr. Barnett?"

I felt exactly like a man clinging by his fingernails to the edge of a cliff and wishing the rope would come just a bit closer so he could grab hold of it. I reminded myself I would behave in a like fashion if put in Mr. Shores' position.

"I take an interest in underdogs, Mr. Shores," I said. "Furthermore, I thought it an attractive position for your business. Think of the possibilities, sir. If my magazine succeeds —and forgive me the vanity, but I am certain it *will*—*The St. Evans Post* will have the dignity of being co-founder."

He was silent for some moments before at last agreeing to my scheme. We set a meeting for three o'clock today, and that is why —an hour or two ago—I was in a wretched, ninth-floor office meeting Calida Harper.

The girl reminds me of a yearling filly—headstrong, calculating, and ready to kick a fellow at the least provocation. You would love her, Maralie. She stared at me as if I was a ghost first, then Winston Churchill, then a free ticket to Easy Street, then a banana peel in a trash-barrel at the West End. I am not sure on what footing this puts us. I'm not certain she's sure. I suppose tomorrow will tell.

I ask myself what I think of her.

She is beautiful.

"Calida"…"Beautiful warmth". Which I must admit is horribly ironic. Miss Harper seems to prefer the cold-shoulder method of communication. She is a perfect cruet, to pardon an odd expression; tall, stately, and full of vinegar.

I have so much to do in the next few days. My yacht will be out of the dry-dock with all repairs finished. I'm thinking of rechristening her. I shall search around for a good name, and ask Dirigible to paint over the old one. Sailors say it is bad luck to change a ship's name, or to paint her a different color. What a mercy Man has more than one chance to change his stripes. 'Give thanks to the Lord for He is good. His mercy endureth forever.'

Give the little ones some candy in my name and assure them their "Uncle B" will come to visit soon.

Ever yours,

   Wade Barnett

Chapter 2

Callie:

I paid the cab-fee and shoved open the little glass door that separated the building I called home from the rest of New York City. It wasn't the Ritz, but it was better than the digs where I'd heard some young journalists camped out. I slipped past the reception desk, hoping Jerry would not be on duty—he always managed to address me in a way I could not ignore. If I did ignore it—and believe me, I'd tried—his forgiving smile berated me for my cruelty. Not to mention he was a Brit, and anything with the flavor of London got gold colors in my book. Still, I wished I had the strength to be impolite now and then.

Blast manners. I wondered what Emily Post would think of me if I told her I plotted my schedule—all my comings and goings—around who was on duty.

My clandestine entry failed. I saw the familiar dusty-blue of Jerry's coat and he whirled about as the faint report of my heels gave my presence away. I wished to goodness I had worn flats.

"Hey, Jerry." I plastered a smile on my lips and tried to look preoccupied.

"Miss Harper! How was work?" His round, jovial face beamed at me. Dear Jerry. I had to share my good news with someone and because Nickleby—even if he was a darling cat—did not exactly count as someone, my manner toward Jerry softened an increment.

I leaned against the desk, limp with all that had happened that afternoon, overwrought with the suddenness and fascination. "Oh, Jerry, it was smashing!"

I sighed, and felt that the world was bright and beautiful. Even the homely interior of the apartment building seemed gentled by my lucky break. The potted palms looked almost vibrant and tropical which they certainly never had before, being uncommonly forthright about their plastic heritage. The scarred, pocked linoleum appeared gold and white—how had I ever thought it a dull pattern of cream and tan?

Jerry leaned an elbow against the desk and sighed. "Really, Miss Harper? A smashing day? I'm glad. You know that, don't you?" I smiled too and our eyes met—the both of us too content for words in our different ways.

Suddenly I realized I'd been smiling *with* Jerry. Poor chap. He little thought that my mind was anywhere other than caring that he cared for me. I removed my smile with deliberation and fished through my pocketbook as if I'd lost something.

"If you don't mind my asking, Miss Harper, what was it that made today so smashing?"

I stopped rifling through my pocketbook, bubble-spirited once more, and clapped my hands together—it wasn't dignified, but I could think about dignity tomorrow. "I got a new job. It's loads better than the other one. I'm starting up a glossy with one of the most famous reporters in America—fancy that, Jerry! Miss Callie Harper: World-famous journalist—oh, it's going to be the making of me!"

"I can fancy anything, Miss Harper. You were born to be a success." His tone had grown humble, softer. I knew I ought to curb his sentiments but I was too happy to care—my good fortune had intoxicated me; besides, I needed human companionship—another person with whom to share this glorious day. But I couldn't let Jerry ramble on in this way, weaving webs of compliments from which he'd need to extricate himself after I left.

"Everyone's born to be a success in some way, Jerry." I smiled and snapped my pocket-book closed, then lifted a hand to fix my hair, keeping an eye on my reflection in the speckled mirror behind him. "Even you, Jerry, are successful as a lobby-man."

"That's right, Miss Harper! That's the spirit." He nodded and started rubbing his brass desk-bell—his pride and joy—with a chamois-leather. The brass shone in the soft light of the lobby. "But...Miss Harper. You won't be...you won't be leaving the building, will you?"

I yawned and sent a dazzling smile past him toward my reflection. "Oh Jerry—of course not. Not now anyway—my lease isn't up." I never was one to mince words and I would not delude him into thinking I planned on staying in this shabby little place once I was famous. Still, it wasn't awful and I had a certain fondness for it. I smiled at Jerry. "G'night. I'm dead-tired. I'll be going up now."

"Goodnight Miss Harper—and may you be a success!"

What a goose. But a dear goose. I waved goodbye as I stepped into the elevator and began the ascent to my twelfth-floor apartment. Gee—Miss Calida Harper and Mr. Wade Barnett. I pictured our names together in seventy-two point type at the top of a newspaper. What a break.

The elevator door eased open at such a tortoise-job that I grew antsy and squeezed through soon as the crack was wide enough. My room was just there, on the left, and I sang a few lines of a jaunty show-tune under my breath as I wiggled the key in the lock. "You're the top. You're the Coliseum. You're the top….you're the Louvre Museum…" It was the world's stiffest lock and I lived ever in a state of consternation lest my key break and I need summon Jerry from the desk. I didn't want him to get any ideas about being my hero.

At last the lock yielded to my joggling and I slipped into my room and slammed the door behind me. Nickleby wound himself in and out and around my feet. I waded through him feeling that he must be at least six creatures instead of a single fat one, and slung my purse, hat, and shoes onto the worn sofa. "It's happened Nickleby—I've got a chance to make it big in the glossies." I picked my cat up and buried my nose in his soft black fur. "And who do you think I get to work with? Mr. Wade Barnett. Gee. Isn't it fabulous?" Without further ceremony I dumped Nickleby onto the pillows and two-stepped into the bedroom to change into my dressing gown.

I was back in the living room a moment later, wearing my beloved, horrid, crushed-velvet robe. Horrid because it resembled a scarecrow's garments, beloved because it was the most comfortable thing I'd ever worn. I filled the coffee pot and flicked the hotplate on, then held Nickleby to my chest. The day's events required further discussion.

"Do you think he'll like me, Nicks?"

Nickleby batted my nose with one paw as if to convince me of the utter ridiculousness of the question.

"You're right, of course, Nickleby," I said. "What isn't there to love about me? Oh look: mail."

I tossed my much-buffeted cat to the side again and stood to pick up a telegram from the floor that I had failed to observe as I came in. I slit the envelope with my fingernail—chipped nails were the best for this job—and unfolded the small piece of paper:

THIS IS YOUR CHANCE –(STOP)- IF GOES WELL YOU MAKE IT BIG –(STOP)- IF NOT YOU ARE THROUGH – (STOP)-

Golly. Shores sure was spending a lot of money on me. Sixteen whole words in a telegram. I felt special and angry. I saw it all now. Shores set me up with Wade Barnett to see if I had what it took to be a true journalist—which he seriously doubted. And it was quite clear this would be it. If I failed Mr. Barnett, there would be no returning to *The St. Evans' Post*.

My jaw clenched. "So be it." Nickleby mewed and blinked his green eyes at me. I tapped the end of his nose and shook my head. "Shores is dead-meat. He thinks I won't last in that office with Mr. Barnett. I'll show him. I'll be famous and glamorous and everyone will love me and then we'll see what tune the *elegant* Mr. Shores sings." My heart pounded in my chest and I pushed the lid of my glass bon-bon bowl onto the coffee table and tried to decide if the moment required raspberry cream or caramel.

I exchanged glances with Nickleby and sank languidly onto the sofa. "This calls for chocolate, Nicks. Chocolate and an appointment with Mr. Dickens. You suggest the caramel? I thought as much." I popped a chocolate caramel into my mouth and grabbed Pickwick off the table, opening to the silk ribbon that marked my place. "Observe, Nicks," I said. And even around the lump of chocolate my voice had a determined edge to it. "I take notes from the best masters." I nodded out the dim window in the directions of Shores' office and sucked my chocolate. "Let that be a lesson to you, Mr. High-and-Mighty. I won't be easily squashed."

I awoke next morning to a street-chorus of blubbering pigeons outside my apartment window. Rolling onto my stomach, I grabbed the dingy alarm-clock in terror, feeling in my soul that I had overslept. The clock chucked and wheezed but showed the time—to my vast relief—as only half-past six. I passed a hand over my eyes—my lashes bristled against my fingers. Drat—I'd been so engrossed with Pickwick I'd forgot to take off my makeup. And I had so wanted to look especially nice for my first day as personal assistant to Wade Barnett. I slung my legs out of bed and unbuttoned my gown, grabbing at my underthings and a blouse and skirt. It didn't matter much what I wore now—if my eyes were puffy and discolored from the effects of left-over makeup, would anyone care about the clothes?

I stumbled into the bathroom, not missing the chance to bang my shins against the stool. Whose stool it was or why I'd not removed it from the premises, I couldn't say. But the truth is, I bumped against it every morning of my existence, and knew I'd rather miss the excitement if I tossed the stool in the nearest dumpster as I'd so often threatened to do.

Nickleby surveyed me as I washed my face and dabbed off the rest of my makeup. I yanked the brush through my hair, put on some more mascara, powdered my nose, and looked at the result the mirror. I tried my dimple on for size, but somehow it didn't twinkle like it usually did. If I was so grown up and self-confident, why did my heart thunder at the bald idea of working for Wade Barnett? Mr. Shore's telegram remained in the wastebasket, mocking me with its yellow face. If it had an opinion—which I doubted not—it would certainly side with Mr. Shores in calling me a failure.

I plucked the telegram from the wastebasket and glared at it. "I intend to eclipse you, Mr. Shores. So just warm your buns on *that* burner." I adjusted the starched collar of my crisp white blouse and slipped into a pair of high heels. Then, blowing a kiss to Nickleby and stuffing Shores' telegram in my handbag, I swaggered downstairs. I couldn't give up the game before it had properly begun.

The minute I stepped onto the lobby-tile I knew I ought to have worn flats. Jerry looked up with that Labrador-smile of his and waved.

"Good morning, Miss Harper!"

I wiggled my fingers in an obscure reply to Jerry's white-gloved salute.

"Going forth to charm the world, are we?" he asked. "Be yourself, Miss Harper. They'll love you for it."

Something in his words stopped me in my retreat through the lobby. Jerry's round, boyish face lit up as I came over to the desk.

"I don't know, Jer." I drummed my fingers on the desktop and bit my lip. "The world wants glamour and glitz. *I* want glamour and glitz. "

"Glamour and glitz?"

"Yes, yes. You know…dinner parties and glittering gowns, and awards and the opera. Gold cigarette cases and mink stoles, dozens of men sending flowers—all that. New York City will know Callie Harper as a dangerous, elegant woman." My heart beat faster at this verbalizing of all my hopes and dreams. Some

23

girls might not state their case quite so frankly, but what did I care? It was only Jerry. Not like I was planning to dupe him anytime soon. "I'll charm my way to the top. That's the way to do things, isn't it?"

Jerry looked doubtful, but I supposed it was his native gentility that prevented him from saying anything contradictory. Instead he smiled again and put his gloved hand on top of mine, squeezing my fingers. "You now, Miss Harper; you'll be whatever it is you make yourself into. Just take care you make yourself into something you'll want to live with the rest of your life. And don't forget me—us. The apartment and me…and the pigeons." His face turned three shades of red and he began polishing his bell with embarrassed vigor.

Pigeons. Honestly? I was angry with Jerry for making me question the merit of my ideas, but something stopped the retort on the tip of my tongue. Even if he was wrong, I supposed he had his right to an opinion. I smiled instead. "Well, I suppose we'll see, won't we?"

I exited the building with chin held high and a war in my breast. Did Jerry Atwood have a right to tell me who I ought to be? It plain as the dimple in his chin he didn't approve of my schemes. And unhappy woman that I was, I *minded* that he minded. Shores had never approved of me, Jules cared for no one but himself, and Bette and Doris followed suit. So there I stood: indebted to Jerry for the only friendship in my life apart from Nickleby. He did have a right to a gentle suggestion now and then. Brilliant. As much as I hated to admit it, I needed Jerry's good opinion. There was a homely comfort in knowing he was my slave. Woe upon woe.

"Goin' where?" The cab-driver's harsh accent struck me full force in the face, accompanied by a black belch of foul-smelling exhaust from the taxi. I stared with some misgiving at the beat-up yellow cab kissing the curb. I still hadn't got over my vague fear of taxi-cabs and their motley array of drivers.

"*St. Evan's Post*, please. Park Row." My voice wavered on the last word like I meant the address as a question.

"*St. Evan's Post*? What are you—a reporter or sumpin'?"

Oh joy. A chatter-box. "Yeah. Or something," I slid into the cab and turned my head so he would get the message I didn't want to chat. I felt tense, and my head ached.

He wasn't the type to take broad hints. "Why don't you write an article 'bout how higher fees for taxis would break up traffic?"

"Frankly, because I don't care."

"Don't you want less traffic?"

I pressed two fingers to my eyelids and choked off a sigh. "How would higher rates fix that problem? This is NYC, buddy."

He blew his nose, chuckling. "We get paid more, we move quicker. Cover more territory, serve more customers, make more dough. Right now it don't pay to hustle so we take the interesting routes." He winked at me through the rear-view mirror. "Miles rack up, hot-stuff."

Startled, I looked down at my gloves. "So you conspire to throw off the schedule of one of America's largest cities just to make more profit?"

"Hey, baby. If it works, it works."

That was why I hated taxis. A sense of profound relief swept over me as we pulled up to the familiar, dull Post building a short while later. I tossed a few dollar bills into the passenger's seat and ducked out of the cab.

In the ladies' room of the office I powdered my nose again, fluffed the hair and set the pillbox hat at a more rakish angle on my head. There. On second thought, I took out my Hazel Bishop "Real Real Red" lipstick and swiped it on. 'Won't eat off, bite off, or kiss off,' they said. I was crazy nervous and my lips were dry as the Mojave Desert.

Cal, you're an imbecile.

With that sizzling remark to boost the old spirit, I sauntered upstairs and entered my office, hopeful—if not confident—that I'd make a good impression on Wade Barnett this time.

Throwing open the door only revealed something new to distress me. Jules sat at a desk—my desk—with Bette and Doris winging him. All three avoided my gaze and kept their eyes on their type-writers.

I swung my arms and swaggered in, hoping to affect nonchalance. "What's up?"

Jules raised his head and frowned. "What's up yourself? Why'd you come around here to bother me?" He never dealt in tact and I quailed under the intense hatred in his dirty look.

"Where's Shores?" I asked. Bette and Doris bent their heads further. I could see dark roots in Doris' hair beneath the smooth blonde. A dye-job. So that was her secret. She'd been hitting the bottle. And I had always admired her golden tresses.

The thought gave me the pluck I was missing. "So what—did he kick me out?"

Jules met my gaze, and I saw a flicker of something—jealousy?—glimmering in his eyes. "Kick you out?" His tone was incredulous, confusing me. "Kick you out? You doofus! You're a hot-shot now—you're working with Mr. Big Bucks himself. He set up new digs for you two on the golden side of the street."

The golden side? That was office-slang for the ritzy left side of The City's old "Newspaper Row." My head swirled and I steadied myself against the dark, cheap paneling of the office. I couldn't believe my luck—first a job with Wade Barnett, then a snazzy new office? I was brought round eventually to the knowledge that Bette, Doris, and Jules were all three boring holes into my body with their steely gazes.

Triumph surged through my veins and I lifted my head, dropping a gracious smile on them. "Catch you kids later."

Once in the relative safety of the hallway I did a Ginger Rogers tap sequence and danced down to the elevator. I collided Mr. Shores who, apparently, was on his way up to see me. His presence had the effect of a Tums on heartburn. I stopped mid-dance and curtsied.

"Miss Harper."

"Mr. Shores."

"I see Mr. Cameron gave you the scoop."

"Yessir." I searched Shores' face, trying to a find a hint of smile, but his expression was in keeping with last night's telegram—irascible and doubting. Unintelligible to me.

"I have given complete authority over you to Mr. Barnett. You take your cues from him now, and if he don't find you satisfying, you're out. Understand?" Shores' balding head shone with perspiration, and a hot breeze wafted over us from the open window down the hall.

"Perfectly." I smiled and fluttered my lashes like Ava Gardner. "Gee Mr. Shores, you're such a great boss—giving me this break and all. I just wanted to let you know how much I appreciate it."

27

"I'm sending you on this job because you're dispensable. Jules can't be spared. I already told you that. Now, if you'd stop blinking like a cat caught in a sunbeam, *I'd* appreciate it."

Shores pushed past me and stalked into the old office. Of all the nerve! Why was he grumped with me for being 'dispensable'? Growling to myself over the unfairness of it all, I fled the office and stopped at the edge of the street. There—just across the constant stream of yellow traffic—was my destiny.

"Wish me luck, Nickleby," I muttered. I took a large breath, drew myself to my stylish height of five-foot-eight (in heels), and dashed across the street in a brief lull between cars. Shores never told me which building I belonged in, but I didn't sweat it. I had confidence in my intuition; my first impressions were usually right and always interesting. I'd know when I arrived.

My step was firm all the way up the sidewalk. The clandestine sensation of treading on the golden side and belonging there teased a corner of my mouth upward. I felt as if I belonged in the top ranks now, right alongside the legends like Ed Sullivan, Wade Barnett, Walter Cronkite, and Maralie Barrymore. I grinned like a dolt at everyone I passed before realizing that sort of a loose, girlish expression ill-suited the image I'd built of the famous Callie Harper. I pooched my lips, dropped into a lazy saunter, and ambled up the sidewalk. There. The Frenchiest French-woman could not look more blasé than I.

"Miss Harper? Are you well? You look a bit faint." To my extreme horror, Mr. Barnett was at my elbow; brown eyes bent on me with concern. "I was just looking out for you."

Look what I got for elegance. I pulled my arm away from his touch and summoned all the hauteur I could manage. "I am exceptionally well, Mr. Barnett. And you?"

"All the better for seeing you—now we can get started." He rubbed his palms in an eager, anticipating way and smiled. "Come, come now. There's much to talk about!"

He tugged me past a pair of delivery men into an office facing the street. It was quiet and cool inside compared to the bustle of Park Row without. I exhaled and found that I met Mr. Barnett's solicitous gaze without any of the former moment's embarrassment. I smiled—somehow I had to make up for being so rude. It would be no good at all to be acerbic with an American legend.

"I'm looking forward to working with you, Mr. Barnett," I said.

"Likewise." His smile was quiet, content, and somehow reminded me of the country summer days of my girlhood.

The sensation gave me a pain in the base of my stomach. Memories, always trying to convince me I didn't belong in Manhattan. I effectually put a cap on recollections by frowning. Maybe if I frowned, *he'd* frown and I'd not be bothered by viewing his singularly attractive smile.

But it was no good—I couldn't keep from grinning like a crazy. Hands on hips, I surveyed the office. One room but gobs of space. Marble tile covered the floor and a potted fern or two brightened the deep front window. The delivery men had just brought in the two desks.

"Is it to your liking, Miss Harper?" Mr. Barnett asked.

"Gosh. It's fabulous!"

"Really?"

I laughed over his eagerness, and tossed my clutch onto the cherry wood top of the smaller desk. "Seeing as you're the boss in this joint, I'll take the little desk." I sat down, removed my gloves, and folded my hands. "So what's next? I'm afraid you'll have to explain some things to me."

Mr. Barnett drew near and perched on the edge of my desk. He fiddled with the leather tassel on the clasp of my handbag. "Right-o. Shoot away. I'll tell you all I know."

"We're supposed to create a family paper?"

"That's the idea."

"News, nonfiction, short stories, poetry, ads, or what?"

"A bit of it all, I suppose. A cosmopolitan paper for the family fireside, if you will."

"Real cute." *Real sappy.* I twisted on my chair to see the time. Eight-thirty sharp. "So it doesn't sound like Mr. Shores has much of a plan."

Mr. Barnett laughed—it matched the elbows of his coat: shiny, worn, genuine. "Not much. The whole plan is mine, actually."

"Yours?" That threw me for a loop. "But I thought this was one of *The Post's* ventures."

"It is. I signed a contract to head up a new magazine for *The Post.* But strictly speaking, it's a personal venture; I wished to test a private theory."

"A theory." I stared hard at Mr. Barnett, but his countenance was as impenetrable as Mr. Shores' had been. I knew Mr. Barnett was not insane but I couldn't make it out. "Excuse me for speaking so plain, Mr. Barnett, but we are supposed to report the news. Not 'private theories.' That's for our farm-team of writers who concoct all those ridiculous feel-good bits."

Mr. Barnett stopped playing with the purse-tassel and looked at me with his head to one side. I averted my gaze and ran my fingers through my hair. Drat—that nail was still snagging.

After what seemed ages but in reality must have been a minute or two, Mr. Barnett leaned forward. "Is that what they teach you these days? Not to have personal theories? Tell me, Miss Harper, what the world would have come to if one wasn't permitted to have a theory?"

"I suppose we'd be…that is, I think society would…"

"Exactly, Miss Harper." Mr. Barnett grinned. "We would have gotten nowhere. If Edison hadn't had a personal theory—a conviction, if you will—that electricity could be harnessed to light the buildings of the great cities, there would have been no groundbreaking news to print in the papers. The very *soul* of journalism is based on personal theories. We sit here in an office on Park Row—what used to be Newspaper Row in the glory days. Most papers have moved on to other places in the city but I chose this office because it has history. So many personal theories have been printed and distributed and read over the years. So many." His gaze roved out the window toward City Hall.

I drummed my fingertips on the desktop—a habit of mine that annoyed me to no end—and fumed inside. First day, first *hour* of the job and Mr. Barnett and I were already at odds. I struggled to contain my pride and stopped drumming.

Instead, I spread my hands wide and smiled. "So what's the theory? I'm listening."

He shifted and bent to look into my eyes. I tried to hold his gaze but it was too open and honest for me. I saw hopes written there, and dreams; I saw a soul and it troubled me. I preferred the cold Manhattan glaze—it saved one the trouble of being involved. I removed my eyes and picked at the chipped fingernail.

"The theory is that America still loves her families. That the periodical of today can print something for everyone—the grown-ups, the children, the in-betweens—all within the same two covers."

I shrugged and pushed back from the desk, suddenly interested. It was a wild theory, if you took most of America at a glance. Even in my own life—and that image of a dusty, dark-haired, tanned little girl rose before my mind. I shoved her away. Even in my *own* life my interests had varied widely. Putting it all together in one magazine? Golly. It was a challenge.

I stood and extended my hand to Mr. Barnett. "You've got me there. I accept your challenge. We'll do it. Though it'd be a job enough for Maralie Barrymore herself."

Mr. Barnett chuckled and walked to his desk. "She could do it."

"Wait." I followed him across the room and folded my arms. "You know Maralie Barrymore?"

His eyes flickered up. "Know her? I should say so. It isn't such a strange idea, is it? We've worked together quite often over the years."

My breath seized in my throat. Wade Barnett knew Maralie Barrymore. It was amazing to find myself tucked in the back pocket of these giants. I pressed my palms against the desk. "Do you think I could…meet her sometime?"

Mr. Barnett pulled a box of doughnuts from a drawer of his desk and offered one to me. I took one.

"Maralie leads a rather private life these days—she seldom makes social appearances," he said.

I swallowed my bite of doughnut. "But it wouldn't have to be a social appearance. If you're her friend..." I smiled my sweetest, most engaging smile. "Gee, Mr. Barnett. It'd only be a few moments. Just so I could soak in her presence."

"You sound as if she was a mineral spring."

"Ohhh," I groaned and accepted the cup of coffee Mr. Barnett put into my hands. "You're hopeless."

"Miss Harper, I won't make a promise I can't keep, but I will swear to you this one thing: if I hear of a good opportunity for you to meet Maralie Barrymore, I will do everything in my power to make it happen."

"You're a fine man, Mr. Barnett."

"Mmm. Well, if I am a fine man, I can also be a task-master. We need to come up with a name for our project—we aren't signing on as ghost-writers, you and I."

"No indeed."

"I want something that embodies a homey feeling. Something classic. Think." Mr. Barnett gestured with his tin coffee-mug that looked like it had seen one too many grenades in the last World War.

"Uhhh...Mickey Mouse?" I ventured.

He grimaced. "Who would buy a *Mickey Mouse Gazette*? Try again."

"Mother Goose?" I quipped.

"Aha! You've hit upon it, Miss Harper!"

I jumped and sloshed half my coffee onto the desk. An hour in his presence and I was still unaccustomed to Mr. Barnett's sudden way of grabbing hold of an idea. "Oh glory." I scrubbed at the warm brown puddle with my handkerchief. "Well, at least it'll smell nice." I sighed and wrung the handkerchief into the waste-basket. It was my only one edged in lace—served me right for being daffy enough to bring it out the first day of a job.

Mr. Barnett tapped my shoulder and pulled the hankie out of my hands. "Never mind that—the name! Think about Mother Goose."

"Honestly, Mr. Barnett, I'm not certain it's a great idea."

"I am. Now *think*."

We were silent for some time. I ran through my cob-webbed, mental collection of mother-goose rhymes. Georgie-porgie, Little Bo-Peep, Little Miss Muffet…nothing inspirational. I looked at Mr. Barnett. His chin was in his hand and he chewed his lip, obviously quite deep in thought. Something was crawling on my arm. I looked down to see a round, red ladybug.

"Ew! Horrid thing!" I flicked it off and was about to stomp it when Mr. Barnett's hand arrested me.

"Hold off a moment, Miss Harper—you wouldn't want to kill our mascot."

I looked from the diminutive bug on the floor to Mr. Barnett and back again. I was sure he'd cracked his head this time. "What on earth are you talking about?"

Mr. Barnett stooped and let the insect crawl onto his hand, then brought it up to eye-level. "Lady-bird, Lady-bird fly away home. Your house is on fire, your children all gone. All but one and her name is Ann and she crept under the pudding-pan."

I peered at the ladybug on his finger. "Sounds a bit morbid, don't you think?"

Mr. Barnett made a face. "Morbid? Not at all. Didn't you ever say that little rhyme as a child to see if it was time you came in for the evening? If the ladybug flew away, your mother wanted you home. If it stayed awhile, you knew you were safe."

I kept quiet—not because I was defeated, but because I was busy trying not to remember those days. I, too, had played the ladybug game and the suddenness of the unwanted memory made me cross.

Mr. Barnett did not seem to mind. He went on studying the red-glossed insect and talking to me: "Concentrate, Miss Harper! Build something off that rhyme for us."

"Ladybird….snippets?" I offered with a shrug.

A puppy-grin pushed his eyebrows high on his forehead. "*Ladybird Snippets.* Do you know, I like it?"

"Do you?"

"I do. Consider: it shows off the childish spirit in us all—the fact that in every person, in every soul, somewhere there is a faint, long-lost glimmer of childhood; however deep they might wish to bury it, however long it has been hidden. *Ladybird Snippets.*"

I tossed my hands. "Well you can certainly sell it if you keep talking that way."

"What do you think? Truly."

What did I think? I sipped my coffee so I wouldn't have to answer yet. I thought it was a name that perfectly fit my growing picture of Mr. Barnett: old-fashioned, out of touch with reality, and pretty darn cute. But I couldn't say those things. Instead, I took another sip of my cold coffee and managed a smile. "Sounds great. So you and I: editors of *Ladybird Snippets.* Where's our team of writers?"

Mr. Barnett watched his bug fly out the door I'd left ajar and dusted his hands. "You're staring at one half of them."

"You?"

He grinned and imitated me—hands on his hips and all. "You? Yes *me*—and a certain young woman by the name of Miss Callie Harper."

I plopped back onto the Underwood typewriter crate and stared at him. "The two of us? Running an entire magazine?"

Mr. Barnett fumbled with his cuffs a while then ventured a look at me with an expression that showed his small store of faith in me was dwindling. "It was another part of the theory. A magazine meant to be an intimate glimpse of American family life must have only a very small production team. It's the best way."

"The best way for whom?"

"Maralie Barrymore agreed."

I pressed my palms to my forehead. "Well then why didn't you get 'Maralie Barrymore' to help you with your blasted scheme? What'll Shores say when we've both worked ourselves to the bone and we still haven't got the proof-copy finished?"

"I have had extensive experience meeting deadlines." His voice was gentle, reminding me of the fact that I stood there arguing with a world-renowned journalist. "I've arranged it all with Mr. Shores," he said, "and he believes he can spare Bette or Doris now and then if we fall too much behind."

I turned from him with the empty doughnut box, needing to get away from this overly ambitious journalist. I'd been told newspapermen were crazy. I'd even believed it a time or two. But never, never as thoroughly as I believed it now. My brain was numb with the very idea of half the responsibility of a first-rate magazine falling on my own shoulders. Even the knowledge that this was how a girl could get famous hardly put a dent in the exhaustion I already felt.

"Miss Harper, you don't have to work with me."

I turned, and saw the soberness in his face. He was on the verge of sacking me, I knew.

"I'd like to see us succeed," he said. "And if you're half as capable as I hope you are, we'll do a smash-up job. But,"

Ah yes. Always a 'but'.

"..You need to choose now. Follow me in this…and more…or leave. I won't blame you for either choice. I know I'm not an easy man to work for, but I need to know I can rely on my partner. Are you in or out? This isn't a game, Miss Harper. It's real life."

What was my choice? Because pretty much, I wanted to know myself. I thought of Mr. Shores' telegram, and Jules' jealousy. I thought of Jerry back at the apartment and the gentle confidence he had in me. Then I knew.

"A smash-up job?" I tossed the doughnut box onto the crate and crossed my arms. "I'd go for that."

"Then it's settled?" Relief spread over Mr. Barnett's face, followed by a grin of satisfaction.

I stuck my hand across the desk and shook his, squeezing plenty hard. "I suppose it is. Mr. Barnett, *Ladybird Snippets* has a pair of wings."

Chapter 3

The next hours were a whirlwind of arrangements. I spent half the time on a ladder, nailing things to the wall, (We had an indecent number of pictures, calendars, and the like) or perched on a bar-stool filing folders. It's funny how much you learn from a person just by going through his files. Even Mr. Barnett's file-folders were odd: for instance, what other man in America has—not one but two—files marked "Things That Make Me Smile?"

I certainly had never heard of it, and I took the liberty of poking my nose into the fattest file while I thought Mr. Barnett was not looking. *Warm blueberry pie, matching socks, rowboats, feeding pigeons, fried shrimp...* I read greedily, not pausing to laugh over the quaint list, though each item brought a flare of warmth to my mood.

"Ah, Miss Harper—you've found my secret files."

I slammed the manila folder closed and stuffed it in the filing cabinet. Caught red-handed. "I like fried shrimp too," I said. "I mean—I think it's a neat idea: making a list of your favorite things."

"I thought so." Mr. Barnett reached into the cardboard box and took out a stack of files. He glanced at the writing on one with a concentrated frown then handed it to me, smiling.

I watched this play of expressions across his features and considered him. He was not eccentric—he was too pleasant and good-humored for that. He was not a crank. He was hardly even a bachelor—any more than I was an old maid...Long ago when my first guy dumped me I determined I'd never get married and I would never be an old-maid—the two are not exactly conclusive. I'd sorted it out in my head this way: spinster-hood is more a condition of the heart than the circumstances. I never planned to let my heart grow bony elbows and graying top-knots and I *certainly* never planned on wearing spectacles—unless they were the cutesy ones with the rhinestones on the side.

So I was no spinster, and Mr. Barnett was not a hermit.

That being decided, I filed the remainder of the folders and pushed the drawer. It closed with the familiar crunching, rumbling sound that never failed to make me feel productive. I leaned against the cabinet and crossed my arms—I'd pinned my hair up but baby curls around my face and neck stuck in damp swirls to my skin. It was hot today, even in our little marble office. The cool of the cabinet's metal body seeped through the back of my blouse—*oh, divinity.*

Mr. Barnett tossed the cardboard file-box onto a growing pile in the corner and dusted his hands. "Was that the last?"

"I hope so."

"Me too. But it's really starting to look like home, isn't it?"

He swept the room with his eyes and I knew just how he felt —a little corner of one's own, chipped out of the heartless stone of a city. A claim staked by you that no one else has a right to. I glossed over the fact that if this was a home than he and I were the...*nothing. Absolutely nothing. Come on Cal—don't be a goof.*

"Where is home? For you, I mean?" I hadn't known how long I'd been wondering that till it came out of my mouth. I could have guessed anywhere from San Francisco to Neverland.

Mr. Barnett loosened his tie and rolled his sleeves higher. His cotton shirt hung limp against his chest. The sun beat down through the front window and lit up the swirl of dust motes with a dozy sheen. "Why don't we discuss this over sandwiches? It's hot as blazes in here. We'll come back when it's cooler— maybe the delivery men will have brought the air-conditioning units by then."

I walked out ahead of Mr. Barnett and he closed the door behind us.

"Aren't you going to lock it?" I tossed him the key I'd filched off the nail by the door.

He made a face, wavered a moment, then locked it. "I always forget—a relic from my boyhood, I suppose."

"So I take it you grew up in the country?" If my own girlhood was any example, country-folk never locked their doors. Ever. If the door locked by accident it was time to break a window because no one could recall where the key was. I scoffed at such behavior now—it was a good thing we'd never had any valuables. The only thing a thug would find in my grandmother's house was an overabundance of ceramic shepherdesses. I hated those figurines.

Mr. Barnett and I walked on for some time in companionable silence up the side of Park Row, then down Spruce Street. I'd never explored this far, finding it felt safer to conduct all my city wanderings in a cab. Neither of us spoke. Generally I felt it incumbent upon myself to keep up a steady stream of banter when I had a fellow at my side. *If* I had one. Mr. Barnett felt different in this respect as he was in every point I had staked him against so far.

We rounded another corner and meandered down a surprisingly quiet side-street edged with small businesses. Mr. Barnett touched my elbow and we paused at the low doorway of an old shop advertising Italian bread (fresh-baked), Italian coffee (fresh-brewed), and Italian lemonade (fresh-squeezed). The outside was painted a faded, respectable, friendly shade of emerald, leaving me to imagine the alarming color it had been when fresh. The paint was chipped in places and adorned with a few stubborn cobwebs in the false pillars at either side of the doorway. All told, it looked like a dilly joint. I already loved it.

"Be prepared, Miss Harper—I want you to meet some of my friends." His eyes twinkled and his voice strained as if he struggled not to laugh. Knowing Mr. Barnett—or not knowing him, as the case may be—I wasn't sure whether to prepare myself for Attila the Hun or Ham Peggotty. I braced myself for whatever might be beyond that door. Upon entry, we dropped into a different world than the dusty, brilliant street outside.

Here it was dark, pigeon-shadowed, and scented with fresh bread. My stomach twisted in knots at the smell—I hadn't been this hungry for ages. It took a moment for my eyes to adjust to the light--until then I listened to a throaty sound. What was it? Humming? Yes—that was what I heard: someone humming beyond the expanse of glass-fronted counter. In a moment I could see again and I gazed about, wondering how I could have worked six years at *The Post* without ever having set foot in this darling café. The walls were plastered with faded newspaper clippings—some of them probably straight out of *The Post* or *Times* or another of our number. Wreaths of garlic and onions hung near the ceiling, tied to hooks with pieces of scarlet ribbon. The glass-fronted cases below the counter were stuffed with delicious-looking sausages, cheeses, and deli-meat. And behind the counter, from whence came the humming, stood a buxom Italian woman.

We had come in quietly without alerting her to our presence. Mr. Barnett's eyes still held that merry twinkle and I saw him as he must have been thirty years ago—a brown-eyed, brown-coated boy with a penchant for mischief. He put a finger to his lips and cocked his head for a moment as if listening to the tune the woman hummed. What was he doing? I tried not to laugh—it would spoil what was obviously a supreme moment in Mr. Barnett's plot against her. All at once Mr. Barnett joined the woman in the chorus of her song. He had a strong baritone, and I recognized the chorus of an Italian aria from the last opera I'd attended for review.

The woman turned around, abruptly stopping her tune. "Ah! Meestah Barnetta!" She raised two plump, floured hands and beamed at him, then bustled around the counter and enveloped him in a strong hug. "What you doin' here today?" It was then she caught sight of me. "Ahhhh!" There was a world of meaning in that "ahh" and its accompanying sweep of my person. "You bringa your pretty girlfriend for lunch, no?"

I examined the clippings on the wall and pretended I hadn't heard. Still, from the corner of my eyes I studied Mr. Barnett. He seemed composed as usual—entirely unruffled by Annamaria's assumption that had caused my heart to try for the Kentucky Derby.

He laughed. "No, no, Annamaria—she's my assistant. I've started a new job and she and I are out to change the world." He motioned for me to come closer and I obeyed—a new sensation of shyness creeping over me.

Annamaria wiped her hands on her apron and shook her head at Mr. Barnett. "Assistant, girlfriend—bah! She's still beautiful."

I bent my eyes on the floor, but Annamaria's thick forefinger was under my chin and she lifted my head so I had to look into her face. It was broad and good-humored, and red as the roses in her cotton-print dress. She wore little gold hoops in her ears, and when she smiled her teeth were parted in the middle. She startled me by planting a hearty kiss on either of my cheeks and patting my back. "You helpa heem, no?"

"Yes ma'am, I...I do—I *try*," I stammered.

"You good girl?"

I flushed. "Not as good as I ought to be."

"Ahhhhh. *He* a good boy." Her tones weighed me against Mr. Barnett and I felt the severe incongruity of the result.

"I try to be good as I can." I turned my eyes to my shoes, wishing the floor would swallow my humiliation.

"Course she tries." Mr. Barnett put one hand on my shoulder and another on the woman's. "Annamaria, of course she does her best. None of us is perfect. I'm not half as good a boy as I ought to be, so help me, Lord Jesus."

Curious, I cocked a brow and watched him, expecting to find an expression of mock piety on his face. There was none, and my stomach clenched.

Annamaria's gaze descended heavy upon me and if we'd been on a see-saw I would have gone sailing from the sudden weight.

Her eyes narrowed a bit. "And what'sa your name?"

"Calida Harper."

"Calllida Harper." She tasted the name, trilling the 'l' as if she savored it. Then she chuckled. "Eet sounds like an opera-singer name. Very good—I like-a you." With that, Annamaria squeezed back behind the counter and continued her work.

Mr. Barnett smiled and escorted me to one of the green wrought-iron tables lining the wall. "Very good—she likes you."

"Yes...yes, I suppose she does."

He laughed quietly and that smile danced still in his eyes. "She mentioned the opera—you're part of the family now. The opera is her obsession, you know."

"Is it?" I felt a desire to laugh too—the idea of that woman having a passion for the theatre was so absurd.

"Very much so. She has a beautiful voice—in fact, she might have been one of today's biggest stars had she not taken a quieter, perhaps *nobler* road." Mr. Barnett's voice thrummed with approval and esteem for that obscurity behind the counter. In fact, strange as it was, he seemed to reverence her.

"A nobler road? Which one is that?" I asked, eager for an explanation. Running a bakery and a café? Was that the nobler road? By whose measure? And why? But his answer was postponed by a thunderous sound of feet outside the door, and a sudden flood of olive-skinned, dark-eyed children. Their voices came to me jumbled and confused; they spoke Italian.

Mr. Barnett said something to them in their language and I stared at him, feeling stupid. "You know Italian?"

"I do." He laughed. "It's another rule in the newspaper business: know at least one foreign language—do you?"

"Pig-Latin. That's about the length, breadth, and width of my vocabulary. Oh—and of course I can say 'hola' and 'au revoir.' Doesn't make for much, does it?"

He laughed and I found myself laughing with him. "Not much, no, Miss Cosmopolitan," he said.

"Guess I paid less attention to French in high-school than I did to writing saucy rhymes about the teachers." I hugged myself and sighed. "Gosh—I'm famished! What's good to eat here?"

"Everything. But I'd suggest a pastrami sandwich and some cannoli—you look in need of a little plumping-up if you don't mind my saying so. I'll not let you work yourself to a skeleton under my watch."

"You're so kind." I scoffed over this man's plan to overthrow my stylish, slender waist, but I was hungry and the food smelled divine. I ordered according to Mr. Barnett's suggestion and one of Annamaria's children tottered over to us, carrying our lunches. Mr. Barnett took one of the plates and shoved it over the table-top toward me. I spread my napkin in my lap and started to eat.

Much to my horror and embarrassment, Mr. Barnett bowed his head to pray before his meal. My bite of pastrami sandwich lodged in my throat and I ducked my head, unable to meet his eyes when he addressed me a moment later:

"Back at the office you asked me where home was. Do you still want to discuss it?" He flapped his napkin and laid it in his lap, then sprinkled salt on his sandwich and red-pepper flakes on the enormous pickle.

"Yes, I want to 'discuss' it." Even to myself I sounded awkward and short. What was wrong with me? *Callie Harper— you're a sad, strange little girl and aren't doing anyone a favor by acting like a wax mannequin. What would Nickleby think of you?* I sipped my glass of water and manufactured a smile, hoping desperately for it to become real. "May I guess where you are from?"

Mr. Barnett nodded and continued in the pressing business of consuming a quarter pound of Italian cold-cuts on a cheese-encrusted roll.

I shifted in my seat and switched my analytic filter to 'on.' I was no Sherlock Holmes, but I'd made a lucky guess a time or two in my life. "You never locked your doors," I said. "That means you grew up somewhere in the country. From the state of your coat I should say you were down on your luck—really, Mr. Barnett, we'll have to suit you up—but I know for a fact you don't lack funding. That cements the country theory. Country gentlemen never live up to their means. Your accent suggests a southern birthright, but it is tinged with something a bit colder than Georgia--Virginia, if I'm not mistaken. So my theory stands thus: you are Virginian, born and bred on some retiring, beautiful plantation home among the oldest of families, and you struck out sometime before your twentieth birthday to make it in the world on your own." I slumped back in my seat, flushed and triumphant. It had to be right. I studied Mr. Barnett's face to see if my hypothesis stood the test.

Mr. Barnett laid his sandwich aside, wiped his mouth with his napkin, and took a sip of water, looking hard at me. Somehow I got the feeling I hadn't quite smacked the truth. "Your theory is a rather interesting one, Miss Harper. Tell me, how did you come upon it?"

He *would* ask. Rather than divulge all my ridiculous Agatha Christie-isms, I shook my head. "I just made a wild guess. I'm wrong, right?"

"Though I hate to prove a lady wrong, I will admit your deduction is rather full of errors."

I rolled my eyes. "Come on—don't try all that chivalry jazz on me. What's the scoop? Where'd you grow up?"

Mr. Barnett smoothed the brown grosgrain band on his hat and gave me an infant-size smile. "In a squalid little apartment, overlooking a sluggish river on one hand, and a prison-yard on the other. We were very poor—my mother and I—and we never locked our door because the lock had been beaten in so many times by my drunken step-father that we would never be able to get back in if we had." He paused a moment, his telling eyes full of distant events. "My own father left us when I was eight years old—he…he was killed." Mr. Barnett's eyes were bright and intent and they flickered over me as if unsure whether he ought to have left off the last part. "Afterward, we moved to the city."

I wasn't hungry anymore and my hands felt clammy. There was the wistfulness of a small, insecure, abandoned child in his voice and my heart thundered sickly. I knew that wistfulness—it was my own. And to hear it echoed in the words of this good man seated across from me caused the world to sway in a dizzy haze.

I reached across the table and rested my hand on his for a split second. "I know the feeling—my dad was killed too." Well, more or less. "My Momma was left with two kids—me and my brother, Tristan."

For my own story I'd reached the end. There hadn't been a happily ever after in my life, and—barring recent circumstances —I wasn't looking for one. Life was life. Men took advantage of women, seduced them with promises they never intended to keep, married them--sometimes--and ditched them soon as they required commitment. It was the old, wearisome story. The recollection of my past solidified the plan to remain single all my life. I spoke for myself, *to* myself, and forgot for the moment that there was anyone in the world besides me and my sorry little history: "Having a family isn't worth the heartache."

"Is that how you feel?" Mr. Barnett's words brought my senses back around and there was the green wrought-iron table, and the salt and pepper shakers, and Annamaria humming to herself behind the counter.

I eyed the newspapers on the wall—stories of another world's successes—and sighed. "It's what I've seen. And a girl's gotta trust her own common sense—it's all we've got."

"If you don't mind my saying so, I've often found common sense and wisdom to be greatly at odds."

"Well I do mind you saying so. Gosh. I don't know why you're so touchy about it." I ignored the shade of amusement lingering on his face and felt the familiar flush of anger creep through my body.

He looked at me over the rim of his glass, grinning. "I'll not bother you with this conversation any longer. Forgive me."

My temper steamed like a hot spring and I knotted my napkin in my lap. There was no way I was done with this conversation.

"I don't see why you'd want a family! I'm never going to subject myself to a man and let him treat me as he will, and leave me the moment it enters his head." I knew my pressure was up. I knew I was pouring these torrents of scathing words onto Mr. Barnett as if he'd just had the audacity to demand my hand in marriage or—or *kiss* me. I knew I was unreasonable and overly emotional and ridiculous, but it would not be kept down. I half choked over the rest of my words:

"Men don't love women. Love may have been alive once—I like to believe it was and maybe it still exists for some people—but life has got to go on and I won't be dependent on some man for my satisfaction and fulfillment. It's stupid and I won't degrade myself that way. If you think for one moment—" my voice shook and I slammed my fist on the table. "If you think for *one* moment that I will ever show my heart to *any* man you must be dreaming."

I would not cry. I would not. But my vision of Mr. Barnett's placid face swam with the hot tears and one plashed down my nose. That was it. I pushed my chair away from the table and fled the bread-scented café.

Once on the street, the shame of my situation hit me in the face like a piece of scaffolding falling from the top of the Empire State Building. I had just lost it in front of America's most famous journalist. Besides that, I had showed him a piece of my heart: shabby and acid-eaten; shattered delicacy. My spirit stood naked, exposed, ashamed. Mr. Barnett could be nothing but unsatisfied with my assistance, and I tomorrow I'd receive Shores' gloating telegram, lurid against that patch of shabby linoleum at my front door. TOLD YOU SO. Okay—so maybe he wouldn't use those words, but the idea was the same. He'd probably be polite, patronizing. And I'd be indebted to him for a last kindness. Despicable.

I continued my flight, weaving through the late lunch-crowd of my fellow journalists, hoping no one saw the tracks of tears in the powder on my face. I wiped my cheek with a napkin that I somehow forgot to leave behind and considered my options:

I could leave the country. No—that wasn't exactly doable: I had no money. Besides, Mr. Barnett had already kindly pointed out that I was ignorant in all forms of second-languages.

Go back to Annamaria's and apologize to poor Mr. Barnett? No. Absolutely not. It was impossible. I couldn't bear the thought of seeing Mr. Barnett's stricken, confused, consoling face. Why did he have to be so kind? Why, why, why? No. Apologizing—especially today—was out of the question.

Then there remained only one option: *Nickleby? I need a hug.*

With that, I hailed a taxi, jumped into the first one that presented itself, and embalmed myself in the relative privacy of the backseat. I felt in desperate need of a favorite book and chocolate. That, or a one-way ticket to the antipodes. Mercies abounding, this cabbie was the taciturn, gruff, "probably couldn't speak English if his life depended on it" sort. I mentally blessed his buttons and settled back in the cab with my pill-box cap tilted over the eyes to shield me from my own thoughts.

I fell asleep—or was so overwrought I'd done a sort of swoony number—for it seemed only an instant later that a loud "harrumph" arrested my attention. I awakened to the sight of the cabbie's ugly face and his leather-gloved palm shoved over the back seat in expectation of payment. I fished around in my handbag—grateful beyond belief that I hadn't left *that* at the scene of the crime—and found a dollar or two. I crumbled them in my hands, tossed it over the seat, and hopped out of the cab.

Don't be on duty, Jerry. Please don't be on duty. I'll die. I'll absolutely shrivel up, split open, and die. I loitered around the front of the building, trying to see through to the inside. Of all the days for that shabby little window-cleaning guy to have done his job valiantly. The glass shone so I could see nothing but my own harried reflection. I looked awful—sweaty and limp with little mascara-tracks in the corners of my eyes. I licked the corner of my stolen napkin, dabbed at my eyes, ran a hand through my hair, and set my jaw. Then, feeling like a first-class, A-number-one martyr, I pushed the doors open.

"Miss Harper? Home so early? Brilliant. And how goeth the new job?" His eyes were friendly, his smile jovial.

I hated for Jerry to have to witness my death, but it was inevitable. I was dead as a doornail. Signed, sealed, and delivered by the Grim Reaper himself.

Chapter 4

Once barricaded in my room—door locked, curtains pulled shut, hat and purse shoved into the diminutive closet—I stood in front of Nickleby like a woeful nun before her Father-confessor.

"I am wretched!"

He blinked and mewed as if to console me on that point. "Well, I *am*. I was having a perfectly lovely day until home came in the picture. Do you remember home, Nicks?" I caught him up and buried my face in his soft black fur.

"Do you remember the day Dad left? I do, Nicks. I remember." As much as cats are reputed to hate getting wet, Nickleby didn't seem to mind the flood of tears I dropped on his black coat. He licked my cheek—sandpaper tongue on damp skin.

"I remember running out the door behind Dad, calling him back. Watching him tear out of the driveway in his car. I wanted to go for a ride—We stood there and I waved goodbye with a stupid smile on my face. I never thought it was a real goodbye—a forever one." My voice had horns and callouses and was hot to the touch.

I was livid with my father for leaving, with myself for remembering, with Mr. Barnett for sympathizing. And it wasn't like I could write *him* off as a nuisance. No—his sympathy annoyed me all the more because he had a right to be as bitter as I. He had a right and he had given it up in favor of something that looked an awful lot like forgiveness. Of all the horrible positions to find oneself!

"Oh, let's forget it. Shall we, Nicks?" I twitched the curtains open. The baring of my darkest memories was complete. I could face the world's stare again with composure, and once more be that cool Callie Harper I'd perfected. I flopped side-ways in the over-stuffed chair and kicked my heels off. One landed by the register, another in the base of Boston fern I always forgot to water. "You'd be ashamed of me, Nickleby. I made a fool of myself today."

He inquired 'how' and batted my gold earrings with a deft paw. I shook my head—Nickleby and I understood one another perfectly. "You are an overly curious beastie, aren't you? But I guess it'll come out somehow—once Shores ditches me and I'm looking for some job as a second-rate typist." I sat up straighter and wiped my eyes, attempting to compose myself.

"I guess Mr. Barnett had a similar childhood to us—or *kitten*-hood, as the case may be. He said his father left him and I started thinking of Dad and it all went wrong from there. In short, since you must know everything--being my only confidante--I ranted to Mr. Barnett and fled the scene of the crime. It was a hit-and-run of the first order. Boy...what a headline that would make."

Nickleby reprimanded me with a supercilious mew and hopped off the chair onto the window-sill. He began the laborious process of cleaning himself and I rolled my eyes. Much a cat could know about the difficulty of restraining one's emotions. "You needn't look so high-and-mighty, Nickleby. But I don't care—I'm ignoring you, you know."

I took *The Portrait of a Lady* from my leaning tower of literature that stood in place of the bookcase I'd never bought. I held it with gentle hands and opened the covers. There were the familiar words printed in the familiar manner—books soothed me like nothing else ever had, chocolate excepting. As I read, I wondered for the hundredth time why Isabel Archer had accepted Gilbert Osmond's proposal of marriage. She'd aced it as a single woman, and if she'd got tired of that, she ought to have married Ralph Touchett.

But I knew.

I knew because her story had foreshadowed mine. She had wanted something more. She had wanted those glittering soirees and a palace in Italy. She'd wanted the glamour.

I closed the book, drowning all the voices that were trying to teach me a lesson. "I've had enough lessons today to last me a lifetime, thank you very much," I muttered.

Annoyed to find the books—my avowed friends—had deserted me, I tipped the lid off the candy-bowl and split a raspberry cream with Nickleby who had come back around at the sound of glass against wood. He knew what it meant as assuredly as anyone could.

I never understood the stereotype of cats ignoring their mistresses.

But even raspberry creams could not minister to a mind diseased. I swallowed my half only because I hated to waste perfectly good chocolate and curled up in a tight ball in the chair. Life was miserable. I was miserable—more so, because I had come to a decision: I would have to apologize to Wade Barnett. I wondered how humble pie tasted? But it wasn't the humility that hurt the most—it was the fact that I was in the wrong. I had always prided myself on having the upper-hand of my emotions in every situation. Not so today. And I had hurt the only man I'd ever met who remotely seemed to care about me.

Just peachy.

I was certainly not a candidate for the Nobel Peace Prize the rate I was going. Action could be postponed no longer. I gathered my pumps from the floor and flower-pot and slipped them on my feet. Just as I opened the closet to dig up my hat and clutch, a sharp knock rapped on my door. I wriggled out of the depths of that closet and unlocked the door, then opened it a crack. Jerry stood in the hallway.

I nearly shut him out, but he put up a hand and beamed reproach at me. "Miss Harper—I don't know what's wrong with you—but don't do anything desperate. You looked fair to be killed when you came in."

I slumped against the door-frame, eyes on the straggly edge of the hall carpet. "Thanks Jerry. But I'm not planning on doing anything harmful. I'm not clever—the worst I could manage would be a chocolate binge and it's so inelegant."

"Oh, but Miss Harper, you are clever. Not to mention chocolates are positively scrumptious."

Jerry, darling, you're such a dope. I danced my foot on the patch of linoleum, feeling my gumption ebb away with each second he stood at the door. "I assure you I'm perfectly well; just a slight indisposition." I started to close the door, but he raised his hand again. "*Yes,* Jerry?"

"Miss Harper, a letter arrived for you just now—hand delivered it was. A gentleman in a brown coat with a brown hat. He looked like he belonged in an English manor-house with a dozen dogs at his heel and a large library of books. He said to give you his regards and that you'd find an apology inside. A perfect gentleman, Miss Harper."

I pounced on the letter Jerry brought forth, almost forgiving him for waxing poetic on the one subject in the world that most consumed me at present.

"Thanks, Jer—you're a darling. G'bye!" I slammed the door, not caring for once if it was rude, and hied me away to the couch where I installed myself with a pillow on either side and Nickleby on my lap. I held the envelope in my hands and felt the address with my fingertips. Mr. Barnett's handwriting: angular, smooth, masculine. I dropped it into my lap and covered my face with my hands. "Nickleby, I am so ashamed."

His mew encouraged me just enough to slit the envelope with a bobby-pin—anyway, I was curious. I shook the slip of paper out of its cocoon and unfolded it with trembling fingers. My eyes rushed down the page and read the contents greedily:

Miss Harper,

I realize it was in no way the manner of a gentleman to divulge my life-story to you over lunch. I should have restricted my replies to the weather, the general area from which I hail--questions pertaining to the moment. Instead I have pained you and I am sorry for that. It was not polite of me, and was, in fact, dashed inconsiderate. I do hope you will forgive me and feel cheered up presently. As a cure, I generally recommend a good book—something about the color of Wodehouse would serve very well. Don't try Hugo—he can be a bit heavy on his feet. I freely give you this afternoon as a holiday—you've worked like a Trojan all morning. Come to the office as usual tomorrow, and we will sign a truce.

I am yours respectfully &c.

Wade Barnett

P.S. Not a word of this to Shores.

I hugged the letter to my chest and felt a wild desire to dance, laugh, sing, anything! Mr. Barnett was not angry with me. He would not tell Mr. Shores. He was sorry for having pained me—and he liked to read. It was the perfect ending to a hellish afternoon.

I jumped to my feet and rushed to the secretary-desk, scrambling about for a sheet of my personal stationary. I found a yellow legal pad, pages crumpled and died with spilled ink. No, that wouldn't work. There were numerous reporting tablets, but I shied from using those either. I needed real stationary for an apology—Calida Harper did not often stoop to admitting she was wrong.

In the very back corner of the cluttered desk my hands met with a slim packet. I pulled the packet out and turned it over. "Bologne, France," the stamp said; the envelope smelled of lavender. Tristan's note scrawled on a piece of paper was all I had left of him:

To Callie—who never has any of her own. Much love from her brother, Tristan.

I laughed in spite of the lump in my throat. Dear Trist. It had been eight years since I'd stood at the dockside waving goodbye to him as he went off, brave and true, to fight in the Second World War. Like so many of our valiant boys, Tristan hadn't made it back.

I took a sheet of the stationary from the packet then replaced it in its quiet, secluded corner. I wished my life was more like that packet—shaded and gentle and not prone to making rash and stupid decisions and generally ruining life.

Despite this, I felt calmed by the scent of lavender. I dipped my pen in the gummy inkwell and dashed off a letter to Mr. Barnett:

Dear Mr. B,

I was in the wrong. Forgive me and know how wretched I feel over the whole to-do. I will be there tomorrow. And I will read Wodehouse— wasn't he a ducky-darling?

Penitently,

Calida Harper.

I signed my name with a flourish, folded the letter, and realized I had no idea where Mr. Barnett lived. Oh well—I'd send it to the office on the chance he'd still be there. The address scrawled, the stamp licked, I rang the desk downstairs.

"Jerry?"

"Miss…Miss *Harper?*"

I decided to ignore the incredulity in Jerry's voice. Hadn't I a perfect right to ring up the desk if I wanted to? He needn't sound so shocked. I gripped the phone. "Listen, Jerry. I need you to do a huge favor for me."

"Anything for you, Miss Harper." His loyalty was touching— really. Even with that astonished edge still sounding in every word.

"Great. Do you think you could slip out and deliver a letter for me?"

"To the post office?"

"Well, no. To my office—my new one."

"I'd love to, Miss Harper but you know I'm on duty…"

Rats. I'd forgotten that, but there was no way I was going to do the dirty business of delivering an apology on my own. I grabbed at the first idea that drifted by: "I'll watch the desk, Jerry! I'll answer the phone and smile at everyone who comes in….I'll even put on a British accent. Won't you take the letter?"

In the long moment of silence, I could hear Jerry's breathing on the other end of the line and I knew he was weighing two sense of loyalty—should he go for me or the desk? Vain creature I was, I certainly hoped I carried more weight than a desk. Besides—that letter needed to be sent. It was imperative: I couldn't think of Mr. Barnett waiting all night thinking I hated him. Then I heard the faint 'hush-hush' sound of Jerry polishing his bell. A sign in my favor.

"All right, Miss Harper," he said, and I could imagine his round face and tender eyes bent on me in sorrowing reproof. "Just be sure you don't let anyone get away with the paintings."

"Jerry you're a doll. I'll be right down." I hugged Nickleby, grabbed the first volume of Wodehouse that caught my eye, and dashed down to the lobby. Jerry was there, his lobbyman's coat and cap folded neatly on the desk. In its place he wore a street suit of the same dark blue.

He took my letter with the grave spirit of a deceased martyr: "Mind the paintings, Miss Harper. And don't worry—I will deliver this letter. Where to?"

I gave him the address and he bowed as if he held in his hand my last will and testament. I watched him out the door and chuckled to myself. Dear Jerry—undertaking to deliver a letter with as much grit and determination as if there were three feet of snow piled outside and a tornado to boot. Besides that absurd caution over those two framed posters he so proudly considered 'art.'

He was a good fellow enough. I had to admit the world felt under control when he was by.

I tilted back in his chair and for the first time that afternoon felt a moderate sense of peace creeping over me. Checking beforehand to be sure Jerry was a safe distance down the street and not likely to come back, I picked up his lobbyman's cap and tilted it at a rakish angle on my head. Then, humming a snatch of "In the Mood," I cracked the spine of *Something Fresh* and immediately felt cheered. Mr. Barnett was right—Wodehouse was as good as an aspirin when you were feeling low. I settled down into the surprising comfort of the leather desk chair and waited for Jerry's return.

The Collected Letters of Wade Barnett:

July 21st, 1952

My dear Maralie and Tobias,

I sit here at my desk in our office—too quiet now that she's gone—feeling like a villain of the deepest dye.

I've wounded her, and the worst of it is, I think I meant to.

No, that is too harsh.

I did not mean to wound her, though I knew bringing up the topic of our childhoods would lift unpleasant memories in her mind. I only wanted to hear how she viewed her past—is it a thing she has passed through, unscathed? Is it a thing that haunts her today? Is it a thing she accepts as a matter of consequence, and thinks little of?

I took her to lunch at Annamaria's as a celebration of our first day on the job. Miss Harper has a remarkable mind—one that is swift to catch hold of an idea and ferret out the reasoning behind it--and I thought our little discussion of personal history might be conducted best over sandwiches and cannoli.

This has little bearing on the brouhaha I will reveal presently, but I will tell you that Annamaria approves of Miss Harper. I am content, knowing this. Annamaria is a courageous, wise woman and her opinion—like yours' (which is another reason you must meet Callie)—means a deal to me.

As we ate our lunch, Miss Harper insisted on guessing about my background. I would have rather told her outright, but she insisted on playing detective. How bright and pert she looked, making so many clever assumptions. She hit far from the mark, of course, but it was her enthusiasm that gladdened me.

Then it hurt, like watching a lame kitten limp away from a fire, when I tricked her into mentioning her own childhood. Her eyes filled with cold fire. She says her father was "killed." More or less that is true, but not in the way mine was killed. She can't know the depth of my sorrow.

God forgive the war raging in me!

It surprised me to feel the depth of my own emotion as I watching her struggle against the powerful, sweeping waves of memory. I wondered how many of our thoughts were similar. How many fierce achings and sharp longings and barren sensations of a childhood stolen by tragedy?

She said having a family isn't worth the heartache.

She surprised me into an answer, for I've always thought the opposite, as you well know. I've always longed for a family, that I might reverse the wretched workings of my generation and pour blessing on the next without fear they will go wrong. She said she holds her opinion because common sense has shown it to be true.

I replied with something boorish and stupid. Something I should have kept to myself. Tell me, Maralie: was I always such an unconscionable oaf as I have been of late?

My manner of reply hit a raw spot in Miss Harper's heart, and she flew on me with tooth and claw bared and gleaming. She ranted for some moments and I was wretched over having brought things to such a pass as this. But it was her last remark that scored my heart with red-hot talons:

"If you think for one moment that I will ever show my heart to any man, you are mistaken!"

Oh, how that blood-strewn remark has rattled the corridors of my soul!

I can see it is my fault. I pried too deep too soon, and I have wounded her in the way so many men have wounded her before, beginning with her father and ending with me. I am one of them —those men who wreck and ruin women's lives for their own purposes.

Lord forgive me in this, and protect her!

I have written to Miss Harper, delivered the letter to that good fellow, Jerry Atwood, and can only hope she will, by some miracle, forgive me. My heart is wretched and sore within me, and I fear I've made a breach nothing can repair.

I pray it is not so. Tomorrow will tell. If you would put in a prayer or two for us, I would be very grateful. No offense intended toward you, Maralie, but Tobias: how on earth do you handle a woman? They don't think in any logical pattern I can see.

Tell the little ones I said hello again. I apologize for writing two letters in as many days—I cannot think where else to take my woes than to you two champions of the faith. Forgive me for the bother.

I am yours always,

Wade Barnett

Chapter 5

Callie:

Jerry's delivery was successful—he'd spoken with Mr. Barnett himself. "A real gentleman, Miss Harper. I feel as if I've met him before."

"That's highly unlikely, Jer, considering the circumstances," I reminded him.

Jerry only winked. "Whatever the case, now I don't worry about you."

"Oh Jerry—as if you ought to worry. I'm a big girl now. I don't need someone to hold my hand and pat my head when I remember to look both ways crossing the street." It wasn't a gracious answer, but it was all I could manage when my emotions were already this overwrought.

Nickleby and I spent a restless night on the couch and here I was this morning, looking especially nice in a blue cotton dress with a blue ribbon in my hair. Men liked blue—didn't they? At any rate it was a tranquil color and might soothe a few remaining ruffles on the surface of Mr. Barnett's temper.

An hour later, I crawled into the office, heart thundering like an apoplectic pigeon. I closed the office door quietly and tip-toed to my desk. Mr. Barnett sat at his with a pencil clamped between his lips and his typewriter before him. He appeared to be absorbed in his work so I took a quick look at the papers on my own desk. At the top of the stack was a note dashed off in Mr. Barnett's neat script:

Take a look at these bits and see what you can come up with. I'd like to see us each manage two short stories, several poems, and two articles by the start of next week. We'll fill in with advertisements this issue.

Well—I could see Mr. Barnett was ambitious, whatever other claims he might have to aid his already stellar reputation. I glanced at the first few pages in my stack—clippings from other magazines. Poetry from *The Saturday Evening Post*, scraps from other equally famous publications. Some of the clippings looked ancient—I scanned one of the oldest and my breath caught in my throat at the familiar words on the page: *Aunt Betsey Trotwood, Mr. Murdstone, Peggotty.*

"Mr. Barnett! This is David Copperfield!" I realized all too late, of course, that it was an absurd thing to pop out with as the first thing you say to a person in the morning.

But Mr. Barnett only grinned. "Ah—Miss Harper. Good morning. And yes—" he gestured with an open hand to the paper. "You hold in your grasp a very old piece of very famous literature, first printed in serial-format in a paper. Fascinating, isn't it?"

I didn't answer because the meaning behind all of this did a job on my ability to think. These clippings from Mr. Barnett...I shuffled through the stack and noted all the famous signatures: Rudyard Kipling, G. K. Chesterton, H.G. Wells, Jack London.

My head swam. "Do you mean to tell me you want me to be a...
a modern day Dickens?" The office rang with my question and
Mr. Barnett cocked his head to one side.

"Don't you want to be?" he asked.

I tossed my head and straightened the intricate openwork of
my starched collar. "Of course I *want* to. I just think it's a bit
loony—I mean, all of these authors were one in a million."

"And?"

"And I'm only a journalist, Mr. Barnett. I've been stuck inside
Shores' office the past five years writing obituaries for Polish
bankers. It's not exactly first-rate experience."

Mr. Barnett frowned. "Does that matter?"

"Doesn't it?" I countered.

Mr. Barnett stood and paced in front of his desk with hands
shoved in his pockets. "The only thing that matters is the way
you view that experience. Everything you do builds you one way
or the other—even obituaries (provided you did your best) could
be just as great an experience as shadowing a famous reporter."

I crossed my arms and drummed my fingers along them. Sure,
at heart I wanted to be a Dickens, but I hated being great on
command. "Whatever."

Mr. Barnett walked to the edge of my desk. "Miss Harper,
perhaps we'd better both get to work. Write with the best that is
in you—that's all I ask."

The best that was in me? I smiled and extended my hand. "I
can do that—though I wouldn't buy any bonds insuring its
sterling quality."

Mr. Barnett shook my hand and dashed back to his desk. "On
your mark, get set, go!"

I laughed to myself and sharpened a pencil; what a nutty guy I'd got myself in with. I took one of the fresh white tablets out of my drawer and smiled. I never tired of looking at those fresh pads of paper, unmarked and unused—it seemed a shame to cover them over in writing. There was always that hanging-in-balance moment for me when it came to paper: I both hated to mar the whiteness and yearned to scribble all over it. Did Mr. Barnett ever feel that way, or was it a sensation peculiar to myself?

I licked the tip of my pencil and summoned all my wits. I would need them to keep up with Mr. Barnett's challenge. But through my panicked complaining I registered excitement, the sense of a hunt. Two stories, several poems, and two articles? I could do that. I *would* do that.

Without further ado, I took up the first of the clippings on my desk and began to read, pencil poised to take notes. The sound of Mr. Barnett's typing was loud in the room. Years of long hours spent at my own typewriter told me he leaned heavily on the left side of the keyboard, and that his 'e' key stuck when he pressed it too hard.

I leaned my head on my hand and flicked through the pile of clippings, never looking up. "You really ought to send that typewriter back to the Underwood Company and get the warranty. You bought them new and that 'e' key shouldn't be sticking that way."

The typing stopped. Mr. Barnett and I looked up at the same time. "How did you know my key was sticking?"

"It's easy. There's an 'e' is twelve percent of all words in the English language. Your keys made an unmistakable thump far too often for it to be any other letter but 'a'. And it thumped toward the right end of the left side of the keyboard." I went back to my reading, but I was seriously pleased with myself. This Dorothy Sayers-wannabe had proved herself right for once.

Mr. Barnett appreciated me too. "Well I'm astonished. Really, Miss Harper, that's remarkable!"

I felt my face grow red and I ventured to look up. Mr. Barnett leaned back in his chair, hands clasped behind his head. A pleasant smile spread across his face—I knew that smile. It had inspiration written all over it, and somehow I got the idea I'd been the muse for this expression. "Do you ever do this, Miss Harper?"

"Do what?"

"Get brilliant ideas from conversing with people."

I felt shy all of sudden. "Sometimes…but the general public's not exactly brilliant."

"No. But it happens now and then that you hit upon a stroke of genius just when you least expect it, and from the least likely candidates. It's brilliant, I tell you!"

I was busy trying to see if that turned out to be a compliment, but whether it was or not, Mr. Barnett was pleased. He gave his pencil a few quick turns in the sharpener and grinned like a little boy. There was a spark of mischief in his eyes.

"You've inspired me, Miss Harper. Keep talking and between the two of us we'll give the families of America a first-rate detective series to rival the fame of Sherlock Holmes."

I left my desk and wandered over to his. "You really have big ideas for this thing, don't you?"

His eyes met mine—brown and true and gentle. "Nothing is worth doing if it's not worth doing well. A much wiser man than I said that and I've found it to be true. Why content yourself with mediocrity?"

"It's a heck of a lot easier."

Mr. Barnett laid his pencil aside and looked at me in a way that made me flick through my mental files to see what had gone wrong. "Do you think that? Truly?"

Yes, I thought that. Truly. Living life on the sunny side of the street—wasn't that ideal? I floundered for a moment, trying to find some answer Mr. Barnett would be pleased with. I did want to make him happy, but at the same time a deep sense of loyalty to myself forbade me to answer dishonestly. "Yes. I do think mediocrity is easier."

"You aspire to mediocrity?" It frightened me—the grave expression his eyes held and the fading of his smile.

I shrugged. "Who *aspires* to unsweetened oatmeal? But I've always been a dreamer—I've always had unrealistic expectations for myself and my life." I'd said the right thing and—even better —it was true.

Mr. Barnett relaxed and his smile shone again—remarkably like thunderclouds passing from the face of the sun. "I am pleased to hear it. Never settle for the pasty, pale, insipid things —they're not worth spending your life on. Reach as high as you can for as long as you can. And invest in people—relationships. The things that will last longer than you."

What was he? My counselor? I didn't like being preached to any more than I liked admitting I found mediocrity easy.

"Don't you think the mediocre things are the easiest?" I didn't enjoy recognizing a whine in my voice. All I wanted was for the case to be closed—but I had to have the last word. I've always been a sucker for repartee.

Mr. Barnett returned to scribbling on his tablet of paper—I wondered if it was the mystery he'd been so inspired over a moment before. "It's easy only in the present. But later, when we look back, we'll see how hard it has made our life."

His attention was fixed on his paper—my attention was fixed on retreating gracefully. I plopped down in my chair, rolled a new sheet of paper into the bar of the typewriter and tapped out a title in the untidy way I had. Title first; story later. The old adage of never judging a book by its cover annoyed me. I always judged a book by its cover. If the author couldn't think of a proper title, how would they manage fifty-thousand words in succession? That was my theory, anyway, and besides—I was pretty great at coming up with titles.

Midnight at Charletain. That was the name staring blankly at me from the bar of my typewriter and demanding I come up with a plot for it. I shifted in my seat and summoned all my mental faculties. Midnight…Charletain. It sounded like a gloomy gothic castle. Something with poison and daggers and velvet gowns, perhaps? I shifted to the other side of my seat and stared out the front window. My reflection showed slim and shady in the glass. I wished I could step through into that cool world where Callie Harper looked poised and in control of every situation. Except for the fact that my reflection mimicked my every move, I could have sworn I was a spectator in a playing out of my dreams. In that world of glass I looked like everything I aspired to be.

"Gathering inspiration from the street-sweeper, Miss Harper?" Mr. Shores' voice shattered my dream world and I turned a vivid scarlet. Even my reflection looked hot and uncomfortable when I glanced at her, guilty. Mr. Shores filled the street-doorway, a hand pressed to either side of the lintel like the old Bible paintings of Samson.

"Of course, Mr. Shores." Why did he have to come here? Mr. Barnett and I hadn't yet spoken of yesterday's confessions.

Besides, I'd racked up two more quarrels on the score-board. So far Team Barnett had the lead on Callie three-to-one.

Mr. Shores ignored Mr. Barnett and instead came behind my desk and peered over my shoulder.

"*Midnight at Charletain?* Intriguing title, Miss Harper. Tell me, what are your plans for this story? Will it be able to keep pace with Mr. Barnett's genius?" His mouth was close to my ear and his hot breath blew my hair against my cheek.

I moved away from him, annoyed. "I'm not permitted to say, Mr. Shores. All work belonging to *Ladybird Snippets* is strictly copyrighted and illegal to share with the public until it comes back from the printers'. If you'd like to file for a special exemption I'm sure Mr. Barnett would be more than willing to help you out." I opened my dark eyes wide and blinked, kitten-wise at him. My voice held all the innocence of a guileless infant. But inside, my heart lifted her hem and danced a highland fling to the tune of distinct triumph. Mr. Shores was vanquished and I, Calida Harper, had been the victor.

Before he got the better of me, I pinned my hat on, stuck a paper tablet and two freshly sharpened pencils in my satchel, and hurried over to Mr. Barnett's desk.

"I'd like to go out for a while, sir. It's such a gorgeous day and I need to do a little research."

Research? More like scrape-together-a-plot-from-the-bits-humanity-dropped. But people-watching inspired me far more than sitting at a desk and musing over shining typewriter keys against empty paper. I'd always done my pieces for college finals while sitting on one of those old wooden benches or prowling—perennially dateless—around pairs of sweethearts at the soda shoppe.

Mr. Barnett raised his head and smiled at me. "I don't mind. Bring me a hot pretzel if you've half a moment."

Mr. Shores prowled about my desk back-stage. Mr. Barnett's smile stuck around brighter and longer than made sense. At least he wasn't cross with me. Then I knew that he must have overheard my tete-tete with Shores. The idea formed a bubble of laughter in my heart. I did something daring and served my employer a wink which was instantly returned. Then, trying my best not to laugh, I ducked out of the door and onto the streets of NYC.

For some time I wandered with no particular destination in mind, enjoying the strange sensation of walking the streets this early in the day. Funny how a city can have a completely different face in the brief hours you take your eyes off it. It struck me that I'd never before seen New York City at nine-thirty in the morning from the view of a Wednesday pedestrian. It was still busy—still chopped up by that uncanny flow of traffic that gave her the title of 'The City That Never Sleeps,' but there was a certain preoccupation that convinced me everyone in the world was going at it hammer and tongs as I was. I mentally crumbled *Midnight at Charletain* in my mind—I wasn't feeling the whole gothic drama thing today.

Two stories, several poems, and two articles? I had reached the relative quiet of City Hall Park, and I plopped onto a bench occupied by no one but an elderly man with a newspaper. I stared at the towering spectacle of the Park Row Building in the distance.

Mr. Barnett was a perfect gentleman, kind, and thoughtful—but I knew now why he had become the most famous name in journalism: the man never stopped. *Ever.* Two people running an entire magazine? It was impossible and, what's more, improbable. I'd never heard of such a thing—how did Mr.

Barnett expect it to work? Because as far as I could see, I needed all my bits written this week so I could spend all of next playing copyist and publicity manager—not to mention the usual tasks of a secretary like answering the phone and filing papers and painting her nails. I glanced at my hands—the polish had chipped and worn off like the metal of a rust-eaten car fender. Brilliant. I fished around in my satchel for the pair of nail scissors I always kept handy and went to work at trimming down the worst tips.

So what to write? What to write? I dragged myself into a mental alley, beat myself over the head, and rifled my pockets for loose change. *Perfect timing for a case of writer's block, Callie! First week of a new job and you can't even manage a story and a couple poems. How do you ever expect to become your ideal if you freeze like this? Hubcap.*

I ignored myself with the admission that I was terribly vulgar at times. No. I would remain composed and self-possessed and I would find something to give Mr. Barnett. Besides, it wasn't uncommon for dead silence to give way all of a sudden to productive genius—at least, that's what I hoped for. I tossed my nail scissors into my satchel and pulled out my tablet and pencils. If I had to start from square one, so be it. This case called for the German-philosopher game: interview myself like I'd interview a celebrity. What is America? What is the American Family? What would interest that family? I wrote the questions on my tablet and felt better at once. I could conduct this like an essay. I looked up for a moment to find my bench-neighbor peering at me over the top of his newspaper. Our gazes collided and he smiled at me as if he'd been waiting for me to take notice.

"Studying for a college exam?" he croaked.

College exam my eye! And me, twenty-seven if I was a day. "No, sir. I am a *journalist.*" Afterward I deemed I'd used far too much emphasis on 'journalist' as if I was announcing my relation to the Queen of England. Still, it was harmful to one's inspiration to think back on those gawky college-days when I labored under the delusion that the world was a delightful place full of stories I'd never tire of reporting.

"A journalist? Aha. And what are you journaling about?" His mild blue eyes—clouded as they were by age—twinkled at me. "Your deepest darkest feelings?"

It was then I realized he had no concept of journalism, thinking it related somehow to that species of sappiness twelve year-old girls call their "diary." It amused me to think what the present situation would look like in a girl's emotion-peppered diary:

"Awkward, absolutely *horrid* writer's block. I felt like a *complete* and *utter* failure. And then a simply *adorable* old man asked me what I was *writing* about—isn't that *too* funny?"

I smiled in spite of myself. "No sir, a journalist is a reporter. I used to work for *The St. Evan's Post.*" I gestured to the paper he was reading, having caught sight of our familiar emblem. I realized—all too late, of course—that I had never finished that obit of the Polish banker. A vague fear crept over me that perhaps this was the banker's twin brother and he might be grossly disappointed by the absence of his relative's official death announcement. "But now I am the co-manager of a magazine: *Ladybird Snippets.*" I tapped my pencil against my tablet and tried to focus, ignoring the old man at my side.

"Are you looking for a story?" he asked.

"We're always looking for stories in my business." I sighed and rolled my eyes. "The trouble is finding the good ones."

"Would you like to interview me?" He cast his paper aside and leaning forward with the eager expectation of a schoolboy.

Rather a presumptuous old chap, assuming I would be interested in his story. Whatever. I snapped my mind to multitask mode and sighed. I could continue to play the German Philosophy game while I made this fellow happy. I flipped to a fresh sheet of paper and shifted in my seat to see his face better. "Name, please?"

"Archibald Scarrowby."

"Really?" *You sound too eager, Cal. Just because an old gentleman has a name that sounds like it popped out of an English pub doesn't mean he'll have a good story to tell you.* Still, my journalist's blood simmered with eagerness at the unexpected entrance of an interviewee. "And what is your profession?"

"Watcher."

"Watcher?" I paused mid-scribble and raised an eyebrow. "Like a bird-watcher?"

The old gentleman laughed and winked at me. "I watch birds. I watch people too. But I make clocks and watches—or at least, I used to."

"Before...?"

"Before the Great War."

I took down his words in my own manner of short-hand and thought hard. Great War—certainly he couldn't mean the First World War? I was still young enough to marvel at anyone being ancient enough to have experienced one of the massive world events before my birth. "When you speak of the Great War, Mr. Scarrowby, do you mean—"

"Kaiser's War. I was already in my fifties when it began. Too old to fight, too young to quit." Mr. Scarrowby's eyes showed a pale, contented blue beneath the brim of his flat cap, and I realized with just how old of a man I was speaking. He neared a century, but despite the tweed jacket and white hair I could see his frame was still relatively robust.

I smiled at him. "What did you do?"

Mr. Scarrowby neatly creased his newspaper and clasped his gnarled hands. "I'd been a watchmaker like my father and grandfather but with the war came metal rationing. It was impossible for me to get the metals I needed to continue. Besides—I longed to be in the trenches with the young men. I was not too young to remember some of the brave men who had fought in the War Between the States. I was only six years old but I still recall a band of ragged, rugged soldiers straggling home to Boston. They'd been through hell—if you'll excuse my language." He tugged the brim of his cap with old-fashioned courtesy.

"No, no. War is hell. I…I lost my brother in the last war." It felt good to have that out in the open—I never spoke of Tristan.

Nodding, Mr. Scarrowby continued his story: "Since I couldn't make watches and I couldn't stay at home, do you know what I did, Miss…?"

"Harper—Callie Harper."

"Do you know what I did, Miss Harper?" His voice captivated me—all the city noise had faded. My imagination had peopled the street with a few elderly men—the city strangely bereft of all young fellows. Mr. Scarrowby appeared too, younger by forty years or so and full of vibrant life.

I was entranced. "What did you do?"

"I ran away to France."

"To...France?" I sat straighter and stared hard at Mr. Scarrowby. "What did you do in France?"

"Watched." He chuckled over his own pun. "I went to work as a civilian radio-technician. I pretended to be a French country-man who fixed clocks for a living. But I sold my services to the Allied forces and fixed bomb-shelled radios for them all across the battle-lines. I was rather a popular figure, I believe, which got me in a scrape or two." Mr. Scarrowby stated these facts of his heroism with humility, but I was delighted. My hand was cramped from holding the pencil too tight as I scrawled notes on both sides of my paper.

I cracked my knuckles and smiled at him. "And after the war? What have you done since then?"

Mr. Scarrowby laughed; a dry chortle that did me good to hear —it had stood the test of time and was still ripe and ready. "Just loafed."

"Really?" It was so unexpected—so wry and short and sudden —so perfect.

"Really. Loafing and watching—the people and bird-sort now, you'll understand—is a first-rate occupation for a man of my years. And what better place to do both that City Hall Park?" He tapped his finger alongside his nose as if the pun was a secret between the two of us, and smiled. I'd never met anyone I liked half so much. The way the smile lines fell around his eyes, the way his voice reminded me—painlessly—of the corn-fields back home when they were ripe for the harvest; all these things made a sort of man I'd never met in my years living in the city.

"You aren't a New Yorker, are you?" I asked. "Where are you from?" I was not too enamored to hope this conversation would not end the way yesterday's had with Mr. Barnett. I braced myself just in case. *Mention nothing of home. Nothing at all. And hope he has a normal family with normal parents.* Mr. Scarrowby had already admitted to having a father and grandfather—that was a hopeful start.

"Here and there. Over the mountains of the moon and back across the farm pond." He laughed, and I laughed, and it seemed even the pigeons strutting in the gutter were chuckling with us.

I stood, my tablet crossed back and forth with notes of our conversation. Priceless notes. Inspiration enough for years. I took one of Mr. Scarrowby's gnarled, dry hands in mine. "Thank you for letting me interview you."

"Letting you? I forced you. And don't you forget it." He tapped his nose again, shook his newspaper out, and disappeared behind it. That was all, and it was quite enough for me. I started back to the office at a half-trot, eager to begin the formation of my findings into something Mr. Barnett would be proud of.

Mr. Shores had just left when I entered the office—I could tell because Mr. Barnett still had that glazed-over look that Shores inspired in every sensible person's face. I tucked my hair behind one ear, tossed my paper tablet on the desk, and waited.

In a moment Mr. Barnett passed his hand over his eyes and shook his head. "That man is enough to try a saint's patience

"If he be waspish, best beware his sting."

Mr. Barnett put his hand behind his head and leaned against them looking as if he was in need of a good nap. "Did you know you are clever, Miss Harper?"

I smiled. "I had an inkling. Only I can't take credit for that ounce of wit—it was all Shakespeare, as any good thing is."

"Where is my pretzel?" Mr. Barnett asked. "Starving a man is cruelty."

The pretzel. That blasted, darned pretzel I was supposed to buy. I ground the toe of my shoe against the floor. "Afraid it's MIA, sir. But I can run out to find a new recruit if you'd like."

He shoved back in his chair and laughed. "Did you eat it?"

My stomach growled. "If only." Since he didn't appear monstrously upset, I nodded toward the street door where Shores' broad back could still be seen a block down the street. "What was his beef? Have you spiraled to Hell in his esteem for some arbitrary reason?"

"Oh, there is nothing wrong with Mr. Shores' opinion of *me*," Mr. Barnett said. A quiet soberness had settled upon him.

The way he pronounced 'me' sent an angry prickle down my neck. There was a world of meaning in it, and Mr. Barnett was too polite to say it outright. Well then, I'd have to say it for him —I wasn't going to be working cheek-to-jowl with a man and not have all expectations laid bare.

"Listen, Mr. Barnett. I know Shores doesn't like me but I do have more potential than he thinks. He's never seen me at my best because he only gave me second-rate assignments. I will pour every ounce of brains I have into this project if you'll only have a little patience." Pleading? Come on. Calida Harper never pleaded. She deigned to give her assent to the outcome of things. Whining, sighing, pleading? What was this world coming to? But there was no help for it. This was my one moment to argue my case.

"Just a little patience, Mr. Barnett, and I assure you: you won't be disappointed."

The corners of his mouth quirked up in that mischievous way he had. "Only a *little* patience, Miss Harper? Are you certain that will remedy the case?"

"Well of all the—" But Mr. Barnett was laughing now and I couldn't stay vexed with him, much as I wanted too. "As long as you convince Shores I'll suit you, you may have full license to tease me."

"There is no question of whether you will suit me, Miss Harper. We mightn't agree on a number of matters, but if I take a liberal dose of Patience every morning and you tame your tigers a bit, we will refrain from killing one another before the first issue goes to print. After that—why, the both of us will be too guilty of a dozen trespasses to extricate ourselves from the web we've woven. No, our partnership is sealed, and in good faith I say."

Trespasses? Guilty? What had I got myself into? An Al Caponian scheme? Mr. Barnett winked at me. " 'Partners in crime or business' she asks?" He chuckled. "Mayhap they are one in the same. I feel like a fugitive for making that bet with Shores."

"What bet?"

"I told him you and I were at one another's throats like rabid catamounts, and asked him which one of us he'd put his money on for the intellectual slaying of the other."

"Oh?" The proposition was too absurd for me to consider. I didn't relish the idea of anyone even thinking about matching my wits against this renowned fellow's—I'd lose before the bell had rung once. Strange to say though, I didn't mind my sense of inferiority. It would be too strange a thing to comprehend my crossing mental blades with Mr. Barnett and scoring the first touch.

Mr. Barnett crossed one leg over the other and bounced it on his knee. "You might be flattered, Miss Harper, to hear that Shores pegged fifteen bills on you."

"On me? He's a damned fool."

Mr. Barnett raised one eyebrow and looked at me in a 'must you swear?' sort of way. I felt myself go red.

"Well he is."

Mr. Barnett put up his hand and shook his head. "No need to convince me, Miss Harper."

"He is some sort of fool, at any rate. Even you'll agree with that."

"I'm afraid I must remain reticent on that point," he said, but there was a twinkling in his eye that vexed me at the same time it boosted my courage.

"Well I think we had better forget Mr. Shores even exists. We'd all be a deal happier if he was no more of a threat than a dime-store dummy." I huffed back to my seat and sat down so hard the chair spun me around once or twice. And it squeaked. I hated chairs that squeaked. It was so undignified.

I made the mistake of looking in Mr. Barnett's direction just in time to see the last, explosive shade of red pass over his face before he burst into loud laughter.

What was so funny? I'd worked myself into a royal rage. I could just see what Nickleby would think of me when I came home and confessed all to him.

"What is so funny?" I asked at last, as the storm of laughter showed no promising sign of abatement.

"You, Miss Harper!" He was making an effort—I could see that much—but it only increased his high humor. He drew a deep breath and wiped the corners of his eyes. "You look like a little old mouse that has got her tail wet and isn't a bit pleased."

"Well I'm not a bit pleased. Now I'm going to play Catholic and take a vow of silence. That is, if you don't mind. We've got gobs of work to do and we won't get famous by sitting here giggling like a bunch of drunken hyenas." It was after I'd scooted to my desk and flipped to a new page of my tablet that I realized Mr. Barnett was already famous and could afford an afternoon of laughter if he wished. The realization only fueled my vexation and I growled to myself as I assembled my notes into a semblance of order.

Not another word passed between us that morning. We didn't break for lunch till three o'clock, and even then there was no time for an official dinner-hour. Mr. Barnett slipped out sometime before three, clapping that dusty-dim hat of his onto his head, and reappeared a quarter of an hour later with a greasy, brown-paper package clasped inside his coat. It had started to rain outside and he shuddered water off his shoulders. The drops fell onto his shoes in dark, damp circles. When he took the parcel out of his coat, I noticed the oil spots it left against his white shirt. They'd never come out. Not for love or money— I knew; I'd tried a dozen times if I had once on my favorite dotted Swiss blouse.

"Mr. Barnett!" I gave him a proper lashing over the evils of hugging brown paper parcels to oneself, especially when they contained...well what did it contain? The delicious smell of fried fish filled the office, and my stomach won over my common sense. What did a spoiled shirt matter when there was lunch at hand? Mr. Barnett wiped all the papers on his desk to one side then sat his package down and undid the string.

"A pound of shrimp, fresh off the piers this morning, fried to perfection and destined to be the lunch of the stunning Miss Harper." He presented one of the shrimp to me on the end of his letter-opener and frowned. "No, no. Something's wrong…oh yes. I forgot. My briefcase!" I handed the leather case to my employer in great confusion and watched as he rummaged in its depths with a concentrated expression. "Aha. Here we are!" He resurfaced with a glowing face and a bottle of tartar sauce, presenting it to me with a bow. "My lady, will it be the sauce for you?"

I stared at him, disbelieving. There was nothing poetic in the moment—least of all in the fried shrimp growing cold on the desk and the bottle of tartar sauce Mr. Barnett clasped in his hand like a golden chalice.

"To Miss Harper—a long-suffering, independent woman who needs no help at all but falls to pieces over an empty stomach. Cheers!" He winked at me, and poured a bit of tartar sauce into the never-used ashtray.

I could have laughed, but it was the thoughtfulness behind the odd moment that disarmed me and swept away the usual words I would have found to use. I cleared my throat and kept my eyes —stupidly—on the small puddle of sauce in the glass ashtray.

"Aren't you hungry, Miss Harper?" he asked.

This was something I could answer. I cleared my throat again, much distrusting words would hold my weight, and answered in a small voice: "Yes…rather."

"Well that's something we can fix in a trice." He was his old, bluff, whirlwind self in a moment, but I stood there like a fried shrimp, telling my typewriter heartbeat that it was my imagination. Or had I seen—wonder upon wonders—the corner of a curtain lift in his eyes and show much more of a man lurking there than I'd ever thought to exist?

Chapter 6

I spent the next few days at the Coney Island Fair—rhetorically speaking. The real thing would have been gobs more fun. It seemed that no matter what I said or did, Mr. Barnett and I disagreed. We never outright fought—I could take that—but there was a constant inner battle with the dozen different Calida Harpers that made up me. Up and down, up and down like a wooden roller-coaster dangerously near to careening off the rails.

Sweet Callie conceded to Mr. Barnett's opinion every half-second. Dreamy Callie replayed every conversation of ours through my mind. Naughty Callie stuck her tongue out—not always *mentally*—while Mr. Barnett's back was turned. Cross Callie contradicted him; Higglety-pigglety Callie recommended a change of opinion at least three times an hour. And on and on till I could never tell from one hour to the next whether I would be laughing or pinching back tears. He maddened me, this man. Why? Why? Why? I asked myself that question (always in sets of three) multiple times a day. Why did I care so much to hear what Mr. Barnett had to say while at the same time hating myself for listening, and him for his conviction?

But somehow through the strain of it all I managed to drum out my assignments. The first interview—all those gems of Mr.

Scarrowby's—I typed up as neat as I could, christened it "The Watcher's War," and left it on my desk, hoping Mr. Barnett might get a chance to look at it. Friday morning my manuscript was gone and in its place a note directed to me in Mr. Barnett's now familiar handwriting. He had not come in yet, and the office was quiet. I dropped my clutch into the chair, took off my gloves, and held the note with shaking fingers.

I scolded myself: "Callie Harper, you're acting like Katherine Hepburn with malaria. Get a grip." But my hands *would* tremble. All I could think of was that inside this little twist of paper was a commendation from the top journalist in all of America. It was worth every tense moment in that office so far—heck, it was worth every tense *year* I'd spent since college—to hold that note in my hands and know what Wade Barnett thought of my work. I was scared to death and euphoric all at once. The thump of the early papers hitting the door as the paperboy rode past startled me into action. I unfolded my note and turned it to the early light streaming through the front window.

"Miss Harper: Please work on your pieces today. I will not be in the office. If you get hungry—or overly cross—trot off to Annamaria's. She'll feed you well and give you advice or coffee. Probably both," it ran.

That was all. Not a word about my war-veteran, not a single warm line. Not even a signature. Nothing except his assumption that I'd get hungry and cross, as if those were the only two moods I was ever in. I crumpled the note in my fist and threw it at the filing cabinet.

"Well then!" I felt the telltale something snap inside me and braced for the approaching gale. "We'll just show Mr. Barnett that we don't need his good opinion. We can make it on our own, can't we—?" I smiled in spite of my embarrassment as I realized Nickleby was back at the apartment and I was speaking to no one. But I had the office to myself—that was pleasant in its own way. I could imagine I was the famous journalist and had sent Mr. Barnett out on an assignment.

"There are worse things than spending a quiet morning by oneself," I said. I lounged in my own chair for a while and tried to focus; the poetry wouldn't write itself at my short stories must be drafted by tomorrow afternoon at the very latest. I wrote for some time but my chair was hard and the words would not come smooth despite the fact I used a full fountain pen. I shifted and tried to refocus. My eyes wandered to the window and I watched the world revolving around itself outside the office. Yellow taxis crawled by and harried businessmen, late for work, chased after them. Shoe-shiners catcalled and newsboys hawked our papers from the stand directly across the street from my window. That small one there—he looked like Oliver Twist, I thought. Pale, thin, virtuous-looking....dirty and smudged. Yes, it was all there. And that man with the red beard loafing by...he was Fagan...

Next thing I knew, it seemed to me that Oliver and Fagan were running down the street chasing me, and Mr. Barnett was running behind them waving a newspaper and shouting something about fried shrimp and Annamaria.

I woke with a start and raised my head. The square of sunlight had already moved to the far corner of the room.

What a stupid dream. But all of mine were—I never dreamed anything I wanted to dream; only senseless rabble that I'd never have thought of in a remotely awake state. Oliver and Fagan and fried shrimp indeed—what nonsense. My empty pad of paper was just there at eyelevel on Mr. Barnett's desktop. I wondered how late it was and how long I had slept. And what had awakened me?

I raised my head and screamed a bit when I saw Mr. Shores standing there, arms crossed and smile mocking—it wasn't a ladylike scream either; I sounded like Genghis Khan on his way to battle.

"Sleeping, Miss Harper?"

"Dreaming, Mr. Shores," I retorted, a bitter foam in my voice.

"Ah. And does Mr. Barnett pay you for dreaming? Did Maralie Barrymore make it to fame by dreaming?" His face had to be the ugliest thing I'd ever laid eyes on. I had half a thought of hurling my pencil at it and seeing if the tip would stick in any one of the large pores on his nose.

My hackles were up stiff and fierce as a she-wolf's. What right had Shores to wriggle into *my* office without announcing himself and start questioning *my* business practices? The string of "my's" tasted sweet when said in that adorable, coaxing mental voice with which I soothed myself. Never mind if sleeping on the job wasn't quite what you'd call sound business practice—I was now under Mr. Barnett's authority, not Shores's. I arched a brow and clenched my fists in my lap.

"I'm sure Mr. Barnett doesn't pay me for dreaming…any more than *The Post* pays you for spying on other offices' employees." Even I was surprised at the steel in my voice, and I watched its effect on my former boss's face. His complexion— ruddy at best—had become florid.

I pushed away from Mr. Barnett's desk and paced the room, hands clasped behind my back. I wore my stilettos today, and towered over Shores, positively dwarfing him—my height fed this new sensation of power. "*Ladybird Snippets* and *The Post* might be sister companies, but we don't want to begin a family feud, do we?" I managed a patronizing smile. "Now Mr. Shores, I suggest you leave straight away. Oh—and please knock next time you come to borrow a cup of sugar." I had stunned Shores into silence for the moment but already my sugar-cube tower of might began to crumble. My stomach felt shaky and that unconscionable desire for tears pinched in the bridge of my nose.

At the door Shores turned around and shoved a kielbasa-finger in my face. "Just because you've got this job doesn't mean you're a hot-shot around here. I could have given the gig to Jules, only he's a promising guy and I didn't want to injure his career. You on the other hand?" He twiddled his fingers as if to let my imagination play out the end of the story. "You're dispensable. I told Mr. Barnett so before he hired you."

Shores stomped out of the office and I was alone again. I stared after him, arms crossed, garlicky language flinging through my brain. I needed to score some vanity-points. I was in the habit of cultivating a good opinion of myself much as the average housewife is in the habit of cultivating ferns and geraniums and other plants on her windowsill. Recently I'd been in a drought—my battered pride couldn't take much more of this whaling.

What had Shores meant by "injuring" anyone's career? So he thought *Ladybird Snippets* an ill-fated venture, did he? The nerve! I growled to myself and stamped my foot. What an imbecile! Well I'd show him and every other jumped-up, bandy-box, suspender-wearing, balding, purple-faced editor out there that Calida Harper was a force to be reckoned with and any man who supposed otherwise had another think coming. "World—get ready to see a real writer!" I declared aloud, shaking my fist at a portrait of Winston Churchill.

"That's the spirit, Miss Harper! Have at 'em."

Mr. Barnett's voice spread warm and heavy upon the otherwise silent room. My arm fell limp at my side and my face flared. *Brilliant, Callie.* Without looking up I dashed to my desk and held a newspaper in front of my face, engrossed—or so I hoped Mr. Barnett would accept—with research. That flimsy paper was the only thing dividing me from naked humility. Five minutes passed…ten minutes…fifteen. My breath slowed to its normal pace and I ventured a peep around the paper. Mr. Barnett appeared to be busy at his desk.

Annoyance mounted. I folded my paper with a deal of noise but the calm, sensible man across the room didn't respond.

"Mr. Barnett," I drummed my pencil on the desktop. "I thought you said you were going to be absent all day."

He glanced up and removed his black-rimmed glasses. "So I was…but I received an invitation that included you and I felt certain you would like to be forewarned."

He used that paternal tone again, but my curiosity was piqued. "Fore…warned?"

"We'll be dining at the Stork Club."

I dropped my pencil, I dropped my jaw, I dropped every thistle I'd clutched to my heart all morning.

He looked at me as if I was asking a rather ridiculous question. "Whatever are you staring at me like that for? You remind me of the wolf in Red Riding Hood— 'Grandma, what big eyes you have.'"

"*The* Stork Club," I pressed, still not believing this twist of events.

"Well it's certainly not the Turkey Club, I can assure you." He chuckled and rubbed his chin. "Have you anything suitable to wear, Miss Harper?"

"To…wear?" I asked, still trying to comprehend my booming luck and thinking repetition might help.

His eyes were that warm, dark hue like melted chocolate—his laughing color. "Though I am no Christian Dior, Miss Harper, I do know that you can't go off to the Stork Club wearing brown cotton and ink-smudged cuffs." His whole face twinkled when he smiled like that.

"Are you teasing me, Mr. Barnett?" Delicious warmth sped to my very fingertips. I was going to the Stork Club. The *Stork* Club. With Wade Barnett.

Mr. Barnett stood and shoved his hands in his trouser pockets. "I'm only giving you a simple suggestion. Of course you could go in that get-up but Grace Kelly might tell tales."

I glanced down at my street-suit and winced. He was right of course. My cuffs were smudged and my skirt had already crumpled itself into a dozen fine wrinkles like an old woman's forehead. "What will I wear?"

If I was any other woman I would have asked the question of my sister or my best friend or my hairdresser…but my only sibling was dead, I didn't have friends, and I was scared to death of the German Amazon who trimmed my hair. There was only Mr. Barnett to ask.

He took a walk around me, head to one side, eyes appraising. "Something for the evening, of course," he remarked. "In a light color, I suppose. Black is rubbishy. You don't want to look as if you're always on your way to a funereal—madness. Men prefer cheerful colors."

"They do?"

"*I* do. I suppose I shouldn't speak for my sex at large." Our eyes met and he held my gaze for a moment. Earnest. That was the word that captured the essence of this man. Everything about him desperately earnest. I wished I could be half as serious myself, but I could not. It was not in my character to be grave.

"Then I shall wear something light blue or pink and make myself look thirteen years old." I said it with a glibness born of gigantic excitement and danced back to my desk. I knew the afternoon would be one long, arduous fight against excitement, but even I—the girl who loved a party better than anything else —knew there was work that must be done and done well before the evening's festivities; therefore, I set to work with a right good will and though references to posh night-clubs, dancing, and evening dresses elbowed their way through my poetry and stories, I managed to finish my assignments for this first issue of *Ladybird Snippets*.

I deposited my work on Mr. Barnett's desk at a quarter-to-five. "What time shall we meet at the Stork Club?" My voice faltered a little over the name of the famed club…it didn't yet taste right in my mouth. But I savored its sweetness and rephrased my question: "I mean…the Stork Club is open pretty late, isn't it? What time should I get there?"

Mr. Barnett removed his glasses. "Aren't you the least bit curious, Miss Harper?"

"Curious?"

"About why we're having dinner at the Club?"

I was so enraptured over going at all I hadn't wondered why. "Now that you mention it, why are we going?"

He stood, stretched, and started to pace the room in that ponderous way he had, a faint smile hovering around his mouth. "It seemed to me that the average American family likes a peep at a celebrity now and then. You know—actors, singers, that sort of thing. A printed form of Murrow's Person to Person, if you will."

"Yes?" I moved a step or two closer, waiting to hear what marvelous thing might fall from his lips next.

"And I had a bit of a case of writer's block this morning. Yes—do gape, Miss Harper, for even the famous ones are only demigods. We do come out of our temples now and again and mingle with the lowly. But this idea—I think there is something to it."

From anyone else the words would have been tinged with unacceptable hauteur. I only smiled and urged him on with my hands. "Well, what next?"

"You and I will be on duty this evening—it's not entirely a pleasure-jaunt. We are interviewing Nalia Crostticini—the Italian lark, to use the papers' pet name."

Nalia Crostticini and the Stork Club in one night? It was too much glamour to swallow all at once. In fact, I rather choked on my admiring comment, and gathered my things quietly. "What time do I meet you?"

"Meet me? No, no, Miss Harper. I will pick you up at the door of your apartment at nine-thirty. No protesting. You may be quite independent enough, but I cling to my odd habits like moss to a rock and I will trail your cab down the street if you refuse."

Put in that light I couldn't protest further. Besides—I didn't exactly want to pay for a cab myself—this way I'd save the difference and splurge on something to pretty me up. "Nine thirty, then," I said, and dashed out the door.

The cab ride was short and once at my apartment building I flew through the lobby without stopping to say a word to Jerry. Jerry and the Stork club did not belong in the same night.

I took the stairs, not wanting to waste a single moment waiting for the elevator.

Nickleby met me at the door with a curious mew.

"Nickleby, darling!" I picked him up and pressed my cheek against his fur, pretending it was the black-clad shoulder of a charming dance partner at New York's finest club. But charming dance partners generally don't have claws, and certainly wouldn't bat your nose to tell you to hurry along with your preparations. Nickleby did all these things so I deposited him unceremoniously on the bed and pirouetted to the closet. "What do I wear, Nickleby? I could do the black taffeta...so mysterious and alluring, don't you think?" I pulled the gown off its hanger and pressed it against my body, then poised my hand on my hip. "Do you like it?"

Nickleby blinked at me owl-wise, and twined through my legs. I remembered Mr. Barnett's preferences not to wear black, but this gown was my favorite. It had such...such...Hepburnism about it. (A word of my own concocting, but a good word nonetheless.) Black gowns were the champagne of the fashion world, as any woman knew—what did Mr. Barnett's taste matter in this case? Not a jot or a tittle.

"I am a grown woman, Nicks." I stared at him, wanting confirmation in this respect. He yawned. "And I can wear what I please when I please it." Another yawn and a swish of the plumed tail. "And Mr. Barnett can just stew in his own juice." – not an elegant assertion, but one that satisfied me.

The brown suit came off, the black taffeta came on, the nose was powered and the cheeks rouged, the hair pinned, and the choker fastened. I was ready in less time than I'd expected and had nothing left to do but bury myself in a play and wait for the clock's sluggish hands to point that fateful hour. Nickleby licked my calves through my hose—he was excessively fond of the lavender sachet I kept in my top drawer. At last the anemic claws of time pointed to twenty-five after nine, and I put on my heels, applied a last swipe of my expensive Revlon "fire and ice" lipstick, and shrugged into my wrap. "Nicks, I'm off. Keep the light on for me—I might come back a changed woman, but I'll still be your darling Callie." He looked so soft and cuddlesome in that moment that I dashed in and dropped a kiss in the air right above his ears—I couldn't kiss him, naturally, because his fur would have stuck to my lipstick. Besides—I didn't want to be late and keep Mr. Barnett waiting.

All the same, Mr. Barnett was waiting for me at the desk, quite engrossed in conversation. With Jerry. This put me in a temper. Why did everyone find Jerry intriguing?

After several moments, I cleared my throat and tapped my toes on the floor. Both turned about, and Jerry's face brightened. "Golly, Miss Harper! You look grand." That was all he said, but for his beaming smile it might as well have been 'eyes like lodestars.'

"Doesn't she though, Mr. B?" He said. "You could pass for a duchess, Miss Harper."

Mr. Barnett's eyes scanned me and his smile was a shade cooler than usual as if his mind worked behind his warmth and chilled it somehow. "You look very....sophisticated," he said at last. Somehow I felt as if he'd been searching for that one word and now dropped it on me from afar, hoping he'd not have to say anything else. He stepped closer and bent, speaking low: "But...ah...where is the funeral?"

The black dress. I stiffened. "Shouldn't we be going, Mr. Barnett? We don't want to keep Miss Crostticini waiting."

"You are right, of course. Jerry? Very pleasant seeing you again. Perhaps you can come up to the office some afternoon if you're free...have a cup of coffee?" The men shook hands and I ground my teeth. Mr. Barnett followed me to the curb.

I ignored him completely—marble, chin-tipped statue—till he had successfully hailed a cab. Couldn't even have a taxi waiting when he'd made a scene about forcing me to accept his chivalry. Mucho bueno, goose-egg. Such a helpful fellow.

The night air was hot enough, but I froze the atmosphere of the taxi until the cabby, Mr. Barnett, and I were in considerable danger of turning into snowflakes. "What anyone finds in that man I cannot see," I muttered. I wanted Mr. Barnett to hear me but feared what he might say in reply; if he didn't hear me I would not repeat myself.

He heard. "Miss Harper, what anyone could *not* find in that man, I cannot see." Seeing that I was silent and like to remain so for some time, he straightened his shoulders. "Jerry Atwood combines good sense, loyalty, and a first-rate mind to form quite an intricate man. I like Jerry and if you knew your allies when you saw them, you'd not lock the door on him like a stray dog."

I scoffed. "And you talked to him for what—five minutes?"

"My first impressions are generally correct—however we've met on several occasions. Don't you believe in intuition?"

"*Women's* intuition."

"Ah."

This infuriated me. "I suppose you'll tell me he's a perfect brick and he's going to star in the next issue of *Ladybird Snippets?*"

"Not a bad idea, there."

"Mr. Barnett!"

He clapped his hand on my shoulder, and there was enough weight to his palm to caution me it was not a playful gesture. "Don't get in a rage. I'm only pointing out that to catch from a man all I caught in so brief a time, he must have the most perfect good breeding and strength of character."

"Breeding is for rabbits," I said. It was absurd, but I had said it, and my hot cheeks melted the ice of my tone a bit when I spoke next: "He's not in the least clever."

"Give me strength, woman! And are clever people the only ones with whom it is worth carrying on a conversation?" His voice rose to a near shout, and the cabby's head turned an inch in our direction. "If that were so, I'd not be—never mind. Better to leave the insulting to your expertise."

"Mr. Barnett! Do be quiet—you're making a scene."

"Am I?"

"Don't be ignorant." I hissed.

"*You* are ignorant," he said, and his eyes snapped. "I am sorry to say it, but you are woefully ignorant."

Woefully? Well that burned. "Relating to what?" I asked.

"Relating to anything and everything estimable. Good sense and fine character mean nothing to you, do they? Miss Harper, you're a journalist and I'm a journalist, and I think it safe to say that I've had the most experience of the two. Do you think if I only bothered speaking with the clever people I came across that I'd be able to fill my quota? Cleverness is not so common you can earn your bread off of publishing first-hand wit—there's simply not enough of it to go around." He nodded at me, gesturing with a liberal hand. "You are the proof to my pudding."

I would not look at him, but raised my chin a bit higher in the air. "That is entirely a matter of opinion."

"Is it? *Is* it?"

I dug deeper with a barbed spade: "A personal theory."

"Not a personal theory—a universal theory, Miss Harper, among sensible people. Everyone knows that so-called 'ordinary' things and people are the underpinnings of life, and therefore monstrously important."

"So you say."

"So I say and so would any sensible person who hadn't false ideas of worth. Miss Harper, don't gentleness, kindness, and humility count for *anything* in your book?" His tone had not quieted. In fact, he was nearer to shouting than I'd ever seen him.

I swallowed the fury. "I view those qualities as perfectly necessary, but I don't agree they compose an interesting person.. Wit, vivacity…even a certain level of arrogance with a smoking-jacket charm about it—those are the things that make a person worthwhile." I watched the streetlights flick by—rapid candles springing up and fading away with the gray night strung between.

Mr. Barnett's palm tapped against my hand on the leather seat of the cab. "I think that Jerry—"

"I think we had better leave the subject of Jerry to the dogs," I said, removing my hand and cutting him off with a curt nod.

There was no answer from Mr. Barnett in his dim corner of the cab.

I bit my lips and dug my nails into my palms. This was not how I'd imagined our evening. This was not how I'd imagined *anything*. And it was all Jerry's fault again. Stupid, plain, sensible Jerry. Why did good sense have to win over charm every day? It was unfair, that's what.

"Mind if I smoke?" I asked. My companion did not answer and I lit my cigarette in silence, rolled down the window a crack and let the smoke trail outside.

I put it to my lips and pretended to draw on it, then dangled the horrid thing out the window. I never did smoke—just kept a case of cigarettes and a lighter in my purse for those moments when words failed me and anyone else would be excused from speaking because of such employment. Besides—it looked dignified and sophisticated, though the smell made me nauseous.

In a moment we approached the brilliant Stork Club building. The mascot—a leggy bird inspecting all who entered through a black-rimmed monocle—occupied its famed place in the center of the sign. Our cab pulled close to curb, and Mr. Barnett paid the fare then walked around to open my door.

A rush of warm evening air fluttered my wrap against my bare shoulders. I got out of the cab with all the dignity I could manage, and Mr. Barnett closed my door and pulled me close as a stream of traffic crawled past.

"Let's not damage the evening by arguing," he murmured above my head, nodding and waving at someone he recognized. His grip tightened on my arm the tiniest bit, letting me know that he would not let me leave till I had given him a reply—that he didn't want to leave this gaping rift between us.

I tugged away from him and opened my eyes wide, fluttering my lashes in the deadly manner of the movie stars. "Who's arguing?" Fatal innocence. That was the way to play these games.

He was annoyed by my answer, I knew. But I only tossed a glib laugh over my shoulder and joined the stream of silk-clad women and dark-suited men who made a lazy, breathless queue, waiting for their turn to enter the doorway of the New York's most elite club. Mr. Barnett caught up with me and grabbed my arm just above the elbow. "Listen Callie—we can't go in here like this."

"Like what?" Arch—that was my tone and the tilt of my head and the way I glanced up at Mr. Barnett from under my eyelashes.

He pulled me nearer and put his mouth close to my ear. "Like this. Armed to the teeth and shooting firecrackers at each other. I am sorry for shouting at you, but I won't take back what I said —I spoke the truth."

"Of all the—"

He stopped me with a finger to my lips. "No, listen to me. I'm afraid we must agree to disagree on this subject, and say no more. You made me angry—furious—but that's no reason we should abandon our mission. I forgive you."

"Forgive me?"

"For being difficult. Look. We can discuss other subjects later but now—here—you must remember that we are in quite a different world. I am a famous man and you are…well…forgive me, but a bit naive. Don't you think the public—yes, especially our fellow journalists—would pounce on a chance to breathe scandal down our necks?

I pulled away just long enough to notice the curious looks already thrown on us by the club-goers who had nothing better to do while waiting than criticize each others' evening-wear and wait for the next celebrity to pass by. I fabricated a smile and touched Mr. Barnett's cheek lightly with my fingertips, trying to convince our neighbors that we were merely have a quiet banter, not signing the Magna Charta. "What scandal?" I whispered through my smile and wriggled my arm out of his grasp.

He let me go and shook his head. "Try this one on for size: America's Top Journalist Having Emotional Break-Down Over

Newest Project. Or better yet—Barnett Working Assistant Overtime: Calling Quits After One Week.—really, Miss Harper, it would be better to stay *out* of the papers at this point."

I saw the truth in his words despite my own vexation, and managed a real smile—not a dazzler, but passable. "All right—as long as we get the scoop with Nalia Crosticinni tonight, who cares about personal opinion?"

"That's the stuff," Mr. Barnett said. He started to whistle a bit of "Little White Lies" then pointed out a few of his personal friends to me. Mr. Barnett was acquainted with everyone in New York City and I found his pace dizzying as I tried to follow his discreet indications of each acquaintance.

"Will Maralie Barrymore be here?" I asked, seized with a realization that Mr. Barnett had not kept his promise to introduce me to the giantess of our industry.

Mr. Barnett shook his head with a queer laugh. "Not tonight."

"Another strike against you—you haven't kept your word."

"What on earth do you mean?"

"You promised to introduce me to Maralie. She was my muse at school."

"She would find that laughable, I promise you. I will introduce you in time. Now, if you're lucky, Miss Harper, you might see Lucille Ball or Marilyn Monroe on the dance floor."

"Do you dance, Mr. Barnett?" The idea was a new one.

"Like a fury."

"Well I make it a point never to mix business with pleasure." I rearranged my wrap. "But at some point in time I will have to see this 'fury' you speak of."

"With pleasure."

This confectionery exchange put an end to our conversation for a time and I was glad for it. Somehow—now that the moment was here in reality, now that I stood in line just two couples away from being indicted into the Stork Club—my stomach took off like a an old puddle-jumper plane and my hands shook.

Calida Harper, look at you. You're dressed to the nines and standing outside The City's most famous club with America's most famous journalist about to interview Venice's most famous singer. Don't botch it by quivering like a schoolgirl at a homecoming dance.

This mental lecture did a deal to cool my nerves as I recognized just how lucky I was to be standing there. But this twitterment of anxiety and excitement was not fated to last long —a moment more and Mr. Barnett and I were standing at the door and the shining, black and white doorman let us through with a smile and a soft word of greeting.

Mr. Barnett checked his coat and my wrap at the counter manned by a slim, blonde young lady with a heart-breaker smile.

"Good evening, Mr. Barnett," she crooned. Her voice had a twinge of the South in its accents, and her eyes were very blue.

"Good evening, Miss Susan," Mr. Barnett tipped his hat off his head, twirled it, and handed it to her with a smile. "I hope you haven't misplaced anything since losing Hemingway's handkerchief."

Hemingway's handkerchief? I'd bet anything she had stolen it. I'd have stolen Hemingway's handkerchief, given the chance.

The girl laughed, seeming pleased at this little attention. Mr. Barnett bowed, wished her a pleasant evening, and took my arm. We walked through a low doorway and the sound of a full band playing something vivid and danceable enveloped us. Here the lights were low but not dim and glowed softly on the burnished wood of table-legs, the folds of silks and satins, and the eager, expectant, or indifferent faces of the guests. I exhaled slowly, but my blood mounted and my eyes started to sparkle—this was what I'd always dreamed of. Here was glitter, and shine, and *beaucoup de elegance.*

I looked about for our celebrity, but my eyes could not stop wandering over the gorgeous couples filling the room with splendor and the smiling waiters moving between. Mr. Barnett tugged me through the crowds and we made our way to the other end of the room. I wondered which table would be ours.

"Mr. Barnett, where are we—Gracious! We can't go in there." I pulled up short and Mr. Barnett turned, surprised.

"Whatever is the matter now, Miss Harper?"

I nodded at the illuminated doorway in front of us. A golden chain stretched across its opening and a grave, respectable man clad in black stood watch over it like Saint Peter guarding Heaven's gates. "That's the Cub Room," I said. "Only celebrities are allowed in."

Mr. Barnett patted my arm and winked at me. "Oh—old Saint Peter? He wouldn't harm you—not when I'm your escort. I am a bit of a celebrity myself, you know."

I had forgotten that vital piece of information, but now that he said it, my heart thundered in my breast. "Of course," I said. "I wasn't thinking."

Mr. Barnett smiled and took a firmer hold of my arm. He bowed to the man at the door. "Hello, Greg. How's the family?"

"Doing great, Mr. Barnett." The man smiled and bowed to me. "Sir, Madam, this way please."

The gold chain was lifted and Mr. Barnett pulled me through into an even more glamorous world than that I'd seen before, a world to which I knew I was born.

Chapter 7

I tried to remember to breathe and smile naturally but all I wanted to do was rush home and tell Nickleby about this change in our fortunes.

The actress in me finally awakened and put a saunter in my steps that had not been there before. I belonged here as assuredly as any woman in the room—Ann Shermane, or Doris Day, or Grace Kelly, or any one of the dozens of cultural goddesses who frequented the Club.

"Mr. Barnett."

"Yes, Miss Harper?"

"I like it here."

He looked at me as if he didn't quite know how to make me out, but I laughed. "It's the most marvelous place I've ever been and—well to put it quite conceitedly—I feel it is my destiny to be here. To mingle with all these people. You know, it's rather like that game we used to play as girls: if you could invite any three people to dinner—living or dead—who would they be?"

"Yes," Mr. Barnett said, and there was an odd shade in his smile. "Yes, I suppose it would feel that way your first time."

What did he mean by that enigmatic statement? But I had no chance to inquire further, for Mr. Barnett spoke to the *maître d'* and we were escorted to table forty-eight. A lithe, beautiful Italian woman reclined at the table and smiled at Mr. Barnett as we approached. She extinguished her cigarette and put out a small, olive-toned hand.

"Wade Barnett, so nice to see you." Her voice was silken and purring with a note of Italy. Exotic. Enchanting. I felt as if I had bony elbows, freckles, and a hunched-back in comparison with this Italian beauty. But she turned those marvelous eyes on me and smiled again. "And you are…?"

"Calida Harper—Mr. Barnett's assistant."

"My *aide de camp*." Mr. Barnett pulled my chair out for me and pushed it in once I sat down. "I couldn't run this new project without her, I assure you, Nalia."

"Really, Mr. Barnett." I protested, enjoying the warmth of the compliment.

"My dear, it is so very nice to meet you, " Nalia Crosticinni said. "To meet any of Wade's friends." She wore black, I noticed, and I was glad again that I'd worn my taffeta and disregarded my employer's wishes.

Once we were seated, Mr. Barnett made light, witty conversation with Nalia while I looked on, entranced. This was an entirely different Wade Barnett than any I'd seen before. Why he was rather…charming. Mr. Barnett, charming? It was a new idea, certainly, but a pleasant one. He questioned Nalia about her American tour, her health, her husband: was Vincent's work occupying much of his time? Was he in good health?

Nalia sighed—a sort of luxuriant, black purr. "Ah, Wade Barnett…I cannot think of anything more pleasing than an evening here with you,"

He smiled, and in this low, soft lighting his features were gentle and handsome. "I can think of many pleasanter things than spending an evening with myself; however, I thank you for your gallantry in saying so. I admit that to spend an evening in your presence is a joy itself. Besides—I owed Miss Harper a treat after working her so hard."

I nodded to that comment but I let my attention wander from their exchange. They were obviously well-acquainted friends. I had no place in the conversation and it wasn't pleasant to be excluded. It was my personal maxim that if one cannot be a part of something, they would do best to remove themselves rather than wait to be removed. Besides—there was much to look at in this glamorous Cub Room. I ate a bit of the Chicken Kiev the waiter had followed us in with, and tried not the stare at the gloriousness of it all.

"Miss Harper, what do you do?" Nalia Crosticcini's satin accents wrapped around my attention and brought it jerking back to the table.

"What do I do?" I asked. "I'm a…a journalist."

"Indeed."

Well that had sounded stupid. I drew a deep breath and tried again: "I used to work for *The St. Evan's Post*, but Mr. Barnett and I were chosen to kick-off a new publication." There—that sounded better… "Mr. Barnett and I"—it put us on the same plane and gave me a sense of belonging.

Nalia smiled and nodded. "He told me a little about it over the 'phone this afternoon. I wish you every bit of luck in your project."

What a gracious woman. I studied her for a moment, absorbing every bit of glamor and grace I could from her gleaming presence. "Mrs. Crosticcini…"

"Nalia."

"Nalia, how did you know you were meant for this life?" I blushed to see the side-ways spread of Mr. Barnett's grin and the flattered surprise on Nalia's lovely face. "I mean, every girl has a wish to be famous and glamorous, but how did you know?"

"Well...I suppose it just...happened, in a way. I am a very determined woman, you know." She laughed, showing a set of white, straight teeth between her red lips. I nodded inside. That was the way I felt about my career. Determination. Grit. Hard work. I could earn all of this for myself if I dug in with my teeth.

Perhaps I would fight my way up in the ranks till I'd come out in the blue-book somewhere between Greer Garson and the last few pages. I caught Mr. Barnett's eye, and he smiled at me, but in the smile there were many things that spoke of our late conversation, of his obstinate opinions, and of my naivete.

"Mr. Barnett there laughs at us destiny-chasers," I said. "He thinks us a species of Tartar consumed with greed and gossip. But I've no doubt he's the Grand Poobah of them all." I dared not watch my employer's face to see his reaction to these Parthian shafts.

Nalia threw back her head and laughed long and loud. "Oh, Miss Harper, you are such fun. Wherever did you pick her up, Wade?"

"It would appear by Miss Harper's assertions that she picked herself up. But I found her in Mr. Shores' office, pegging away at her latest bit of genius...wasn't it a Polish work, Miss Harper?" He words belied no mockery, but a devil danced in his eyes.

I found myself speechless at this sudden resurrection of the Polish banker and his unfinished obituary. Those days seemed so long ago, though only the space of a single week separated me from them. "I'm not...certain."

"Really? I could have sworn it was Polish," he pressed.

Devil take that mischievous man. I lifted my chin and looked at Nalia. "It was nothing, really. I was more than glad to agree to a partnership with Mr. Barnett."

The *bella signora* sipped her champagne and sighed. "I would think having Mr. Barnett for a partner a fortunate situation."

"Nalia," Mr. Barnett chided, but his new humility irked me.

"As a partner in business, I confess I find him exacting," I laid my napkin in my lap and smiled with uncanny sweetness. "But I've had it from his own lips that as a dance-partner he is unrivaled. I look forward to seeing if he represents himself rightly, for he seemed so determined on that point…It would be a great pleasure to prove him wrong."

Nalia clasped her hands and tossed back her pretty head. "I declare, Mr. Barnett, she is a *gatto spiritoso!*"

"A clever puss indeed." His tone was dry and my courage quailed under the weight of his consideration. Perhaps I had gone too far in my wit. Mr. Barnett stared at me a moment longer, then turned to Nalia, with a pointed ignorance of me. "Do you intend to be in the City long?"

"A few weeks at least—giving a handful of private concerts, performing at the Opera—you know."

"Then I hope to see you again before your stay is up." We were leaving? I ventured a glance at Mr. Barnett but his brows were drawn together as if he stood in deep consideration of something.

Nalia sipped her champagne again and fluffed her hair with her fingertips. "Wonderful! And please bring Miss Harper with you. I have never met a more clever young lady nor one with such *fascino vivace.*"

Mr. Barnett rose and I too, close behind him. He bowed to Mrs. Crosticcini, and she gave him one of her beautiful smiles.

"Goodbye, Nalia," I said.

She pulled me close and kissed me on both cheeks. "Come visit me soon, *bella! Arrivederci*, goodbye, darlings."

We hurried out of the Stork Club, and soon the bright lights and soft music were out of sight and hearing and we were in our taxi-cab once more. I had not dared to speak since my last witticism, and I wondered just how angry Mr. Barnett must be with me...he hadn't even remembered to get the interview. My stomach knotted like hammock strings and my palms started to sweat. Mr. Barnett remained silent as an anchovy, which did nothing for my nerves.

"I'm sorry," I said at last, since something obviously had to be said before he or I indulged in spontaneous combustion.

"For what, Miss Harper?" Polite as usual...even abstracted.

"For ruining our chances for an interview with Nalia."

"Ruining our chances? Whatever are you talking about? I got everything I need." In the half-light of the cab he flipped a slim tablet out of his coat pocket and showed me several pages filled with his close, neat handwriting. "Didn't you get anything?"

"But how..."

"If you had paid attention instead of trying to be clever you might noticed how I conducted an interview."

"But you didn't interview her for one second! You made conversation and chatted about the weather and her family and her schedule and everything else."

"Exactly."

Well this was it. Mr. Barnett had not acted like himself this evening. He had not been old-fashioned or odd or pokey. Instead he'd been charming and…and clever and roguish and proved a foil to my own high spirits. I was not used to being challenged, nor did I enjoy the sensation of being vanquished by someone wittier and smarter than myself. It made me question my own superiority, and that was not the way things were wont to go when Callie Harper's reputation was concerned.

"Mr. Barnett," I said. The suddenness of my decision to speak neither surprised Mr. Barnett, nor seemed to affect him in any way. "You were…not yourself at the club."

"What do you mean I was 'not myself'?"

He was going to make me speak? So be it. "You were taunting and clever and made me look a fool."

"It was not my intention to make you look a fool, Miss Harper."

"Well you certainly did a heck of a job not intending."

"You can never make a person out to be something they aren't," he answered with that cool causality that was so maddening.

I turned to him and slammed my fist into the leather of the seat. "What is it with you?" He looked mild and amused at my display of temper. "You're acting ridiculous and mysterious, and altogether strange."

He crossed his arms behind his head and smiled. "Miss Harper, it just so happens that you have learned me backwards."

"Backwards?"

"Yes. You have come to know me as I am in private—in the office. But that man is not me as I generally am—by necessity, you understand. Indeed, Miss Harper, were you anyone else you might say I was finally behaving with some vestige of *normalcy* again. What you are calling strange is, in reality, my general aura."

Well of all the ridiculous people to have on my hands, a personality-shifter had to be the worst. That was my game—no one else had a right to play it. "You mean to say that this...put-up job was you?"

"Or *I* was *it*, yes. We can't have all our secrets known to the world, Miss Harper. There is, after all, a certain level of privacy even the most successful cling to."

I thought I was beginning to understand. At least, his labeling in my head had oozed from First Class Nut to Slightly Dotty; of course the man had to have some measure of professionalism when dealing with the public. Daft of me to assume he would never change tactics when he changed from office clothes to tuxedo.

The darkness of the cab enveloped me and I leaned against my seat, rather cherishing the fact that it was dark and Mr. Barnett would not see the evening's confusion written on my face. Nickleby will get an earful tonight, that's what. For a long while we sat in silence. I listened to the swish of other cars passing us, the occasional blare of a horn, and the Metropolitan Opera twining in static threads through the speakers of the radio.

We pulled up at my building and I got out. I'd almost made it to the door when I heard Mr. Barnett's door open and close. I almost wished he'd stay back in the car—I wasn't quite ready to match wits with him again. He'd given me too much to think about.

"Callie?"

"Hmm?"

He handed me my clutch. "You left your pocketbook."

"Ah…thanks."

He seesawed back and forth on his toes for a moment and I pointed my face in the opposite direction so that I wouldn't see his smug smile. "Callie, I owe you an apology."

I turned. "You…do? I mean—of course you do. I mean…"

He raised his hand to still my confusion and shook his head. "No, I was too hard on you back at the Club. I teased you."

I fished in my clutch for my keys and sighed. "Oh please, Mr. Barnett. I was the hell-cat."

"But I am accustomed to it—you are not. You had no idea I wouldn't be 'myself'. I ought to have warned you."

"And I ought to have kept a civil tongue in my head. I believe Nalia was the only one of our table who was remotely decorous." I laughed grimly and took a deep breath. "So what do you say to forgetting it ever happened?"

"I say we do it again, as soon as possible."

"Mr. Barnett!" This side-blow knocked me over, tumbled me, and picked me back up again. "Whatever do you mean? Have you been drinking, sir?" It was the only explanation I could think of for such a dippy remark.

"I have *not* been drinking, Miss Harper. Think about tonight from a professional perspective: Nalia loved you—our little tiff has earned you a new friend already. If we both continue on clever as you please, our little partnership will take off in no time."

"It sounds an awful lot like a set-up," I said. "Still…it might be fun."

"Might be fun? By Jove, Callie! To see your eyebrow arching higher with every jab and to see you parrying each thrust like a master swordswoman—anyone in Society would pay good cash to see a match like that. We'll sell the act, Cal."

"But it wasn't an act," I reminded him. "I was angry with you."

"And I with you, which is half the fun. Listen. The magazine needs this sort of spunk. From now on no independent assignments unless we make the choice together—we'll go in a pair and put on a little show while we gather our crumbs. We want America to know that *Ladybird Snippets* is a vibrant, witty, clever publication run by a veritable Benedick and Beatrice."

"Well I do believe you're making much ado about nothing," I quipped, my wit revived.

Mr. Barnett clapped his hands. "Much ado about *something*, rather. There—you see? You and I were meant to be together, Miss Harper. We're fire and gunpowder. We're flint and steel. We're...we're the North and South with Dixie whistling and Yankee Doodle dandying. Great Scot, woman—it'll be a masterpiece."

And standing there at midnight with the yellow streetlamps gilding us and Mr. Barnett's tie askew, I did think it a golden scheme.

The Collected Letters of Wade Barnett:

July 26, 1952

Dear Tobias,

The woman maddens me. Please ask Maralie to forgive me for not addressing this letter to her as well, but I thought what I have to say on the subject of women might anger rather than please her.

I pride myself on being master of my feelings, and keeping a close eye on my temper. The average journalist can't afford excess displays of emotion—we are already on the bottommost rungs of professional Society's ladder. A notable journalist certainly must keep a lid on it.

Callie Harper is a witch.

It began with a discussion in the office this afternoon. I had spoken to Nalia on the phone earlier today—she is warm and friendly as always. Perhaps more so than in the old days. I attribute this to the fact that she and her husband have been in Italy the past nine months and have only now returned to America.

"I have a new assistant, Nalia," I said, feeling around for the proper words. Hard enough in English—twice as hard in Italian. "She's very new, and I would like to…introduce her to people."

"People meaning me," Nalia said. She laughed her tinkling, crystal laugh—you know the one. It was good to hear it again— Nalia is an old friend, of course. "For you, Wade, I could clear off any schedule."

I wished she wouldn't talk so particularly of me. "Could you? Well that is very kind. I was wondering if we might meet tonight —at the Stork Club."

"Oh, darling! That would be wonderful. I shall be so glad to see you."

I frowned over her European enthusiasm. "It will be a professional interview, you understand."

"Of course, Wade. It is always business with you. You are so like Vincent. You never have time for fun."

"Vincent is an excellent man of business." Too much so, I added to my myself. The man neglects his wife sadly, as anyone with eyes can see. But I do fear her appetite for excitement brought that to a head. Vincent Crosticinni is a practical man in every sense of the word. Still, he is a good man. I asked her why she didn't bring him along.

He was too busy, she said.

I cannot say I was surprised to hear it.

When I told Callie this afternoon about our trip to the Stork Club, her face lit up with the biggest smile I've seen on it to date —and that is saying something. She's a great one for smiling. Womanlike, her happiness quickly faded to anxiety about what she would wear.

I almost laughed, which would have done murder to her good mood.

I tried to convince her not to wear black—overmuch musing on Nalia turned my stomach sour on the subject of black dresses. I effectively silenced Callie on that point and coaxed her back into one of her kittenish, playful humors. This is her finest mood, and the one I love best, for then we have at it like boxers and exchange banter as if we were a pair of Wall Street brokers.

I was to pick her up at her apartment around nine-thirty. I arrived a few moments early and decided to wait in the lobby so I could fore-go paying the cabby extra for waiting at the curb. I may have plenty of money, but I'm far from a spend-thrift. Perhaps that is why I have plenty of money.

I am ashamed to admit it, but I had spent the afternoon puzzling and fretting over Nalia. Tell me, Tobias, why these women get under a man's skin like burrs? I began to think it was not a good idea to have her meet Callie. I am quite sensible of the fact that Nalia's life has been full of drama, sentimentality and heartbreak. I am not certain after all that a close acquaintance with her will be a good thing for Calida Harper.

I stepped into the lobby of Tarleton Apartments in a dim, dull humor, heart heavy with these thoughts. Jerry Atwood—that paragon of goodwill-toward-men—turned to me with a smile and stopped polishing his bell. "Mr. Barnett! How very very good to see you. Are you here to collect Miss Harper?"

"I am," I said, and felt my tension ebbing away. Here was good humor! Here was helpfulness. Here was a man of good sense and gentle qualities. "Is she down?"

Jerry smiled at me bravely. "Not yet. Not yet." It was a brave smile chiefly, I believe, because it was a generous one. I mentally shook hands with him for his noblesse oblige in letting me whisk away the woman he is as devoted to as if he was her Labrador Retriever.

We chatted for some moments and my opinion of his sense and my estimation of the fact that here, at last, I'd found another man of character (like you and me) deepened with each sentence. It was then in restored good humor that I found Miss Harper standing by.

She had turned herself out in black. Black dress, black shoes, black purse—and her eyes snapped black as if daring me to comment.

I took the bait. I admit.

That began what will certainly go down in our partnership as our longest, fiercest, and blackest argument. I lost my temper. I shouted. Wade Barnett and shouting don't pair in the same sentence. It just doesn't happen. Perhaps I am only getting old and this niminy-piminy chit shakes me up. She made me furious, and I made her furious, and I believe it's the most fun I've had in three years.

That woman has a spine.

She has a heart.

She gives me a run for my money, and jerks down the oddest mental alleyways right when you think you've got her pegged. I was forced to lay my heavy hand of "position" upon her before she entirely blew our cover at the Stork Club. People were watching us. They were noticing me and my impudent little scapegrace and you know how they talk.

Nalia was tame enough at the Club. Or perhaps I was absentminded—I am not certain which had the upper hand, though I managed to conduct the interview in whatever state we were in. Miss Harper's temper flared again toward the end, and I whisked her away earlier than usual.

I had had a brainstorm. I am a clever man, but such inspiration comes once in any man's life.

To cut a very long and winding story to a swift end, Tobias, Miss Harper and I forged tonight a 'Flint and Steel' compact— an agreement to use our wit and our brains in harmony to set a blaze in the country for *Ladybird Snippets*. I am not certain of anything, but I do have a suspicion my key motive was in legalizing the pleasant bantering so I could enjoy it without fear of neglecting more 'important' matters. Am I wrong in this?

Miss Harper, though evidently surprised at my proposition, agreed to it. We are, as I announced to her, 'Dixie whistling and Yankee Doodle dandying.' Fire and Gunpowder. I wonder how long before the explosion?

Your devoted friend,

Wade Barnett

Chapter 8

Callie:

The birth of our golden era was not unlike how I imagine a chick would feel while hatching from its shell—cramped into impossible positions, folded in on ourselves in a nature-defying manner, chipping away bit by bit till a pin-point of daylight showed into our darkness. One would assume that by "Golden Era" a person means a time of plenitude and wealth and ease. Not so for us. Our Golden Era meant that we spent a deal of time digging and panning and polishing what bits we did chip from the rocks of the professional life. When it came time to cash in—or send our first issue to print—my partner and I dropped the packet off together. We swaggered into the print-shop and handed over the final draft with much pomp and circumstance.

"Take care you pay attention to the page-numbering," Mr. Barnett warned the man at the desk.

"Of course, Mr. B."

"Oh—and make sure the margins are straight—the last proof copy was crooked," I added.

"Of course."

"And don't use glossy," Mr. Barnett said.

"Of course."

"A glossy publication always sours my stomach." Mr. Barnett turned to me. "It seems to make a great show of promising everything and delivering nothing. Besides—it's impossible to draw in afterward, and I know how disappointing that is to a child." He laughed. "Did you ever flip through magazines just to draw mustaches on the women and bouffant hairstyles on the men, Miss Harper?"

My cheek muscles were sore from smiling so much already. "Of course I did." But I failed to add to it that I still doodled on the pictures when the mood arose.

Mr. Barnett tipped his hat far back on his head, rubbed his forehead with his cambric handkerchief and grinned. "Thanks for the help, Badger. We'll see you around."

"Right, Mr. B." The man, Badger, grinned at the two of us. "You'd think you was a young married couple sendin' your first kid off t'school the way you're both grinnin'."

Startled, I stared at the paperweight on the print-shop desk and dared not look up.

Mr. Barnett chuckled. "I think I would feel a deal less nervous if it *was* a child. A child need only please a small pool of people…*Ladybird Snippets* needs to please the world."

"And I'm sure it'll be great," Badger smacked the desk with his palms and stood. "Well, I'd better get this down to the boys. You have a nice day, Mr. B. You too, Miss Harper."

Mr. Barnett and I sauntered out of the building. The sun lay warm across my neck as we turned back onto Park Row and ambled up the sidewalk toward City Hall, out of sync with the rest of the world's go-getter pace.

"I'm glad that's over," I said. My heart continuously shredded and patched back up again with anxiety and euphoria. I wasn't sure how much longer I'd have been able to last. For better or for worse our magazine had gone to print and there was nothing left to do but wait. Besides—happiness had the top-hand at present.

Mr. Barnett shrugged out of his coat and draped it over his arm. "I'm glad too."

Euphoria fell to the bottom and nerves rose to the top again. "But I'm sure I'll find some dreadful mistake when it comes out," I fretted. "I'll have spelled a dozen words wrong in one paragraph, or have broken all the most elementary rules of grammar..."

"Tell me, Callie, are you in the habit of spelling poorly?"

"Well...no." I wouldn't say it to him, but I rather prided myself on my ability to spell words like "different" and "separate" and "independent" without replacing the E's with A's and vice-versa.

"And do you often slip up with your grammar?"

"...yes."

"Well, I suppose that can't be helped." Mr. Barnett laughed. "But at present I feel merry as a wedding bell over our prospects. *Ladybird Snippets* is an official magazine now, and I do believe she'll have a fabulous take-off."

Taking off wasn't my concern. But how long she'd manage to fly...now that was the rub. The longer we spent assembling the magazine—collecting bits of news, writing our stories, rummaging for fillers—the more I wondered if this conglomeration would appeal to anyone in America. A biologist himself would have a difficult time classifying our *magnum opus*. It wasn't a men's magazine, it wasn't a women's magazine, it wasn't a children's magazine. It wasn't for the outdoors, it wasn't for the indoors, it wasn't for the old or the young or the in-between.

"Do you think anyone will buy it?" I asked.

"What an idea, Miss Harper." We walked past the City Hall buildings and into the park, fenced by its wrought-iron palings. Mr. Barnett pulled me toward one of the benches—the same I'd sat on with Mr. Scarrowby. "I think everyone will buy it because…"

"Because it's for no one?" I finished.

"Well, yes and no. It's not *particularly* for anybody, but that makes it all the more appealing. We'll reach such a wide array of people."

"And you think it'll sell." I sat beside him and slung my arm across the back of the bench.

Mr. Barnett shifted to look at me. "Why the doubts now?"

I smoothed my skirt and gave a short laugh. "You know as well as I that if I wanted a paycheck I couldn't afford to have doubts. I had to go along with your craziness."

"Aha. Well, I suppose we'll have to see. For now—charity."

"Charity?" I watched with an eyebrow raised as Mr. Barnett fumbled in his coat pocket. He brought forth a small, greasy paper bag and unrolled the top.

"For the birds." He grabbed my wrist, tilting my palm upward and pouring into it a handful of seeds.

Birdseed? No way anyone in New York City was gonna watch me scattering crumbs to fat, overfed pigeons—or whatever they were. I couldn't think of anything more ridiculous. I tried to dump the mess back into the bag but managed to do nothing but spill it down my shirt and into my shoes. The lines at the corners of Mr. Barnett's mouth tightened and he rolled his eyes.

"Callie—"

"I'm so sorry!" I brushed the seed from my skirt and watched in desperation as it followed the rest into my high-heels.

Mr. Barnett took my hand in his fingers, and I realized just how warm and vibrant his touch was. How I wished some of his vividry would ebb into me! In his presence, I gloried in the warmth of our clashes and battles of wit but the moment I was alone my heart chilled.

The introspection brought the blood to my face, and I tried to remove my hand from his.

The response of his touch was just strong enough, just gentle enough to make me want to linger there. "Now, Callie, let's try this again. I thought they'd have taught you how to feed birds back in grammar-school."

How strangely the lightness of his tone contrasted with the confusion of my mind! He poured the seeds and nodded at a curious band of sparrows and pigeons nearby. I kept my eyes on the varied hues of brown, unable to withdraw myself from the oddity of this moment.

"Are you going to make the poor creatures attack you for it?" He winked at the bold, brassy cluster of birds. One pert fellow took a hop or two forward and considered me with his head to one side.

"Attack me for—?"

"The food, Mary Poppins. I doubt you need a lesson in throwing seeds?"

"Of course not." I straightened and tried to recall the last time I'd sat in a park feeding birds. Funny. I couldn't recall ever having done such a thing. I hesitated a moment, took a pinch of the food and tossed it away with an awkward gesture, then hid my hand in my skirt afterward, feeling ashamed and exposed.

Mr. Barnett tossed his seeds and laughed when the little creatures overcame their polite hesitation and began to scrabble like heavy-weight champions over the food. He gave me a sidelong look then sat back. The brim of his hat shaded his eyes but I could see the laughing-color lingering there. "What's wrong?"

"Wrong? Why should anything be wrong?"

"Because you look horridly angry."

"I've a right to look anything I want." I felt that vexing desire to cry and refrained from doing so by tilting my face away from that warm, fascinating man and setting my jaw.

"Are not two sparrows sold for a farthing? And one of them shall not fall on the ground without your Father's knowledge."

Mr. Barnett's words came to me from afar and inspired some vague sense of familiarity deep within me which I rebelled against. We were speaking of fathers…*again*. Something I never wanted to waste a thought on for a single moment more in my life. I hated that subject with a perfect hatred, and my horrid mood simmered a degree or two hotter.

"Miss Harper—what is the matter? Admit it, or risk a personal admission that your usual state is a foul humor. I must have the one or the other, for if you're not all right than you certainly must be all wrong."

"Your philosophy does you credit." I felt ridiculous, using that haughty edge in my tone. "You've firmed up my opinion of you as a man entirely out of touch with reality and ignorant of every concern of normal people.

He pulled back and the laughing-light died. "I see you feel free to express your opinions of me. I like that." (It seemed to me that he didn't like it at all.) "But whether they are correct appraisals, or merely honest ones, remains to be seen."

"I think they're both," I said, my nose in the air.

"That is merely your opinion."

"Aren't I entitled to my opinions?"

"You may be, but that in no way makes them infallibly correct."

I tossed my head. "They are a great deal truer than you'd think."

"Well I don't think about your opinions. My own occupy my time sufficiently," he said, and the hint of humor in his voice was laced with sarcasm.

So now Mr. Barnett was angry with me. How miserable could a girl get before she died? The sparrows twittered around us and squabbled over the food. The remainder of seed in my palm was sticky and damp from the tight clamp of my fist. I dumped it onto the concrete and brushed the last bits from my skin. "I don't know about the sparrows falling," I said half to myself, half to him, "but my Dad always laughed when I fell."

My heart seized and I hiccupped—the precursor to a storm of weeping if I didn't take care. I saw my father bleak and handsome with that eternally smudged flannel shirt he'd been so fond of...*laughing*, one hand extended toward me to help me from my tumble. "He'd pick me up, but he'd laugh first."

I hugged myself and bit back tears. I don't know why the memory killed me, but it did. A hot, pulsing ball of pain rose in my stomach and burned under my lungs till I had to fight for breath enough to go on. "Dads are supposed to be sympathetic, right? They're supposed to feel your hurt. Not make fun of you."

Something told me I'd never tell Mr. Barnett any of this if I was in my right mind. Something warned I'd be sorry tonight for this outburst of furious confidence. But for now I had a need to spit that bitter memory from my mouth and reach out to the simple warmth of this man beside me. *The guy you just read the Riot Act to. You're such a charmer, Callie. You're such a beautiful girl, aren't you? So smooth and winsome with the men.* And the gargoyles of my past pointed fingers and laughed like my father at the irony.

"Mmm."

We fell into a deep, bottomless silence. Any words I ought to have said lodged in my throat and would not come out.

He bent his head over clasped hands. "What would you say if I told you….that I understand how you feel?"

"I wouldn't believe you."

"All right." He drew his breath between his teeth and held it for a moment, then let it out with a whoosh. "What if I told you I was praying for you?"

The idea took me so much off guard I glanced over either shoulder as if frightened God Almighty might have heard my wretched thoughts. "Right now?"

"Well, yes. And later. If I told you that I will be praying for you. What would you say?"

It wasn't a challenge, just a quiet question—quiet enough that my heart only thumped a little faster instead of pelting away like a frightened rabbit with a fox on her tail as it usually did when any mention of God came up. "I…don't think it'll work."

"I do."

"Why?" The question came out before I had time to catch it and pull it to a stop. I felt like slapping myself and would have if it wouldn't mean looking utterly stupid.

Mr. Barnett smiled. "Because prayer is the best way to set a wrong thing right again. Admitting I don't have the answers. Asking the One who does for a bit of clarity. Putting myself back in my proper place in the universe."

He certainly put a lot of stock in a few whispered words. We were silent again for a bit. I twined my fingers in and out of each other and made the motions for the little 'here is the church' game I had played as a baby long ago. So many questions. So many things unexplained. I fought against the one question that had bothered me for eons. I'd never spoken it aloud…never dared. I had a vague fear of electrocution if I allowed the question to escape my lips. But perhaps Mr. Barnett would know the answer and I'd not have to lay awake at night over it any longer. Well, it would have out sometime:

"Why on earth do people believe in a myth?" I asked. "Religion is a waste of time."

Mr. Barnett reacted nothing like I supposed he would, having his god insulted to his very face. He tipped his head to one side, puckered his eyebrows, and nodded his head. "I agree with you. Religion is a waste of time."

If I'd been standing I believe I would have taken a step or two backward. As it is, I leaned forward and clasped my hands till my knuckles popped. "What?"

"Religion as such—for the purpose of feeling holy and following a list of rules because some dead, obscure god says to —is a terrible waste of a man's time and resources."

My mind reeled with so many questions and startles I could find nothing to say. I kept my eyes fixed on Mr. Barnett's face, waiting for an explanation.

He inclined his head with a fleeting smile. "But we've lost sight of the true bottom-line of Christianity. We are wretched. He is glorious. We've ruined it and He's willing to put us back together. It's not a religion formed on useless practices."

"It's…not?"

"It's wonderfully complex—we don't need to go through it all now, but you must realize that there is as much relationship mixed up in the religion as there is religion in the relationship. You can't extricate one from the other in Christianity— impossible. Every other 'religion' on the face of the earth is one-dimensional and entirely devoid of personal contact with the deity. The god sits in the corner of the house behind an offering of molding bread." He motioned at the stone figure of a Greek maiden inhabiting the park fountain. "Or the god is a vague, twisted shadow-thought only to be reached by deep, tortuous meditation. Jesus—Christianity—on the other hand…well quite frankly, it's radical. A Trinity. A three-stranded cord that is apart from and…and above and under and *in* everything of this world and out of it. We are able to have a personal relationship with Jesus because He is. He was. He will be. I know it's hard to imagine."

That was the understatement of the century.

He shifted an inch or two closer. "But just think. Why do we love stories? Why are we addicted to knowing what happened? Because we are part of a Story. A drama. We were made for something more than this—we are always seeing glimpses, hearing news, feeling breezes from the Ever-after. And because we do not acknowledge that we are beings—souls—created for eternity, we are left with an empty ache. We refuse to see our

Story and thus we lead empty half-lives, under the shadow of a longing for something—*Someone*—we push away."

"See? Sounds like a Greek myth," I said. I had to say something. I didn't enjoy this enthralling monologue. I found myself curious and it bothered me. I would not ask another question. I wanted this interview to end. I would not. I would—

"But how do you know it's not all a story made up by some deranged philosophers ages ago?" *Great going. You've just prolonged the torture. You know he's going to explain.*

"'Faith is the substance of things hoped for; the evidence of things yet unseen.'" His smile softened as if he laughed in some deep, inner place in him that I'd never discovered within myself. "It's a concoction of proof, faith, and a bit of 'if not this, what then?' I take it on faith that God cannot lie and what He says in His word about Himself is unerringly true. I look at the history of the Christian church—surely something built on myth would have died under the pressure and persecution the Christ-followers have endured over the centuries? I look at Paul—author of many books of the Bible—and how he is considered one of the greatest philosophers of all time. I look at my own life and the changes that have occurred. What do I see?"

He paused and the concerto of the city played around us. Taxis and horns and thousands of voices. Somewhere a dog protested to its owner and behind that someone practiced a violin. The sparrows twittered on the grass nearby, and the water poured from the Greek maiden's jar into the stone basin at her feet.

Against my better judgment, I took a breath and asked the question: "What do you see?"

"I see a life so much fuller, sweeter, more purposeful than any other that I wonder why so few embrace it. We humans worry about our lives and our plans for our lives—to know Christ loves me. Has a plan and guidance for me? It comes with a peace the wealthiest of us can't buy. To know there is an After? An epilogue to my story? Or—and this is the best part of it—to know there is *a story to come*. Perhaps, Miss Harper, we're only living the prologue. Fancy that."

I didn't fancy it. I didn't like this uprooting of my old prejudices and replacing them with new thoughts and ideas and questions...things I'd rather not have considered at all because they upset the already ticklish regime of my philosophy.

Moving on from this discomfiting world of uncertainties, I thought now as good a time as any to both show him I had not adopted his thoughts on the matter, and to bring up something about *Ladybird Snippets* that had been shifting in my mind for some time. I repositioned myself, smoothed my skirt, and assumed a light, almost jovial mood. "Mr. Barnett, I know this sounds horrid to say out loud—especially after our late conversation—but I meant to speak of it before and forgot. I found a problem with our magazine."

He cocked his head and raised an eyebrow. "A problem? I wish you'd told me before we sent it to the printer."

I blushed. "Not that kind of a problem...a problem in content."

"Well?"

"Well...we don't have anything remotely....racy."

"Ah." Displeasure throbbed in his tones, but I saw he made an effort to conceal it.

I tossed my hands and shrugged. "I mean, we don't have anything popular. Why—even that little romance I wrote could hardly be called exciting. There's not anything in *Ladybird Snippets* that would...well...raise an eyebrow."

I anticipated an explosion, but Mr. Barnett said nothing for some time. We sat in the park and the world whished around us with that strange concert of city noises.

"Miss Harper, do you ever wonder?"

"Wonder what?"

"What our generation has come to."

"Goodness." I fanned myself against the midday heat, to no avail. It was almost as hot as my old office. "I'm hardly old enough to be speaking of 'our generation' as if it was a thing of the past. I deem it a good idea never to question the present; it muddles one's head so."

I chipped at the bench's green paint with my nail and made bold with my eyes at Mr. Barnett. I was certainly not going to be coerced into discussing philosophy yet again, not five minutes after I'd sat through a lecture on Christianity. He chewed his lip for a moment, made as if to speak then paused. A soft, hot breeze ran between us and beads of sweat stood out on his forehead.

He tried again: "Callie, if you never think of the present then you can never do a thing about the future. The future's just made up on dozens of right-nows strung together."

"Let's not be disparaging, Mr. Barnett. I am not in the mood." The jaunty tune of Glenn Miller's popular song of the same title sprang into my mind. It reminded me of Mr. Barnett's boast about dancing. "However, I do think we must do something about that dance you promised me."

"Now?"

I rolled my eyes and stood. "Of course not now. What do you take me for? Doris and Bette dropped by the apartment the other day—they said Jules and some of the other kids are going dancing with them tomorrow night. It'll be fun!"

"Are you sure you want to go dancing? We might quarrel again." But his eyes twinkled at me and I knew I'd won him over.

I put my hands on my waist and my lips quirked into an arch smile. "First off, you claim you're a wonderful dancer, and I am tired to death of men with two left feet. Second, we'll research for a piece about innocent diversions like dancing so that all those prudish, proper Nobodys who are sure to buy our magazine will have something to amuse them. Third and most important, I find that appearing at a nightclub on the arm of Mr. Wade Barnett will silence all those little backbiters at *The Post* more efficiently than would any number of critically-acclaimed articles."

Mr. Barnett stood too and wandered to the gate of the park with his hands in his pockets. I trailed behind and slipped through the gate when he opened it. "Miss Harper, seeing that you have made your intentions so clear—and because I know how it is to be the food of local gossips—I will consent to go out dancing tomorrow night."

"Good!"

We wandered toward Annamaria's café, and as we neared the place, my common sense caught up with me and showed me what a bold stroke I'd taken.

I swallowed the lump in my throat and tried my voice: "I daresay you think me a bit of a fast girl for asking you out." I avoided my companion's eyes, but a moment of silence forced me to look up.

His smile was gentle but had that lurking mockery about it that had started to make my heart flop like a dizzy goldfish. "The thought did cross my mind," he said.

"Well it's not that way, Mr. Barnett. You know that. I was only…" I turned my eyes to my adorable red sling-back heels and blushed.

"Making a suggestion?"

"Yes." There—he knew what I meant. He was only provoking me. What an ogre.

"I agree to go dancing tomorrow night on one condition." He caught my arm and swung me around to face him.

The boyish laughter in his eyes disarmed me. He wasn't America's most famous journalist, nor was he my employer. He was just a normal fellow with his tie askew, his hair blowing in the city-breeze, and a joke up his shirtsleeve.

"What are the conditions?" I asked.

"You simply cannot wear black."

"Provoking toad."

"Nefarious chit."

"What color would you have me wear?"

He held the door of Annamaria's open for me and I stepped backward over the threshold to keep an eye on his face, so absorbed was I in hearing this man give fashion advice to a sophisticated young lady like me.

"Wear yellow," he said.

"Yellow?"

"Yes, yellow. Why not yellow?"

I laughed. "You are incorrigible."

"Why *not* yellow?" he persisted.

"Because no one wears yellow."

"All the more reason to wear it then. Upon my life I can't understand why everyone wants to be so blasé. If I were a woman I would never wear dark, drab colors. They drag a person down—add years to her life and make her look altogether used-up. I already told you that, though you thought me an old stick in the mud for it. Miss Independence must do things her own way, even to the ruination of an otherwise perfectly pretty face."

I took my seat at our customary table. "I'm glad to see your thoughts on how half the women in New York City dress," I remarked with some measure of coldness penetrating my voice. It was stupid and senseless for a man to attempt to understand these things. Who did Mr. Barnett think himself anyway? Kay Thompson? "And what about Nalia Crostincinni? She wore black and you seemed enamored with her."

His voice was grim: "Black suits Nalia. It fits her profession, her complexion, and her life."

"Her life?"

"It won't come as a surprise to you, Miss Harper, to realize that most women of fame and fortune have led somewhat... dramatic lives." Before I had a chance to think that statement over, Mr. Barnett had unfolded his napkin and he pointed a fork at me. "But you, Miss Harper. You're a rare one. You ought never to wear anything but brilliant colors. What are you trying to do? Squirrel yourself away in obscurity? Hide the real Calida Harper from the world?"

Ah, now Mr. Barnett, you hit too close to the mark. I spread my napkin in my lap. "I'll wear yellow," I said, "But only because I want to."

"Oh, of course. We must have our independence, Callie, mustn't we?"

This man would eat the very heart out of me. Why must he be so shrewd? It gave him such a villainous advantage over me in our sparring-matches. But I would not let him put me in a foul humor again—the triumph of sending our first issue to print still flavored the very air I breathed and was not much tainted by that momentary quivering of spirit in the park.

I raised my glass of tonic-water and smiled at Mr. Barnett. "To independence, to Ladybird Snippets, and to the fashion sense of a journalist," I teased.

Mr. Barnett raised his glass in reply. "And to Miss Harper, who views the world from all angles and never tells a man where she'll lash out next."

"L'Chaim!"

"L'Chaim!"

We clinked glasses and downed the sparkling water.

"You two actin' stranger and stranger dese days," Annamaria remarked. Her breath came in short, comfortable wheezes as she trundled from the area behind the counter out to us carrying our lunches. Already the worthy woman had learned that what I liked to eat I liked best, and what I liked best I chose every time.

"I believe we're somewhat intoxicated, Annamaria," Mr. Barnett said.

She rolled her eyes. "An' it's only lunchtime."

"Not in that fashion." Mr. Barnett laughed. "We've tasted the giddy wine of triumph and it's gone to our heads."

"Though we're not certain it's a triumph," I reminded him.

The puppyish furrow returned to his brow and his eyes crinkled in a smile under it. "No. We're not certain...and that's half the fun. The lure of the hunt, right, Miss Harper?"

I raised my glass a second time. "To the hunt. And may the odds ever be in our favor."

Chapter 9

My daffodil-colored skirt brushed against Mr. Barnett's leg as we entered the front door of Alegre Noches the following evening. I wore so many starched petticoats under this gown that I stood out in all directions like a cupcake—impractical, but cute. And what was fashion for but to assure that you were pleasing to the eye? "Sorry—this skirt…"

"It's fine."

The Latin-music from the band on the floor sped into my veins and set me to smiling. Mr. Barnett hung back, waiting for me to lead the way. He might be the dark-haired child of the Stork Club, but Alegre Noches and I had a long history together. It was the first club I'd ever been to when I came to live here, and that faint strain of Spanish heritage that helped me get a good tan sprang to life each time I entered the club.

I handed a waiter my light wrap and fluffed the cluster of buttercups at my waist. "They're lovely," I said, noticing his eyes upon them. "Thanks."

"Well, I had to think of something to complete the audacity of your evening-dress. No one wears yellow, Miss Harper? Well I can assure you that you are the only woman in New York City wearing common field-flowers for a corsage."

"I'm becoming quite a rebel, am I not, Mr. Barnett?"

He only smiled and nodded toward the dance-floor. "Where are we supposed to meet these friends of yours?"

I took in the room at a glance, and shrugged, chin high and breast swelling. This was my element. Here I was known and knew everyone in return. I had everyone under my finger after a fashion. A knot of young men wandered by and tipped their hats.

"Lookin' sweet, isn't she boys?" the tallest of the trio said.

I laughed. "Thanks, Will."

The short one with the Irish accent winked at me. "Make sure you save me a dance, sweetheart, aye?"

"Oh, go find some other girl to bother, Jamie."

"Aye, but you're bein' the only girl worth dancin' with in the room."

"In that case I suppose I must reward your gallantry." I tossed a buttercup to him which he caught, kissed, and tucked in the band of his hat.

I tossed my head and caught Mr. Barnett's eye. My cheeks burned under the curiosity of that gaze. "What? Stop looking at me like that."

"Like what? I'm only curious."

"Well don't be. Try to box up your journalistic curiosity for one night and enjoy yourself."

"I *am* enjoying myself."

I ripped my arm out of his and rolled my eyes. "Then let me enjoy myself and stop staring at me as if you'd never seen me before. You've spent weeks with Callie Harper."

"Not this Callie Harper."

"Well, you played your little trick at the Stork Club, and I'm playing mine here. You certainly aren't vain enough to think you're the only human alive who can play the charmer on occasion?" I wrested myself away from his presence and darted forward to meet Doris and Bette. "Girls! I'm so glad you're here, darlings. I've brought you a surprise."

"A surprise?" Doris opened her eyes wide and blinked them in that sleepy, sultry way she had.

Bette bounced on her toes and giggled—I hated giggling. "Gee, I love surprises. Is it flowers?"

"Better than flowers," I said. I caught sight of that old cad, Jules, close on the heels of his devotees. "I've brought you Wade Barnett."

"Wade Barnett?!" I wished Doris didn't have to squeal in that insipid manner, but her eyes flew open wider than ever and she turned them over my shoulder to where my companion waited, a few yards away. "Is that him?"

"Yes, but hush, Doris. You don't have to shout about it."

Bette linked arms with Doris and they pressed close to me. "*Gosh* he's handsome."

"Look at those eyes."

"And he came with *you?*"

"He came with me." I laughed but somehow my discomfort grew at a rapid rate alongside their excitement. "Look, girls, I'll introduce you but you have to promise me something."

"What?"

"You won't commandeer him."

"Who's talking about commandeering? We're not that silly."

"Indeed." I motioned for the miniature fan-club and Jules to follow me then delivered them to my companion. "Mr. Barnett, you know Jules. Here are Bette Flannigan and Doris Delaney."

Mr. Barnett said all the proper things, complimented the girls on their appearance, and exchanged a cold stare with Jules whom, I assumed, was none too pleased with this transfer of his ladies' affections. We chatted about nothing for several minutes before the band struck up an especially danceable tune. I turned to Mr. Barnett with a brilliant smile, intending to catch an invitation for the first dance. After all, he'd only agreed to come tonight to prove me wrong about his penchant for dancing. He nodded his head and started forward when Jules slipped in front of him.

"Hey Cal—how about a dance?" Before I had a chance to answer—indeed, before I'd even got over the astonishment of Jules asking me—his arm was around my waist and he'd twirled me out to the floor.

"What do you think you're doing?" I hissed.

"Dancing with a very fortunate woman."

I could cope with this. I composed myself and smiled into his eyes. "How polite of you."

The lamplight shone on his well-oiled, waved hair, and obscured the depths of his eyes so that I could not read what lay in that dark blue haze. The girls had always been crazy about Jules—funny, how I'd never found him much to my liking. His arm was warm around my waist as we wound through the other couples on the dance floor.

He bent his eyes on me with a sultry smile. "I read the proof of your magazine this morning."

"Yeah?"

"Yeah. It was pretty good."

"Thank you." This was puzzling; Jules was never known for his diplomacy—even among notoriously undiplomatic reporters. "What's the game, Jules?

"The game, Cal?"

"Yeah the game. You don't do polite. You don't give compliments."

"Can't a fella change sometimes?"

"Doubtful…in your case."

"Cruel Miss Harper, trifling with the heart of every man who swears devotion to her." His eyes caught a glint of the lamplight which then burned there as if his very soul had kindled with something fierce and unnerving.

I pulled away, but his determined arm still held me fast. Instead I met his intense gaze with a stone-weighted stare. How I despised his handsome, ad-ready face. "What are you getting at?"

"You know as well as I do. Shores ought to have given the job to me."

"Isn't that Shores' business?" If only Jules knew the reasons behind Mr. Shores' choice of me, he might be relieved he'd not been the chosen one.

"You could have refused, Callie."

"Oh, now come off it, Jules. You think I would have given this job over to you? You were already Mr. Shores' favorite. The editor's pet. The golden boy who got all the gigs." My breath was a tight knot in my chest. The Latin-beat pulsed through my body as we swung toward the band and then away from it.

"I'm *The Post's* lap-dog, nothing else, Cal."

"And I suppose that's my fault as well."

"I see it that way."

"Well, what do you want me to do?"

"I want you to rescue my career."

"Your career."

"Mine...yes."

"Oh...I hadn't noticed it had grown big enough to get into trouble. My, how time flies."

His cheeks were passion-red and from the sharp angle his jaw made, I knew he was clenching his teeth with all the fierceness of a crocodile. "You're cozy with Barnett. I want you to find dirt on him," he said.

"On Mr. Barnett? Honestly, Jules, you are a mad-man."

"I want you to find out anything you can about him. Anything at all. And when you do find something, tell me."

"You aren't a very good gambler, are you, honey?" I drew closer to him so my mouth was at his ear and I could pour every ounce of malice I possessed straight into his soul. "Because if you think I like you well enough to do any favor for you, much less that one, then you belong in Bedlam."

I expected some retaliation, but Jules only swung me out to the fierce rhythm of the dance, twisted, and pulled me close again. When I looked into his face I found a frightening calmness etched on the chiseled features. "I knew you'd say that. But you aren't holding the aces this time."

My stomach was being stuck with a thousand needles. My heart took a plunge over Niagara Falls. I clung to Jules only because the anticipation of what he might say took all the strength out of my body and left me trembling like a cottonwood leaf. Golden was the lamplight, brass were the instruments, yellow was my dress, and Jules' smile was twisted with bronze as he bent his head toward me.

"I know all about your father and Fleetwood…the whole deal."

Chapter 10

It was moments like these the tragic poets sang of. Moment like these that made Dickens and Tolstoy the men they were. The correct response to a threat was, I thought, to retort with something witty, make a gay repartee and continue on as if nothing had happened. But time had suspended movement and Jules' words seemed to come to me from an ancient distance, bleached a brittle white. I pushed against his chest, willing him to let me go.

"You are too bold, Jules," I managed to gasp out.

"Ah. So this does seal it. You'll give in?"

"Never."

"Never's a long time, honey. You just think about it." And he let me go and cut in on Bette's partner so that I stood by myself on the dance floor with my world shattering around me. He knew? How could he know? But there was a horrible gravity in the announcement of his knowledge that caused me to understand this was no petty bluffer I dealt with. Jules knew and suddenly my tattered past rose up before me, mocking.

"Callie? Are you okay?" Mr. Barnett's voice was the only bit of reality that seeped into my numbed mind.

I turned to him and caught his arm for support. "I don't feel well."

"And no wonder with that fellow spinning you like sixty. May I have this waltz?"

"No. Really—I need to go."

His face fell but he recovered quickly. "Right. Shall I call a cab?"

"No—no thanks. I think a walk will do me good."

"Then let me walk you home."

"Really there's no need."

"If you don't let me I'll shadow you."

I managed a weak smile past my whirling thoughts. "You're a darling. All right—so you can walk me home."

As I waited for Mr. Barnett to fetch my wrap I watched the easy-running crowd of friends I'd made in Alegre Noches. All of them so carefree and extravagant and bent on pleasant pastimes and pleasanter people. Jamie O'Toole approached, hands spread and head cocked. "Will you be givin' me that dance, luv?"

"Not tonight, Jamie. Sorry."

We exchanged a few further pleasantries but my mind continued on its hamster-wheel. If only Jamie knew everything. If only every person in this room knew from where I'd come and what my family was like. It was a thing I'd buried upon arriving at college, and a thing I'd since slaved to erase from my own memory. It was why I spent all my time buried in the heart of the city and why even the sight of those wilting buttercups at my waist chilled me now.

"Jamie?" I paused and smiled at him—so jolly and puckish. "Have you ever wondered what it would be like at a masquerade if everyone suddenly removed their masks and could see each other for who we really were?"

"Not much. And what would you be wantin' to see the real person for? The whole point of the game is to be appearin' like someone else."

That was the point wasn't it? Life was just a ten-penny masquerade—mine more than most—and if I didn't give Jules what he wanted he'd tear my mask from my face and let the world see the woman who truly lay behind the mask of Calida Harper. My lips trembled and I bit them to keep the tears back.

"It's a masquerade, darlin'," Jamie said with a wink. "Everyone's actin' like someone else." He stepped back onto the dance floor and the crowd consumed him.

Mr. Barnett was at my side a moment later and draped the wrap around my shoulders. "Are you ready to go, Miss Harper?"

"Yes, thanks."

The doorman let us out onto the relative quiet of the darkened street, and the dusk proved as an antidote to my rattled nerves. A night breeze had blown away the day's heat and the city was quiet in this hour when everyone was either abed or about his own business. We were in no hurry as we walked the mile toward my apartment, and our feet made gentle echoes against the hushed buildings along the sidewalk.

"I hate that man," I said at last.

"Which man?"

"Jules the Conqueror."

"Ah. Him."

Somehow I felt protected from my past with Mr. Barnett at my side and the city slumberous and quiet about.

"I did notice," Mr. Barnett said a moment later, "That he took possession of you in a bold manner—I didn't like that."

"Yes, he did rather, didn't he? But it is Jules' way to be dictatorial: he never fancies someone might have wishes other than his own."

Mr. Barnett tipped his hat far back on his head and shoved his hands in his pockets. "We never did have that dance, did we, Miss Harper?"

"No."

"There's a masquerade at the Stork Club in two weeks—want to go then?"

I laughed—the cold mass where my stomach should have been grew heavier still. "We'll have to see about that. It seems I'm not much good at a masquerade."

Mr. Barnett looked sideways at me and bumped me with his elbow. "Why the singularly morose tone of voice?" The lightness of his own tone told me that he was relaxed and happy—content, even. Such a paradox to my own mood. But I couldn't tell Mr. Barnett about Jules' conversation. After all—it closely concerned him and I still hadn't made up my mind on the point. I needed a chat with Nickleby. A chat and a load of chocolate.

We stopped at the front of my building and Mr. Barnett took his hands from his pockets. "I'm sorry you didn't get your chance, Callie."

"My…chance?"

"To find some dirt on me."

My heart froze and the blood drained from my face. How could he have heard? "What are you talking about?" I asked as a cover, dreading to hear the inevitable.

"You don't recall your boast to prove me a liar about being a good dancer?"

"Oh, that?" I shrugged and manufactured a dazzling smile. "We'll reconcile that point later." I stuck out my hand which Mr. Barnett took in one of his own huge palms. "Thanks for walking me home."

"Thanks for inviting me."

But I fled from his presence without another word because I could not meet the honesty in his face when so much of my heart and mind calculated the price of exposing him.

The night watchman had relieved Jerry of his duties so I didn't have to run that gauntlet, but when I reached my room I bolted the door and leaned against it, breathing hard. Nickleby looked around and gave me a cold stare, then returned to the all-consuming business of grooming himself. "We've been exposed, Nickleby."

He continued aligning every hair just so and ignored me.

"Jules gave me a cruel either-or back at the club. Now I have a bit of sympathy for Marguerite Blakeney. Jules says that if I don't play tattle-tale with Mr. Barnett and give him something to sink his fangs into he's gonna tell the world about Dad and Fleetwood. How would that color my career? Pink. I'd get the pink slip, Nicks."

At last I'd got Nickleby's attention. He dropped to the floor with a drubbing purr and joined me where I had sunk into my battered armchair. "Life is so unfair."

Nickleby pushed his cold nose against my face and started to clean me.

I pushed him off. "If I was famous already the world might wink at my past. But now? It'll ruin all my chances. And what will Mr. Barnett think of me?" That idea hit me with the force of a nuke bomb coming down on my head. Either course I took would gain his displeasure. If I did give Jules what he looked for I'd earn Mr. Barnett's contempt. If I didn't help Jules then everything would be spilled and I'd still earn Mr. Barnett's contempt.

"Do you know, Nickleby, I think it a very hard thing to have to choose between being despised by one person or despised by the world? I'm not used to being thought of as a drub."

I pulled off my earrings and my necklace and stashed them in the chocolate-dish, then went into the bedroom and changed into my pajamas. After a glare at myself in the mirror, I returned to the chair and hugged my legs as if all the security left in the world was that little space between my arms. I closed my eyes and despite my horror of reliving the old days, my mind took off down that path and I knew I could not deter this parade of memories any longer. They swarmed over me like so many ants, stinging and biting as they came...

My mind winged back to my girlhood and the familiar mountain settlement. It was always autumn in my memories—bright, copper-winged autumn with wood-smoke purpling the distances and the cloying scent of windfalls fermenting beneath the trees. I thought of the bluff, strapping boys half-grown to manhood who had been my playmates in the manner a pack of wolf-pups might frolic with a kitten, and of the dangerous give and take of our parents as they maneuvered the tempest-tossed waters of backwoods friendships.

Dad had left when I was two—yes—but it was not till I was eighteen and leaving Wexford for college that Tristan told me the truth of why he left.

In the keeping of mountain tradition and the growing demand for bootleg liquor during the Prohibition-era, Dad and many of the other men of Wexford settlement had been moonshiners. I knew that, though it was never spoken of.

But I recalled perfectly every inflection of Trist's voice as we sat on our grandmother's cabin porch and discussed our plans for our lives. Eighteen years old and naive as an infant, I sat on the porch in the light of noonday with a glass of honey lemonade in one hand and my college acceptance letter in the other. Tristan lazed back in a rocker behind me but he held a strand of my long hair in his fingers and he twisted it now and then as if it was a cord that connected us.

"I'm gonna miss you, Cal," he said.

"Yeah. But if I wasn't goin' off to college I'd have to see you join up and move out with the Army."

"So you're letting me say the goodbyes."

"That's right." I shifted a bit so I could see Tristan's face, and he smiled at me, holding that strand of my hair and looping it around his fingers like he'd never let me go. A shadow passed between us in that moment and it struck me all I'd miss when I left our mountain. Beads of ice-sweat dropped off my glass onto Tristan's knee like tears and made damp spots on the worn cotton. I placed my fingers there and looked up at my brother. "Seems like people don't stay the same anymore. We're always moving away or getting married, aren't we?"

"Seems like, Callie-girl."

"I'll be sorry to go…y'know that, don't you?"

"Maybe." But his blue eyes were full of smile-bits and they laughed at me.

I punched Trist's leg and frowned. "Don't you laugh at me, Tristan Harper. I do like it here…but it hasn't exactly been an easy life."

"Life ain't easy, chicken. But it's what we've all gotta live through."

"I know that well as you, but it might have been a heap easier if…well…" I hated to speak of it, knowing that any discussion of Dad made Tristan angry. Mother had married Gerald Tallivore—a bum who did nothing but drink brandy and shoot turkeys—when I was fifteen, and ever since conversation about Dad had been rarer and more painful. But the words had to come out. I didn't know when I'd get another chance with me going off to college and Tristan joining the military. "Things wouldn't have been so hard if Dad had stayed around."

Tristan plaited my hair and formed it like a ring around his finger. "But he didn't stay. He couldn't."

The way he said the last bit made the hair rise on my arms. It was like a mirror in an old house clouded with cobwebs and dust, and I felt an urge to brush it all away and summon a reflection from the glass. "What do you mean he *couldn't?*"

"A man can't just stay around after a murder. It'd be suicide." Tristan's eyes grasped my own and forced me to look at him. My breath stopped and roiled in my chest cavity till I thought my breastbone would shatter. Everything familiar about the porch and the afternoon and the mountain and even Tristan tumbled in a pale, ghostly distortion.

"Who'd he murder?" The question was bitter on my tongue. I'd hated Dad plenty the last few years, blaming anything and everything on his decision to leave. But I'd never thought this.

"Bark Fleetwood."

It all started to come clear. So that was why the Fleetwood boy had beat Tristan to a pulp. They'd told me Mr. Fleetwood had died of pneumonia. So this was why Mother told me to take the long way to town and not go by way of the creek-bend. Why Tristan always came to get me from school in the winter when the days were short and night fell early. Then the Fleetwoods had left the valley—when I was six or seven—and had never returned.

"Why'd Dad kill him?" I asked. Yes, the world as I knew it was shattered, but a white mask fell over the real me, and I was a mannequin interrogating my brother and receiving blood-stained answers.

"Liquor."

"Oh. *Liquor.*" Our mountain life's blood and the cause of every problem in our tumultuous history. Seems like hundreds of times I'd watched our men and women dissolving with each tankard of ale into a deeper shade of drunkenness. Like a creature drowned in its own tears.

Tristan's face reddened. "Don't look at me that way, Callie."

"Why are you still brewing?" I smirked to myself at Tristan's shock. Oh, I knew about the late-night pilgrimages to that secret spot in the woods, and his dealings with the strange men who loaded the moonshine into hay-filled wagons and spirited it away like wraith-things.

Tristan let fall the twist of my hair and with it seemed to draw back into himself. "It's a living, Cal."

"A *killing*, Tristan, as Dad proved. *If* what you say's true."

"It's true. I've read the trial papers and I watched the hanging."

My heart raced, then jerked to a halt, then raced again. My spirit retched. "They caught him?"

"Caught him, tried him, and hanged him all within a month of the murder."

"Effective," I said, still sick over the idea that Tristan had seen it all.

"Damned lawmen."

"Don't curse, Tristan."

He spat over the porch-rail and I knew the conversation was at an end. My heart had turned to slivered bone, Tristan would continue on as a bootlegger, Mother would continue slaving away to that drunkard of a husband, and nothing I said would change a thing. I knew that from that moment there would be a rift between us all. Tristan saw things differently than I and how well did I know his stubborn-streak. Wexford men weren't born of flesh—they were carved from the breast of the mountain and stained with a curious black wash of Northern steel and Southern pride.

Still, I was glad I was leaving Wexford. A hour before I had thought I'd spend four years at college and maybe settle in one of the gentle cities at the foot of the mountains. But now as I looked out onto the blue-scarved ridges and the hollows between, I hated it all. I knew I'd never come back and I'd try to erase every scent and memory and habit of this place from my marrow.

Now—nine years later—sitting in my moth-battered chair with Nickleby on my lap and these murderous memories throbbing in my temples, I wondered how Jules could have known all this. Tristan had died in the war and Mother a year afterward—the only time I'd gone back to Wexford. I'd thought then that I'd buried the guilt-ridden secrets of my life with every spadeful of dirt the grave-diggers threw onto her coffin.

All these things had happened, and yet my past still rose to haunt me with the cloistered scent of dead mice and threatened to bash everything I'd done in the last ten years. Could I bear to have the world—everyone from Nalia Crosticinni to Jerry Atwood—hear and know these things? I could not.

I pulled my cat onto my chest and squeezed him until he mewed in protest. My eyes burned but not a tear came, though I willed them to flood me and ease this scorching ache. Anger and betrayal shifted to despair. I would have to bend to Jules' threat. There was no other way. Then the tears let loose.

I tried to reason it out within myself for hours. I watched the slow round of the clock through the dusk of my darkened apartment for three hours, the whole time laying my options out on the table and turning them over, willing a new possibility to come to light. But Jules had done his work effectively. He had given me an either-or and I could not drop my mask. It had grown into my very skin and the pain would be more than I could bear. Besides—what had Mr. Barnett done to have such a hold on me? I could surely find some petty gossip about him that would satisfy Jules and protect my hide without exposing Mr. Barnett to too much humiliation.

So this was it then. I'd take on the role of a spy and add espionage to my expansive resume.

My course of action decided, I pushed Nickleby off me and crept into the bedroom, not bothering to turn on the light.

Chapter 11

"Somewhere beyond the sea, somewhere waitin' for me...."

I heard Mr. Barnett singing the Bobby Darin tune from half-way down the block. What put him in such a fine mood? Personally, I had awakened with a migraine the size of Alaska and the patience of a flea. I would not give myself the indignity of reviewing last night's plight. I had resolved within the course I would take, and now the only thing was to take that course. The less said about it the better.

"My lover stands on golden sands and watches the ships that go sailin'."

I had reached the office door at this point and I poked my head through, wanting to be sure my employer was quite in his right mind. I wasn't expecting to find Mr. Barnett where he was: lounging just within the doorway which one hand in his jacket and the other holding an open pocket-watch. He startled me so I jumped and nearly tumbled back into the street.

"Ah. Miss Harper—there you are." He grabbed my arm to keep me from falling and dusted off my sleeve where I'd brushed against the dubiously-clean wall.

"Am I…late?" I peered at the watch but he snapped it shut and stored it in his pocket.

His answer was not conclusive: "Not late—only I've been waiting for you for half an hour."

"Oh."

"What's wrong, Callie? You're looking glum. Pardon me for noticing, but I'd almost say you looked…cross."

"Well, and if I am?" I pushed past him and tossed my purse and hat onto my desk.

"And what reason on earth would you have for being grouchy…today of all days?" He crossed his arms and quirked an eyebrow.

"Why wouldn't I be cross 'today of all days'?" I retorted.

He pursed his lips, but his eyes twinkled and I hated him for it. I had already made a martyr of my pride for Jules' sake as well as to save my own hide—Mr. Barnett need not culminate the difficulty by laughing at me.

I took up a pencil. "Why don't you go read the funny papers if you feel like grinning?"

Mr. Barnett said nothing, but wandered to his desk and continued the song I'd interrupted. "Somewhere beyond the sea, she's there watchin' for me. If I could fly like birds on high, then straight to her arms I'd go sailin'…Miss Harper?"

I jumped at this sudden introduction of my name and the tip of my pencil broke. Joy. "What is it?"

"I was only wondering what it was that made you so cross…it isn't anything I've done?"

Well it is rather, Mr. Barnett, isn't it? If you weren't quite so… quite so…if you weren't the person you were I wouldn't have a single hesitation in helping Jules build a little intrigue. But I only spread my mouth in an attempt at a smile. "Now why would you think that? I assure you I'm fine. Just out of sorts is all."

"Ah."

He wasn't convinced. I sighed. "You know…it's that time of — "

He put out his hands to stop me. "No! No need to explain. We're all friends here…you and me and the pencil sharpener. Secrets abounding and all that sort of thing. But come—I have to show you something."

His smile beamed such good hope and affability I couldn't refuse. I shrugged and stepped around my desk. He pulled a stack of telegrams off the side table where he perched, and fanned them out like an experienced poker-player would fan his hand of cards. "Do you know what these are, Miss Harper?"

I crossed my arms. "Telegrams."

"Very good. What sort of telegrams?"

I couldn't resist: "Complaints about your singing?"

"Wicked girl. I'm not at all tuneless." He reprimanded me with a wink then continued: "These yellow slips of paper contain the goodwill of our country."

I drew one of the telegrams from his hand, hoping it wouldn't be the old-maid, and Mr. Barnett smiled as I read the contents. It was a simple note, but one that toasted and cozied-up the cockles of my heart. "They really liked it. They actually liked it!" I handed the telegram back to Mr. Barnett with gleeful astonishment.

"*Ladybird Snippets* is taking off with a smash," he said.

"Seems like."

Mr. Barnett scattered the telegrams on the nearby desk and spread his hands with a humble smile. "What can I say, Miss Harper? We're a team—we work well together."

I returned his grin and shook my head. "It's a marvel!"

"A miracle."

"A relief."

"That too." Mr. Barnett chuckled. "Come now, Callie: doesn't that bring back the sunshine—seeing the effects of our slavery?"

"It does."

"Oh—incidentally, you cost Mr. Shores fifteen dollars this morning."

"What?"

Mr. Barnett winced, and shook his head. "Mr. Shores said the bet was dead—it seems I have effectively won you over."

"You have not!" I retorted.

"Haven't I? At any rate, Mr. Shores seems to think so. He paid up this morning and he told me to tell you he sees his threat was unnecessary. Tell me, what was that about? Has anyone threatened you? Has Shores threatened you?"

I laughed shook my head. "Just some silliness. It doesn't matter now."

"No, it doesn't. Because we've done it. By golly we've done it."

We shared a long smile—the smile of marathon-runners or a team who has just swum the English Channel. It held as much exhaustion as exhilaration, and in my private mind I wondered whether we'd be able to pull it off again. But there was proof in that pile of yellow messages littering the desk. If people had enjoyed the magazine enough to pay for a telegram to tell us so, it must have affected them. Mr. Barnett's eyes were still full upon me, so full of goodwill and pleasure I thought I'd break under the pressure of the unsullied happiness.

"It worked, Mr. Barnett," I said at last, tearing my own eyes away and fixing them on the window and the street outside. I brought my gaze back again and blushed to see him still staring at me with the same euphoric intensity.

"It did work," he said.

Silence fell again and I bit my lip. "So…what's next? What's your assignment for me?"

He didn't answer in that vein, however. "Miss Harper— Callie…I want to thank you."

"Consider me thanked."

"No, really. You don't know what a help you've been. You've worked like a galley-slave and born it all like a Spartan. You trotted out the impossible load I asked of you and never complained…well, not unjustly. I'm glad Shores sent you."

I cleared my throat and started back toward my desk. "I'm glad I was sent."

But he toyed with the button on his cuff then made that puppy-look with his eyebrows. "You've been good as a second right hand for me. I can…well, it seems extraneous to say, but I feel that I can trust you. And you don't know how solid that makes a venture like this."

I froze in my retreat and wished his generosity had stopped at thanking me for slaving away to his will. He trusted me. Nauseating thought, that, considering certain circumstances over which I had no control. I turned to him. Jules. What had I got myself into? "We're in this together—like you said. I want to see the magazine succeed too."

The magazine, yes. Myself? Of course. Him…well…he already had enough success to spare and then some. A few revealings couldn't hurt him that much.

Leaving his side I started to hum "Mambo Italiano" to divert the several different Callies inside me from tearing each other to shreds. I was disgusted with my own weakness and yet proud that I'd come to a decision. It was shameful, and it was my choice. I would stand by it. At my desk I fed a new sheet of paper into my typewriter. Jules could wait—he knew he had me in the palm of his hand, and I would not gratify his arrogance by hurrying to him with the payload. I'd take my time and do my job well and carefully.

We worked for some time together—Mr. Barnett and I—and as the morning wore on my uneasiness dissipated. I could almost imagine the events of the previous evening to be an ill-favored dream and myself just waking from it to the knowledge of reality. But the cold knot in my stomach was still there when I looked for it, so I hurried to draw my mental curtains around the temple of Memory, so   I would not have to see.

I thought of many things while I wrote—none of them having to do with the article at hand—and had to scrap several sheets of paper because I'd written "Jules" by accident.

"Don't forget we have a party to attend tonight." Mr. Barnett's voice came lazy and unconcerned from his corner of the room.

"We…do?"

"We do."

"And why wasn't I forewarned?" I shook my head and continued to beat out my article: compiling all the notes I'd scribbled on what a well-read person should read, and which books were my personal favorite, and where one might catch hold of a copy if they were interested.

"Lesson One you've already learned," Mr. Barnett said. "Remember? The heart of journalism is theories."

"Don't remind me."

"Lesson Two happened with Nalia—you don't get good interviews by giving your celebrity the Spanish Inquisition."

"I bow to your superior knowledge."

He twined his fingers through each other and rested his chin on them. "And now we come to Lesson Three."

"Tell me Teacher, because I'd like to get on with my work." But I couldn't help the wry smile his manner jerked from my lips.

"Lesson Three: A journalist must be ready at all times. We never get fair warning."

And I used to wonder why there were more fellows in journalism than girls. I shook my head. "Now that isn't fair. All you've gotta do to go anywhere—from Annamaria's to Buckingham Palace—is put on a clean shirt and fix your tie."

Mr. Barnett craned his neck to view my blouse. "Don't you have any clean shirts?"

"Oh…" I threw my heavy eraser at him and laughed as he dodged it. "Don't be a pickle."

"I'm not being a pickle. We don't care what you wear so long as you look nice. But we do know the difference!"

"We?"

"Men in general and famous men in particular."

He was impossible. I added a sentence or two to my project then stopped typing. "So where are we going?"

"Jersey."

"Aha. What's the scoop?" I gave my red pencil a few turns in the sharpener and circled a section of my article that would have to be re-worded.

"Ribbon-cutting for a new opera-house."

"Nice. Who's the bigwig?"

"There are several, actually. Nalia will be there—you can be your saucy self again while I do all the work."

"You are incorrigible, Mr. Barnett."

"And you are a vixen, Miss Harper—splendid. We shall work ourselves into a regular fury by the time evening comes around. Remember the game: flint and steel."

I winked at him. "Fire and gunpowder." But after Mr. Barnett resumed his work I stared at my own paper, seeing nothing. Fire and gunpowder…little did he know I was the firebrand and intended to light the fuse when I'd got what I needed.

At eight o'clock Mr. Barnett and I pulled up to the door of the opera house somewhere well-beyond the borders of the Hudson. He had driven and I rode shot-gun. Truth be told, I had spent the whole ride in deep introspection and hadn't bothered to ask exactly where we were headed.

Mr. Barnett roused me from my brown study with a rap of his knuckles against my arm. "We're here. Now remember what I told you. Be charming and engaging—like you were at Alegre Noches last night—but keep your eyes and ears open. Take notes on what they do tell you, but also on what they don't. You must learn to tune your ear to suggestion and to ferret out the cause of that suggestiveness. But whatever you do, don't be pushy."

I stretched and reapplied my lipstick, then stepped out of the car. The evening was dim and cool about me now that we were away from the pressing heat of New York City. I took note of the looming gibbous moon shrouded in white mist. "You know, Mr. Barnett, your theories are a little strange."

"So you've told me."

"But didn't you go to college?"

"Princeton, thank you very much."

Made my small-town school sound worse than ever. "Well, you certainly don't speak as if you'd been taught by any proper sort of professor."

"Why?" He stopped off short and I paused beside him, thinking it ridiculous that he felt the need to cut off like a guttering engine every time he had something to say. "Do you say that because I'm wrong, or because I'm not a poll-parrot?"

"Well…" When he put it in that blunt light I got thistle-spears under my skin.

Mr. Barnett sighed. "Miss Harper, you're very…passionate. I'm sure you were an eager and vibrant student in college. But sometimes I fear you are just repeating what you've been told as if you'd never thought for yourself."

"I think for myself all the time."

"Yes." His voice was dry. "So you've told me. Independence and liberation and all of that—we've discussed it. But if that is so, then you shouldn't think it strange that I have my own ideas —that I don't subscribe to every point my professors might have made. I hate to bring it up and dangle it over you, Miss Harper, but my methods and 'strange theories' have taken me a deal farther than many a man's. I think there might be something you could learn if you would listen."

He was right, of course. Stubborn and mule-headed and right. It angered me to have to concede the point, but I could not do otherwise.

"All right, I give up," I said. "I'll try it your way."

"Good. Now come along—the other kids will be swarming over this place like germs in the Bubonic Plague. Can't let competition get in the way." He summoned me to follow him with a jerk of his head and I obeyed.

"Miss Harper!" Nalia Crosticinni sauntered toward me as Mr. Barnett and I entered the marble reception room of the ornate building. She wore a black sheath gown and a heavy diamond tiara.

Overkill.

"I am so glad you have come," she said.

I glanced from her elaborate corsage of roses to my costume-brooch and wished I'd worn the pearls. "Likewise," I murmured. I drew a heart on the marble floor with the toe of my shoe and tried not to look out of place.

Nalia smiled and grasped Mr. Barnett's hands in both of hers. "Wade."

Again I had that prickling, green sensation of being left out of something that had been going on longer than me—longer than I'd been alive, probably. I wondered how intimately Mr. Barnett and Nalia knew each other...

"I see you haven't killed one another," Nalia remarked with a glance at me.

I bridled like a mare ready for the running. "I, for one, would never intentionally harm Mr. Barnett." But my blood sizzled as I remembered the mission Jules had forced me to take on.

Nalia only laughed and linked her arm through mine. I stiffened and tugged in the opposite direction, but she laughed and pulled me close. "Are you trying to avoid me, Miss Harper? Why? I want to hear all about how you get on with Wade."

Again I stiffened—rigid as a pencil. Was this how a diamond-studded opera star ought to treat a journalist?

Then again, why did I care?

Maybe one or another of the rumple-suited photographers lounging in the corners among the carved pillars would take a snapshot of Nalia and I and it would end up on the cover of LIFE Magazine—no other way to get my face up there in a hurry.

"I have a question for you, *mia cara*," Nalia said. It was half a whisper, wholly confidential.

"All right." I flipped a page in my mental note-book and poised my imaginary pen to take down notes. What was it Mr. Barnett had said? You must learn to tune your ear to suggestion.

"Over here—let us be comfortable." Nalia summoned a waiter with a flick of her diamond-spangled wrist, and had him dip two glasses of frosty punch from the crystal bowl across the room. We both sat on the damask settee and Jenny Lind stared demurely at us from the painting above. Nalia crossed her long, elegant legs and took out a cigarette, lighting the end. She offered one to me but I declined.

"Miss Harper, I wanted to speak with you on a matter that is very…important to me." Seeing that I made no objection, she drew on her cigarette and continued: "I like you, *mia cara*. You have a certain natural vivacity about you rare to find among women these days. Tell me, what are your aspirations?"

"Aspirations?"

"Yes, *bella*. What is it you want to do with your life?"

I put the crystal cup to my lips and the glass was cool against my skin. How to phrase this so it wouldn't sound crude? "I want…prominence." Nalia's dark eyes searched my face, and I continued. "I want to be a glamorous, poised woman who can keep up with any man in the business. I want to live on Fifth Avenue and wear nice clothes and know famous people." There —that was an honest assessment.

Nalia pursed her lips around her cigarette, blew out the smoke, and ran the tips of her slender fingers through her hair. "So you want my life?" She laughed. "Yes, it is…what did you call it? Ah—glamorous."

I took refuge from her intent gaze in sweeping an eye over the foyer of the opera house. The domed, concave ceiling was painted with beautiful scenes from popular operas—some I recognized; others I did not. Below, crossing the crimson and gold tiles were a couple hundred people. I wondered, idly, what would happen if the lives of those painted on the ceilings were traded for those socializing on the floor. What tragedies might that cause? Or would it only be a different form of tragedy than those spinning out their cobweb-threads in this life?

I felt Nalia's hand warm on mine and jerked my attention back to our corner of the room.

"Miss Harper," she crooned. "Let me ask you one thing: do you have any aspirations for marriage?"

Marriage? I frowned. "I'd like someone to be fond of me."

Nalia laughed again—musical, trilling notes like an aria. "Well I am fond of you, *mia bella*. But I do not think that is the same. Do you have plans to have a family?" She looked out onto the main floor and I knew without looking whom her gaze was directed toward.

Frankly, I didn't want to see her eyes bent tenderly on my boss like a black widow spider hanging above her unfortunate beau.

"I haven't thought seriously about it—mostly 'cause I've never got the chance," I replied.

"But you will," Nalia said, her face grave and troubled.

This sudden change from gentle inquiry to somberness unnerved me. I felt that somehow I had stuck a knife in a gaping wound that I was unaware of. I hastened to set things right: "I don't think anyone could love me anyway. No worries."

"I am sure someone could. But, my darling be careful. Marriage can be lonely. Men are not what they sometimes seem. Because one has a husband…does not mean one is happy." I watched her twist the heavy ring on her left hand with a bitter smile. "Attachment to a man can be a lonelier place than independence, *bella*."

Boy—news to me. I smoothed my skirt. "You needn't worry about me. Come to think of it, I don't intend to stick my head in the noose after all."

This strangely emphatic woman was not finished with me yet. She had not released my hand from her own and again those dark eyes studied me. "Calida—I may call you that, may I not?" I nodded my assent. "Calida, I have no doubt that you will be that glamorous woman you speak of. But the men take advantage of that. They want you for it. They do not care for your heart and your intellect. They want your beauty and glamour. Do not give it to them." Her fingers clutched at my hand with an urgency that must have been deep rooted, for the pressure left indents in my skin. Her gaze had wandered again, and this time I followed it and met with the sight of Mr. Barnett and Mr. Crosticinni deep in conversation with a knot of men.

"Do not give it to them," Nalia repeated, then released me.

I drew my hand back into my lap and Nalia smoked for a moment in silence. My thoughts tumbled like a handful of earrings dumped into a jewelry box. The way Nalia watched Mr. Barnett…the obvious familiarity of their relationship…the mention Mr. Barnett had made of her "somewhat tragic" past….could it be that Nalia's words were a warning to brush me clear of the man she saw as her natural due?

I marked these things in my memory and thought how Jules would be delighted if they were true. And could they be? Would Mr. Barnett take advantage of a married woman in that manner? Had he taken advantage of Nalia, or were they lovers and the fear of ill-treatment lurked beneath her veneer of happiness? I hated to believe it.

My eyes locked onto the knot of men and I despised the lifting of the veil I'd thrown over all questions of Mr. Barnett. He had seemed different from other men. I had believed him to be different from other men. Different from Jules, standing to one side with a sneer on his face; different from Jamie, puckish and funny but shallow and tied to his drink.

Calida Harper, nothing is proved. A jealous woman—yes, Nalia could be jealous—stops at nothing. You have to give him a chance, knuckle-head. Like a court of law—innocent till proven guilty.

Mr. Barnett himself approached then and burst the soap-sud thoughts with a bluff comment on the stubbornness of men in general and journalists in particular.

167

"Do you mean to say you've finally found another man with a head as hard as your own?" I asked, rising to join him and leaving behind the touchy thoughts as best I could.

"Harder, I'm afraid." He rubbed his head with a rueful smile. "Fella nearly brained me with his camera when I asked if he'd move over so I could hear a little better."

I waved a goodbye to Nalia and leaned in. "What were you listening to? Something scandalous, I hope?"

Mr. Barnett clapped his hand against my shoulder in a chummy gesture. "So asks the woman with an ear for gossip… classic."

"My trade, Mr. Barnett. Now stop teasing. What did you get?"

"Ah-ah. Not till you tell me what you and Nalia were whispering and simpering about in that corner. I certainly hope you gathered something that will be more than a brief line in print—that is what we're here for, contrary to popular belief."

I bit my lips to keep an exasperated sigh from escaping. Blast and wretch. I still hadn't gathered anything to report—anything much. Nothing outright. But then…Mr. Barnett seldom gathered anything outright. I thought I'd try my hand at his methods and see if I had learned anything. "Nalia is unhappy."

His eyes danced. "An unhappy celebrity? Tsk, tsk. What next?"

"No—she's really unhappy. I think she's been hurt by someone. By a man." I stared hard at Mr. Barnett, but if I hoped to detect any hint of embarrassment on his part that might affirm my convoluted suspicion, I was deprived of it.

He gave a mere hint of a shrug and fanned himself with his notepad. "Sheesh—it's hot in here. Callie, let me give you a few pointers: every celebrity in every city in every country is unhappy six out of seven days in a week." He turned away and rolled his fingers at me in farewell. "That is hardly news."

Without another word he left me standing dumb and trivial, dwarfed by a potted palm and frowned upon by the portrait of a maestro across the hall. I watched his retreating figure and the way the other journalists parted for him and followed him with their eyes.

Well isn't that just the crème de la crème? A journalist so great all the other journalists follow him with their tongues lolling and their eyes bugged.

I crossed my arms and tried to organize my thoughts. Obviously a relationship with a celebrity—like mine and Nalia's —was detrimental to getting any real information. I needed to join any one of the knots of reporters decorating the hall and somewhere beneath the rumpled surface of those knots I'd find another celebrity and could grab a story out of them. It wasn't as if Nalia Crosticinni was the only famous human being present. I caught a glimpse of a tall, slim redhead that looked an awful lot like Jo Stafford. Was it her? A crumpled, punch-stained program balanced precariously on the edge of a trashcan nearby. I plucked it out and scanned the names. Jo Stafford, Nalia Crosticinni, Louis Armstrong. So it was she. I could form some story off of her, I was sure.

Resolution made, I started for the nearest group of shabby-coated, camera-bearing, pencil-licking reporters. A hand grabbed my elbow and pulled me short. I whipped about to find Jules' face close to my own, and his eyes bent on me with that mocking light that had haunted me since the dance. The creeper.

"Hello, Callie," he purred.

"What are you doing here?"

"Working." He rolled his shirt-sleeves up and sneered at the assembly. "Same as all these snot-nosed kids-outta-college that think they can make a living in this business."

"Easy, Jules. We were snot-nosed-kids-outta-college five or six years ago."

"More's the pity."

I pulled away from him and tacked on a smile—a pretty good one, I thought. "Well, good luck story-hunting."

With one warning frown Jules pulled the tack out of my smile and it slipped to the floor, trampled under a torrent of panicked thoughts.

"Callie—you never gave me your answer."

Though my mind was made up—quite firmly—I stalled for time: "I haven't seen you since the dance—how was I supposed to tell you?"

Jules kept his hand on my arm and quirked one brow in a warning expression. "In case you aren't familiar with this century, there's a marvelous little invention called the telephone. Or even if you have got stuck in the more primitive customs of your hometown, one can always fall back on pen and paper."

I shushed him, fearing that someone might hear this allusion to my past, but Jules arched that thunderous brow and squeezed my arm—hard. He steered me into the corner by the punch table and blocked my view of the room by placing himself directly in front of me, forcing me against the wall. He towered over me—his chest inches from my chin, the knot of his tie at eye-level. I felt crushed by his presence so close to me, pressing me harder against the wall. His hands touched the wall on either side of my head. The dimples of his smile flashed with pleasure at having cornered me thus. He was so close I could see the dark, sandpaper look of his five o'clock shadow over his strong jaw. His lips curled into a sultry smile of a singularly dark nature. The smile that had captivated so many girls but never failed to make my stomach turn over with nausea.

To any one of the other people in the room we must have looked like an enamored couple enjoying a *tete-a-tete*. I felt sick, being this close to Jules. I'd better give him the answer he wanted and get the heck out of there.

"Jules—I'll do it."

He relaxed—even the stressed wrinkles in his white shirt appeared to iron out. "Good. Sensible, beautiful girl."

"Don't call me beautiful."

He traced the sweep of curls against my forehead with his pointer finger, and those deadly dimples showed again. "Don't you like it?"

I tried to calm the outrage—and panic—rising in my chest. "Not from you."

"Pity. If you hadn't been so keen to join up with Mr. Wade Barnett we could have had a lot of fun together…gone dancing. Gone ice-skating."

"Ice-skating?" My voice was cold and light as tin. "Jules—you're a fool." With a sudden burst of ire I shoved him away from me and into the punch-table. He knocked over several of the crystal cups. The shock on his face and that of the tuxedo-ed man who lorded over the punch kindled angry warmth inside me.

"Don't try to kiss me again," I hissed, pretending ours had been a mere lovers' quarrel. The words were a joke—or were they? Had he been about to kiss me? The thought punched holes in the lining of stomach and the acid poured through.

"And you can take your darn ring back, lover-boy!" I added for good measure, hoping the Lord of the Punch would take that explanation for my flight and Jules' murderous glare. I hurried to join the main crowd and felt a sense of profound relief—Jules had what he wanted now: a promise extracted with the tender care of a dentist from a defenseless woman who happened to have a murderer for a father. Brilliant—but at least he would bother me no more this evening.

Still, I attached myself to the main group so as to avoid another interview, and took notes on the size and architecture of the building while everyone else clustered around the VIP's. I, for one, had had enough of people to last me decades.

I was still poking around the marble columns with a crick in my neck from gazing up at the frescoed ceiling when Mr. Barnett came to collect me. "Ready to leave, Sherlock?"

"For the last hour."

"You look as if you'd been through the wringer—what's wrong? Another headache?"

I would not give him the satisfaction of being always right. "Actually, I am quite well. I'm ready to leave because I've collected all the information I want and all I want now is to get home and get to bed."

"And I have no objection to obliging both our wishes in that respect." He bowed to the ladies and gentlemen, and the hum of the room suspended for a moment as the crowd within watched him leave. I could not attempt to deny that Wade Barnett was a man of some consequence—everyone seemed magnetized toward him. Even I: a woman who was actively plotting to undo him.

We wandered to the car and I let my wrap fall. The breeze stroked my bare skin with gentle fingers. The moon and stars swung around our heads in their childish way. I found myself wishing I could tell those carefree stars and that merry moon what a horrid world it was they danced over. What a mad, sorrowful, mysterious world.

"Thinking poetic thoughts by the moonlight?" Mr. Barnett's voice had that pleasant, lazy note in it again and isolated me on my own island of dismal forebodings.

I left his question unanswered and he did not seem to mind, taking it for granted, I supposed, that my silence affirmed his inquiry. We slipped into the car without further conversation, and I spent the ride home with my hat tilted over my head, hoping Mr. Barnett would think me asleep.

The Collected Letters of Wade Barnett:

August 12th, 1952

Dear Maralie and Tobias,

Jules Cameron concerns me.

That might sound ridiculous, but I can't shake the feeling that he is a villain.

Our evening of dancing—I'm not vain enough to think it was a date—began pleasantly indeed. Callie regarded my preferences this time and showed up in a stunning dress. It was yellow and light and made her look like the little girl I remember. I always knew she was an attractive woman but I never saw it so clearly before.

She doesn't remember me the way I remember her. That is the end of the matter. Any feeling I would be inclined to have in her direction would only be met with horror if she knew.

We arrived at the club and Callie astonished me by showing that she has a social life—a lively one. The men flocked around her till I worried I'd never get that dance. I was introduced to several pitiable women to whom I couldn't have been attracted less if they'd applied warts and fake mustaches. The idea that caking a face with inches of power and plucking the eyebrows and drawing new ones at impossible angles will make the woman more attractive to a man is quite beyond me. I'm glad Callie doesn't paint herself in that way. I'd not be above handing her a bar of soap and my handkerchief and asking her to remove the clownish stuff before getting down to business.

The dancing began and Callie had just turned to me with that smile of hers when Jules Cameron sliced in—he's an odious fellow I have never liked even before last night's events.

If I had seen the face she made in a picture at the theatre, I'm sure I'd have thought we were coming at last to the climax of the danger. I lost sight of her in the crowd of people and those intolerable women kept clawing at me. I pulled myself away and waited for Callie to return. She came back a moment later looking as if Jules had kept a gun to her head the whole time. Her face was white and when she touched me her fingers trembled. Calida Harper does not tremble. It's contrary to everything I know about her.

That was the first clue.

I asked if there was anything I could get her—anything she wanted—but the only thing that seemed to make her the least bit steady was the idea of going home. Of course I was disappointed—being promised a dance with Calida Harper and finding she's indisposed is not quite flattering—but I could see she was in no shape to endure an evening in Jules' presence. He frightened her. Yes. I am going out with an accusatory flavor and pegging him as the fellow who turned what had been gleaming beauty a moment before into haggard fear.

I was livid.

Perhaps I was wrong to keep my anger to myself—perhaps Callie would have told me what affected her so if I had expressed displeasure with that man. But of course I didn't know then what I knew now.

The following night—last night—we were to attend the opening of the Opera House together.

As I changed that evening, my phone rang. I answered, and was more than a little surprised to find Nalia Crosticinni on the other end of the line. She greeted me warmly and we carried on a conversation in Italian, though my mind was working behind the scenes. Something in her features at the Stork Club had bothered me—something when she looked at Callie. I have known Nalia for years—well enough to recognize that scheming jealousy in those dark, sultry eyes masked, of course, by wit and charm of which she has a great deal.

"Nalia," I asked. "What do you think of Miss Harper?"

"Calida? She is pretty and clever but nothing rare. But I will like for your sake."

Ah—there it was again. That possessive note in her voice—if you've heard it before, Tobias, you will know what I mean.

"How is Mr. Crosticinni?" I fumbled for my cufflinks and wished I didn't have to face this again—from this woman of them all. I like Nalia and feel a deal of pity for her. But in recent days she seemed to be getting…attached.

I heard her draw on her cigarette. "He is…distant and stiff and well-pressed as usual. Oh Wade…he has no time for me."

'Oh Wade' nothing. I couldn't let her carry on in this crawling manner. Intolerable. "Tell him I hope to discuss the races with him tonight."

"Didn't you want to discuss my agent with me?"

With a wince I remembered my promise. "Nalia, with all due respect, I think the races are more pressing. Barnaby Vick can hang on your coattails for another week, can't he? Cold Command and Blue Man—the runners up of the Derby Winner

—are racing against each other and I want to see what your husband thinks his chances are."

"Well if you don't have time for me either…" Her tones were pouting, and I could almost hear the tears standing in her eyes. I did pity the woman, but what could I do? Her husband married her for her money and looks—she possesses plenty of each—and she married him because she was lonely. I do believe loneliness was the downfall of the Grecian Amazons for all the emphasis and excuses placed on it today. Say it was from motives of "loneliness" and the Modern Age will let you get away with anything from petty larceny to murder. Maralie, tell me I'm wrong.

"Nalia," I said, "If you would kindly give Vincent my message, I would be greatly indebted to you." Wrong word choice, I suppose, for she cheered up immediately at that remark and rung off in a good humor.

I had no time to worry about Nalia. The Opera opening was the soup du jour. Callie and I were working the joint, but I planned to enjoy the ride to and from the assignment. I thought, perhaps, we might swing by a coffeehouse on the way home.

We argued on the way over.

I am growing more accustomed to Callie's vehemence, but it still amuses me. I think my amusement throws her into a deeper rage, like a bellows blowing on a flame.

I cannot help it. If she only knew how it makes me…ah. But of course there isn't a chance of that in this case. And Maralie, please don't smile like that. Tobias will be more sensible. He's a man. He knows we don't...

The evening was spoiled from the start.

The moment we stepped in the door Nalia descended on us like a murder of crows. She looked beautiful and sensuous and tragic as usual—the quintessential primadonna. I was afraid she might make a scene, but the worst she did was shake my hands with her usual fawning warmth. I hated the fact that she'd given me reason to wish her away. I will have to give Vincent a sound piece of advice in the near future—he can't behave to his wife in this manner and expect her to stay with him. Goodness knows I won't be the man to steal her off his hands—Lord save me—but another day he might wake up and find his bed empty. I pray that is not the case, but I have seen it many times. So many times.

This is what concerns me when Callie speaks in her wild, free way. Her dreams are the things I see falling to shambles around me. The rich and famous are like the whitened sepulchers in the Scriptures. Not all of us, not all the time—but far too often for me to wish this life on my precious, precious girl.

It is no use denying these feelings—I have tried since the day I met her in that wretched office: I love Calida Harper.

If any two humans' stories could be more incongruous than ours, let me be shown it, for I feel we two are players in a whirl-wind game of cat's cradle. To complicate the knotted mess, a dark master is further tangling the threads.

I speak of Jules Cameron.

He cornered Callie at the Opera House. I saw him back her against the wall, leering. It had not taken me long to assume Jules had discovered a bit of Callie's life and threatened her with it the night of the dance. I know the lengths Calida Harper has gone to disguise herself. I know she despises her roots, and I know she has become a different woman because of them.

I recognize Jules' game to be a straight-forward case of blackmailing—what the stakes are, I cannot possibly determine without directly asking him or Callie.

Neither would tell me.

Neither trusts me.

She wears a mask. At moments I see behind the mask and it is that girl I love. But how can I be certain the real Calida Harper is the creature behind the veil? What if the shallow, glitter-loving magpie is Callie and the peeps behind the mask are mere whimsies of mine?

Tell me if you know, Maralie, for my mind is a fog on this point.

These rambling are useless. I love Callie, and she does not love me—not yet. If she does, she loves a shadow-thing and cannot see that I too wear a mask.

Oh, to be done with this ten-penny masquerade! I would lay my past before her if I was certain it would not mean the losing of her. But I am not certain. I am not certain that she would not back away in horror and dread from the thought of me.

So I wait.

I wait and I pray the Lord will prepare her heart to hear, or prepare mine to give her up. The gypsy has stolen my heart away, and I find the idea of tearing it back bloody and painful.

Lord help us.

I would ask for your prayers. Advice and wisdom will also not returned unopened.

I find being in love a heck of a briar-patch.

Also, if you would not mind, I will send her to you, Maralie. Please examine her, pet her, and above all be careful with her. I want you to rub off on my 'beautiful warmth', but gently.

Ever your loyal friend,

Wade Barnett

Rachel Heffington

Chapter 12

Callie:

"Uncanny, Miss Harper."

I glanced up from my perusal of the ads scheduled to go into this month's issue of *Ladybird Snippets*. "Whom?"

"You."

"Am I? How clever of me." It was a Monday, and I was not renowned for extreme wit on Mondays—especially this late in the afternoon.

"This piece... 'When the World Came Tumbling'...it's first-rate literature." Mr. Barnett flapped the slim stack of papers I'd finished only yesterday. "How came a queer idea like that into your head?"

"The opera house-opening...it jumped me." The image of the opera-characters' dramas swapping with our own hadn't left me that night. The only way I could eclipse that idea was by spinning it out to the tune of a tale, as I did with anything that unnerved me. "I was looking at the ceiling-frescoes," I admitted.

"Aha. Well, I'm glad to see something came of that ordeal," he said.

I winced and returned to sorting the advertisements.

"Really, Callie, I'm beginning to see a trend here—you cannot write nonfiction."

"Excuse me?"

He raised his pencil to indicate I ought to remain seated, then smiled. "But you can write stories like nobody's business. I wondered what you were doing. You looked like a sneak-thief, rummaging in all the odd corners of that building."

"I was trying to decide if they'd decorated in the neoclassic or Italianate style."

"And what did you determine?"

"Nothing at all."

"Ah yes—they're all pillars and columns and naked statues to me. But really, Callie, I propose we divide the work in two directions: you will fill all the orders for the literalistic half of the enterprise, and I'll stick to reporting."

"But Mr. Barnett!" I let my breath out in one shaky flood. He must have known I was watching him and Nalia. Must have got wind of the fact that I was a tinkerer in the fine art of espionage.

"Callie," He shook his head. "You've hit upon your forte— why give it up?"

"Can't you give me one more chance?" I needed this. If he relegated me to writing stories and poetry I'd never get to…in the old days I would have been complaining about the loss of a chance to meet celebrities. Now I panicked as I faced the possibility of not being able to keep an eye on Mr. Barnett. Not being able to watch him and to be sure he was....all right. "I need you to give me one more chance," I repeated.

Mr. Barnett had paused for a moment, picking at a loose thread on his cuff, his head bent so I could not see his eyes. But I heard the smile in his voice: "Only one more?"

"Only one." I clasped my hands beneath my desk and pledged by all I held dear to please him in this last interview. I couldn't bear the idea of sitting here at this desk while Mr. Barnett danced at the Stork Club with Nalia. *Not without me. I need to keep an eye on you. For Jules,* I hastened to add.

"I may be able to arrange one last chance for you, Callie. I wonder if you'll like this assignment."

"I'll do anything—go anywhere, please. Just let me have one more chance," I pleaded. My knees felt wobbly and I was glad for the support of my chair.

"Fine—one more chance because you used your magic words." He winked at me. "You'll be interviewing a marvelous, great woman. One of the best women I've ever known—the one I admire most of all."

The moment of crisis over, I rolled my eyes. "Your mother?"

"No—she's dead, unfortunately."

"Oh." I stomped on my own toes with my high-heels as penance for making such a stupid blunder then waited.

"Her name is Nancy Moffat—she lives in Oxthwaite, Pennsylvania now, though she is an old acquaintance of mine from her days in the City."

"Pennsylvania? So far?"

"Well you certainly didn't think a journalist could afford to stay in an around New York City her whole life, did you? I've bought your train tickets and you'll be leaving for Philly... tomorrow."

"Me? Tomorrow?"

"You said you wanted an assignment; I would have gone but you were so adamant." He was mocking me. Eyes taunting, lanky body thrown back in his chair, arms crossed behind his head— or maybe it was my mood that portrayed him thus.

I crossed my own arms and summoned enough courage to glare at Mr. Barnett. He appeared unaffected by this change in my humor, and that in itself maddened me. "Well if you're going to be that way," I huffed.

"What way?"

"Shribbly on you. Tell me about this Moffat-woman and why you think I won't like her.

"I never said you won't like her. I said I only, said I wondered."

Darn his subtleties. "You are obnoxious," I said. "Who do you think you are? Albert Einstein?"

Instead of answering, Mr. Barnett began to sing a tune just low enough that I couldn't catch the notes or the words. "What are you singing?" He ignored me a moment longer but I repeated my question.

In a voice strained with something—I suspected laughter— Mr. Barnett sung to me: "My luv she's but a lassie yet, my luv she's but a lassie yet. We'll let her stand a year or twa; she'll noo be half sae saucy yet."

If he'd taken me like a tea-kettle and stuck me over the coals I could not have felt more enraged than I did at that moment.

I muttered something murderous to myself and completely froze him for an hour till the clock indicated it was time to go home. He made no effort to solace me. I gathered my things to myself and managed a vaguely apologetic goodbye which was returned with an affirming grunt and an absent wave of the hand as Mr. Barnett continued his own work. Dear man, always working later than I and arriving earlier. I wondered when he slept—if he slept—and where he lived. Funny I'd never asked him. I supposed I could look it up in the phone-book if I really wanted to know—not that it mattered where Mr. Barnett lived.

I couldn't imagine what that had to do with me.

It was not till I stood on the curb awaiting a taxi that I thought over the afternoon's argument. A sudden wave of joy poisoned with anxiety washed over me...Mr. Barnett had sung to me that song with the strangely befitting words...and in that song he'd called me...his *love*. I blushed the next moment for being such a loony, but my thoughts would be capricious and return to that teasing line: "My luv she's but a lassie yet."

"What a nuisance that man is," I muttered. "He turns irresistible just when I've made up my mind to double-cross him." A hard film seemed to crust over my heart as I mused over the thing. Not only was I going to betray him, but I had good reason to believe he was following the footsteps of every celebrity cad: seducing a gorgeous VIP and ignoring everyone else.

Oh, Mr. Barnett. I forgot you were a man.

That was why I'd vowed to avoid men—a woman wouldn't fall for glamour and glitz. We knew better than that...most of the time.

I stepped onto the platform of the miniscule Oxthwaite train station and took a long, hard look at this—my illustrious destination where Mr. Barnett had assured me the best woman in the world resided. A cardboard town with a cardboard ticket-station and cardboard people no doubt. I'd always been a fan of snap and color and life. This place looked like Great Aunt Sal had forgotten to dust it last Saturday and didn't intend to remedy the situation in any particular hurry. I clutched my travel case and waited on the platform, wishing the stares of the local fellows weren't quite so…intense. What? Hadn't they ever seen a city girl before? Poor rubes.

Well, I certainly couldn't stand here waiting for a miracle. Nancy Moffat was not here to meet me—Mr. Barnett had not said whether I was to expect that grace—and I would have to go to her myself. I stepped to one the round-eyed attendants. "Excuse me, mister. You wouldn't happen to know where Mrs. Nancy Moffat lives, do you?"

His eyes swept me up and down and I felt my face go hot. "What's a sweet city-mouse like ye'self doin' way out here?" His voice was low and drawling as if the two of us had nothing better to do than stand on a rural platform reciting a girl-boy catechism.

I smiled and flipped a card from my silver case. "Callie Harper —Ladybird Snippets—Journalist."

"Journalism shmirmalism."

"Listen, Mr.….what's the name?" He slurred his answer so I couldn't hear. Was the man drunk? "Pardon?"

"Carter."

"Ah. Well, Mr. Carter, could you direct me to the Moffat household?" How many Moffats could there be in this little dump?

"Not till you give me a kiss, sweetheart." This man was most definitely three sheets to the wind. He leered at me and put his face forward. I pursed my lips—in defiance, I hoped he realized —and crossed my arms. I was not about to kiss anyone, let alone this goblin.

"Now come off it, Gus." One of the other men—a porter, I supposed—had come to his sense at last and pulled Mr. Carter away from me. "So sorry, Miss Harper. You're lookin' for the Moffats? Which ones—the Elder or Younger Moffats?"

"I suppose the younger…Mrs. Nancy Moffat?"

"Aha. Nan. If you'd like, miss, I can drive you there."

I had secret misgivings about getting into a car with a strange man whose authority on the subject I could but take in faith— taxis being the demons of the lot—but I couldn't see there being any cure of it. I was weary with traveling and—unlike another very earnest young lady—I had forgotten to bring my diary and therefore had nothing sensational to read on the train.

"Well, then let's go," I said to the fellow.

In a blink we had climbed onto a hay wagon parked nearby and rumbled away from the station. Well, this was a relief: if mine worthy host tried to make a move I disliked I could always pitch out of the wagon into a weed-filled ditch and plead injuries to Mr. Barnett when he asked me why I hadn't brought him an interview.

"You related to us?" my chauffeur asked after an interval, and followed the inquiry with a stream of tobacco-juice into the weeds.

"…Us?"

"Nan 'n me."

"You're related?"

"To you?"

"To Nan."

He chuckled and clicked his tongue to make the stout mare go at a faster walk. "Married t'her." We drove in silence for some time as I processed this. "I'm Tobias Moffat," he added a bit later.

After this, there seemed to be nothing to say. Mr. Barnett had not given me instructions to interview Mr. Moffat, and furthermore, I felt the odd one out. I was not Mr. Moffat who was married to Mrs. Moffat, and I was not Mrs. Moffat who knew Mr. Barnett, and I was not Mr. Barnett who knew all of us…I was merely an interloper who had no business traveling four hours just to prod in someone's business. I watched the Queen Anne's lace and goldenrod spin slowly by as we passed— a halcyon of bronze and white like honey whirled in cream. There'd been flowers like this in Wexford, I remembered.

Perhaps Mr. Barnett was right—perhaps I wasn't cut out for this sort of busybody's work.

But my steel-strong pride would not admit defeat. It was ridiculous to doubt my entire career just because I'd left New York City and didn't know my way around. Mentally, I began assembling my questions and Nancy's probable answers. I wanted to enter that little house with my head screwed on right.

"Mr. Moffat?"

"Did you see that bull in th'pasture?" he asked, as if I hadn't spoken. I followed the indication of his square forefinger to a massive, black creature dwarfing the other cattle on a bronzed hillside. "If'n ye're lookin' for a good country-interest piece y'might do a story on him. Eh, he's a rare one."

"He is?"

"Gots 'imself a crumpled horn, he does. And takes tobaccy on occasion."

"He *does?*"

"He do. Take my advice—write about th'bull. Them city folk'd like t'hear 'bout it."

This observation and advice silenced me again. What a queer person this Mr. Moffat was. Of course I'd never been married so I couldn't say, but I'd think one's sense of curiosity would not be entirely squelched by wedded bliss. Why didn't he inquire as to why I was here? Was it every day a big city reporter-gal came out to Oxthwaite to talk with his wife? I started to wonder what sort of woman Nancy was. Mr. Barnett had said I wouldn't like her— no. That I wouldn't like the *assignment.*

Mr. Barnett….my thoughts took off on a trail of their own that does not bear repeating, for it only brought ticklish happiness well-flooded with venomous guilt so that I was in quite a state by the time the wagon jolted to a stop. We were on a circular drive divided in two by a track of short grass. A low, white farmhouse peered at us through a circlet of currant bushes.

"This be the place," Mr. Moffat said. "If you jest go—"

"Tobias?" The clear, strong voice sailed out the kitchen door and held my escort mid-sentence.

"Did you have need of me, luv?"

"Buy some soap-flakes in town."

"Soap-flakes, Nan? When you could ask me t'buy diamonds and you know I'd fetch 'em for you." He sounded sad— offended, even.

"Yes, well I have no need for diamonds at present—I do have need of clean dishes, else you won't get your supper." At this point the speaker—a sturdy, tall woman wearing woolen trousers, a faded blue cotton shirt, and an apron—appeared in the kitchen doorway. She dried her hands on a white towel and, upon catching sight of me, waved. "Be that Mr. Barnett's little lass?"

"Aye, Nan."

I smiled over this quaint give and take, spoken with a quiet mix of British and country accents that gave me the sensation of plum puddings paired with fried chicken. I supposed the Moffats were of a family that had come over from England some years before. It was obvious the two were fond of one another, though Nancy spoke so brisk and laughed at her husband's vows of affection.

She swung the screen door open and beckoned with one hand. "Miss Harper, we are glad to have you. If you'd just set your bags here at the door I'll get you a cup of tea."

I hopped off the wagon and took my case from the wagon-box. "Tea sounds divine."

"Soap-flakes Nan. Anythin' else?" Mr. Moffat warbled from behind.

Nancy winked at me and tossed a reply over her shoulder as she closed the door behind me: "Get the soap-flakes and if there's a bit of money left over you can see about those diamonds."

I had paused at the entrance to the kitchen, fascinated by the Currier & Ives aura of the room. It was white without being dingy, blue without being cold, and brushed over with feather-strokes of sunlight. The blue gingham cloth was pushed back from one half of the kitchen table, and a hefty typewriter lorded over a myriad of closely-written papers.

"Did you have any trouble with the fellows at the station?" Nancy's voice thrummed with deep tones, gentled at the edges.

"Nothing a kiss wouldn't fix."

"They're all fools—just as bad as some of the fellows in New York.

I thought of Jules with a wince. "I heartily agree on that point."

Nancy took my hat from me and set it above the pie-safe. A silence settled upon us like a feather-bolster and I found the tranquility to my liking. This kitchen was as different from my dingy apartment as a painting of a sky is different to the blue spread above.

I did wonder what the typewriter was for. It occurred to me that this was not a social visit; I ought to be interviewing Nancy.

I took out my tablet from my satchel and bit the end of my pencil. "How long have you known Mr. Barnett?"

Nancy sat down at the type-writer. "Wade? What's a year when he's around?"

A strange reply to a serious question, but I wrote it down anyhow. "Well, approximately how long?"

"I can't remember a day when we didn't know each other—that's for sure."

That was an answer more to my liking. Nancy pushed a cup of tea toward my elbow—the fragrant steam curled upward and wrapped her face in a benevolent ghost of a wreath. "If you don't mind, I'll type while we talk—I'm wonderful at multitasking."

"What is it?"

"This?" Nancy tapped the top of the stack of papers with a wink. "My life's work."

"But...I thought you didn't have a job. I mean—Mr. Barnett mentioned you used to work in the city and now you live in... Oxthwaite. What happened?"

The keys of the typewriter beat a clicking echo to my question.

"Can thinkers abandon thinking just because they've got a child to raise? Does a gardener stop growing roses on his window-sill because he is no longer a professor of horticulture?" The amusement was cool and blue in her eyes as I watched her glance flash down to her papers, over to her flying fingers, and back up to my face:

"Don't make the mistake of thinking the jobs of a writer and a mother can't be combined—out of necessity if not pleasure."

I molded my hands over the teacup. "Then you're a working woman?"

Nancy paused, and the sound of typing cut out, leaving nothing but the stillness of the kitchen. "I am—a three-stranded cord if you will. Mother, wife, and author all rolled into one. The farm hit a rough patch a few years back and is still taking its merry time coming full round again. I thought, why not write a bit on the side like I used to, make a little money, indulge my creativity, and make it easier on Mr. Moffat? I knew people who would be willing to help me—Mr. Barnett for one. I didn't leave the City because there was no place for me, you know. I could have stayed."

The way she said that last part—with a bit of pride tucked in the words—made me smile. This was a woman to be reckoned with—an iron-clad specimen. I spooned some sugar into my tea. I had so many questions now, but somehow my mind wouldn't form up the way it ought to have in the presence of such an interesting woman.

"I never was very sorry I left," Nancy said, taking up the topic and her typing again.

"But you liked it while you where there?"

"I used to be his assistant." She gestured with her head out the kitchen-door and in the general direction of New York.

"Wade's—I mean, Mr. Barnett's assistant?" He hadn't mentioned that in the briefing. I wondered why.

Nancy laughed, and the type-writer ribbon shuddered under the force of her fingers. "One and the same. Mr. Barnett and I are cousins after a fashion."

"Of course." After a fashion. As far as I could tell anyone could claim cousinship with anyone else. Go far enough back in the family tree and we're all a Noah. First Nancy. Then Nalia. Then—

"Our mothers were cousins," she added.

"Do you ever go back?" I asked. "To the City, I mean."

"Twice a month to deliver my finished assignments and pick up new ones. Now and then I'll be sent on a few days' trip to cover a hand-tailored story Mr. Barnett sends me."

"Mr. Barnett sends you on assignments?" I didn't know why that surprised me. It was just the thing I could see a man like Mr. Barnett doing for an old acquaintance. I wished he'd have told me—or maybe I didn't. I don't know…"Excuse me if I sound pretentious but…I've never come across any of your pieces."

Nancy chuckled and shifted the papers on the table, peering at the writing scrawled on them. "My handwriting has gone lazy," she remarked, then looked at me. "It's no surprise. I don't write under the name of 'Nancy Moffat'—I never did. Wade calls me by my *nom de plume* like everyone else who knew me in those days."

"And that name is…?"

"Maralie Barrymore."

My stomach clenched and turned eight somersaults before making itself into something like physical moan. Nancy only laughed and pushed the plate of gingersnaps toward me. "Have another cookie and get your brains together, honey."

Nancy Moffat was Maralie Barrymore? I could hardly imagine it, but all the pieces fell together now like one of those Chinese tumbler-puzzles. The way Mr. Barnett referenced her with the utmost respect and said he knew her well. The reason he'd told me not to seek her out on my own, but to wait till he introduced us. The way Maralie Barrymore had gradually stopped making her legendary public appearances. I looked at her now and noticed behind the apron and cotton blouse the stylish, classy woman who had stolen the hearts of the stubborn New Yorkers fifteen years before.

Nancy removed a finished sheet from the typewriter, blew on it to dry the ink, and studied me. "You're a fresh little thing— where'd Wade pick you up?"

Why was it the one question everyone asked of me? Made me feel as if I didn't belong here, there, or anywhere. "I was working for *The St. Evans' Post.*" It sounded like admitting to a crime in the presence of Maralie Barrymore.

Nancy, however, was gracious: "Well then, let me congratulate you on your promotion. Any woman who is Wade's assistant is fortunate indeed. He speaks warmly of you."

I smiled into my cup, wishing that I wouldn't feel quite so wonderful and loving that I did.

"I know that smile, Miss Harper." Nancy winked at me and I blushed. "Every girl feels that way about Wade."

Even Nalia. Of course Nalia felt that way about him. We all did. Everyone. Every woman he met felt…My tea tasted bitter in my mouth so I swallowed quickly and took a bite of a gingersnap from the plate Nancy had uncovered in the center of the table.

Nancy placed a new sheet of paper in the machine, set the bar, and started typing again. "Never have I met a kinder and a more thorough gentleman than Mr. Barnett. Save Mr. Moffat, of course."

Couldn't we be finished with the topic of Mr. Barnett? I hadn't traveled four hours to discuss the man who complicated everything in my life. It would do no good to be ungracious in Maralie Barrymore's kitchen, but neither would I stoop to leniency.

"He's a terrific firebrand," I said. "He always contradicts me."

Nancy tossed back her head and laughed—it was the infectious sort that one can only meet with on a sunny afternoon in September when the taste of autumn is on the air. I laughed with her, and the words from her typewriter jigged across the paper black and strong. A large gray tabby stalked into the room and, upon sight of me, wrinkled her nose and yawned. I watched her.

"Nancy…you left the City. Why?"

"Why does anyone leave the city? I was tired of it—and it of me, I'm afraid. I was too radical for the New Yorkers."

"Too radical?" Now that was a difficult accomplishment in New York City.

She smirked. "I'd made great success as a writer. The only other career I was bent upon was denied me."

"Horrid men."

"Oh. It wasn't the men that denied it to me." Her smile flickered and her fingers paused on the keys. "It was the women. Say you want to be an actress, they love you. A politician? By all means. But a mother? Ah—you're Marie Antoinette and ought to be sentenced to the guillotine. *Not*," she corrected, "that I think every woman ought to have no career except that of a housewife. But they wouldn't allow me my own choice in the matter. They told me I was a traitor to my sisters."

The frankness of Nancy's answer and the quiet of her kitchen recalled to me the first time I'd stepped into Annamaria's café. Mr. Barnett had mentioned that Annamaria had aspirations to be a famous opera-star but had given them up for "a nobler road." I had been confused then, but with Nancy echoing similar thoughts, I felt out of place—a rhinestone tacked onto a strand of freshwater pearls. Many thoughts ran through the tea-scented silence till it felt not silent at all, but palpable and soul-stirred. And Mr. Barnett seemed to stand on the edge of it all looking at me with his chestnut-colored eyes—daring me to disagree that these were finer women than Nalia.

I sipped my tea and smiled at Nancy. "I admire you," I said, though I didn't know I told the truth till I listened to the burden of my own words as they shattered the small silence.

"Sometimes I really believe my job as Maralie Barrymore was easier," Nancy said with a laugh. "But I find this sampler of careers far more challenging and rewarding."

Our interview was brought to an abrupt end by the entrance of five or six small children tumbling—one on top of another— into the kitchen.

"Mama—did y'make us ginner-bread men?" asked a young chicken with blonde, fly-away curls.

"Can I lick the bowl?" her identical counterpart—in male form—added.

But the older four of the group elbowed the twins into some state of orderliness and the next moment I found myself inspected by six pairs of round, blue eyes. Nancy looked from her children to me and back again, but did not reprimand them for staring so. My face went hot and I suddenly did not know what to do with my hands; I looked down to find my fingers crumbling a gingersnap onto the tea-cloth.

"Howdy," the eldest of the group finally said. She was a ginger with a crop of freckles and might have been eight years old.

"Hey." My voice was peculiar and high-pitched. I didn't know how to behave to children anymore.

"Gee, you're pretty!"

"Ain't she though?"

"Isn't she," Nancy corrected, crossing through a line on her paper with a red pencil.

"Mama—where'd you get her?"

Nancy stuck the red pencil behind her ear and stood, smoothing her apron. "Don't be over-curious, chicki-biddies. I've made you your ginner-bread men, Mary, and you can eat them under the willow if you promise not to bother Miss Harper. She's come to stay the night."

"She has?"

"Did she bring her nightgown?"

197

"Does it have lace?" the ginger asked. Her eyes quite sparkled as she spoke of a nightgown trimmed with lace.

I smiled. "I'm afraid it does."

"Gol-lee."

Nancy walked to the pie safe and brought a battered tin crock off the top shelf. She peeped into it, smiled, and handed it to the ginger. "Be good now. Lana—you're in charge of dividing up the 'ginner-bread' people. And before you come back in for supper I want you to wash up. Miss Harper is Mr. Barnett's special friend and we want things to be nice for her."

"Gol-lee," the ginger said again, and I recognized that star-struck, distant look in her eyes. Eight years old and she too had fallen for this peculiar man. What was he—a wizard, that he charmed everyone he passed? And again that lump of pain spread like cancer through my chest till it hurt to breathe. I was nervous about spying on him like I was a gumshoe of the Gestapo. It didn't feel right—I knew it wasn't right. But what could anyone do in my position?

The children filed out into the yard and I sighed. "They're darlings." Simple. Unspoilt. A far cry from me at that age.

"Darlings? Sometimes. But as a whole I prefer to call them…" she stood and gestured with the empty tea-cups, "…rapscallions. Are you laughing at me, Miss Harper?"

I stood and helped her carry the tea-things to the counter without answering right away. "Nancy…what made you want to have this career? Understand I don't think there's anything wrong with it, but as Maralie Barrymore…the world was at your fingertips."

Nancy put the sugar-bowl and plate of gingersnaps into the Hoosier cabinet, then crossed her arms and leaned against it. "Despite the cliché, you are right. The world *was* at my fingertips.

But I was tired of being at its fingertips—the social life wears on a woman, Miss Harper. I couldn't take the pressure anymore. I was always running back to my mother with another tale of woe, another difficulty. Then Mr. Moffat came along and I married him and suddenly…well, suffice it to say, journalism lost its allure. Then Mum fell ill and I realized just how much she'd meant to me. All those years of bringing me up and pointing me in the right direction…being there for me whenever I needed her. And I thought, if Mum had been a working woman always running after her own career, I'd never have had that. I don't look down on women having careers, Miss Harper."

"But?"

"But we must be careful we are not following a certain path out of selfish motives. Assigning myself to any career—actress, writer, mother—just because I wanted it, would be just as useless as trying to convince the world that the sun revolved around me. We humans need direction, wisdom, and purpose. We can't make that for ourselves. Our stories aren't our own. There is Someone whose plan must be consulted."

"You begin to sound like Mr. Barnett," I said after a pause wherein Nancy mercifully removed her keen gaze and fixed it out the kitchen window where her children played beneath the willow.

Nancy turned round and the corners of her mouth quirked. "Not surprising—we are related."

"Yes…but till I met you, Nancy, I'd thought Mr. Barnett peculiar to himself."

"Him? No—though I wouldn't put it past being a peculiar of those of us in the faith, perhaps. We are always upsetting the apple-cart, aren't we?"

I ought to have known. How could I not have known? Christianity had something to do with even this. My head ached. I disliked my old opinions participating in this widespread upheaval of all I'd known. Christianity—at least the sort one met with in Wexford—was for weaklings and clingy old women. And Mr. Barnett's variety was too radical for my tastes. A God that was in and of and apart from everything? A God that meddled in your business? How could I accept that?

Independence my foot. If you had that sort of God you weren't your own.

My eyes traveled over Nancy's strong, upright figure and rested on her capable hands. Hands that had wiped tears and struck important words out of a typewriter, taken down dictation and fastened buttons. Fingers that had belonged to the glamorous Maralie Barrymore and the humble Nancy Moffat. Fingers, in short, that had seen the world and carved out a very unique path.

I looked at my own hands, small and crumpled in my lap. The fresh coat of apple-red nail polish was so shiny I could see the curve of my lips in their reflection when I raised my hand to brush back my hair. So different from Nancy. Nancy Moffat—Maralie Barrymore—knew exactly what was what in her life. I, on the other hand, didn't know what I wanted. I didn't know why I chose what I chose. What were my reasons—if I had any?

I sighed. Well-played, Mr. Barnett. Well-played.

Chapter 13

"I like you Calida Harper. Don't let your spark burn out." Nancy folded me in her arms, brushed my cheek with her rough palm and released me. "And *don't* over-praise me in that paper of yours. Goodness knows it'll all be apple-butter. I said it wasn't worth it, but Wade insisted on you coming all this way to talk with me."

A brisk wind gamboled across the railway platform and I rolled my eyes in accord with Nancy's complaint. "If I didn't like you so much myself I'd probably give him a ribbing when I got home. But it's all part of his theory." I quirked my fingers quote-unquote on the last word and grinned. "That man is ridiculous."

"Yet we all love him."

I shook my head. "Vexing."

"Shameless."

"Horrid."

"Bad news." Nancy broke into one of her brightest smiles. "But we'd never trade him."

I didn't answer that one. "Maralie—Nancy, thank you."

She spared me the embarrassment of explaining why I was thanking her by embracing me again then waving me off. That amazing woman somehow held half a dozen kids by the hand—keeping the little Moffats from falling onto the rails or disappearing in the luggage-room. I blew a few kisses in their direction, winked at the Lana-the-ginger, as I'd come to call her, and stepped up the narrow staircase into the train. A brief time later the train and I pulled away from the station. I hated the thought of going back to the City; the Moffats' farmhouse—with nothing to vex one but the cat getting into the cream or the hens hiding their clutch of eggs—had awakened memories of my girlhood. But these memories were somehow a balm to my frenzied nerves and though I reminded myself in front of the white-iron mirror that I had accepted the assignment only so I could return and play a foil to Mr. Barnett, I couldn't help but enjoy myself.

Nancy grew smaller and smaller like the fading of a morning mist: a bright dream of cotton and iron dissipating with each turn of the wheels. At the last, when even my hopeful eyes couldn't discern the slightest smudge on the horizon that might be the railway station, I turned back to my seat, flipped open my pad of paper, and started work on the article I'd been composing in my mind since my first moments at Oxthwaite.

"There. Signed, sealed, and delivered."

Mr. Barnett looked up when I dropped the slim folio onto his desk. "It's an Evergreen, isn't it?" he asked.

I crossed my arms. Why'd he send me all the way to Pennsylvania if he didn't plan to run the story right away? Oh well—you can't trust jelly in a sieve and you can't trust a fellow to follow a logical system. "Guess so. What are you working on?"

"Touching up the bright about the gala."

"Gala?"

"The one at the Ritz-Carlton."

"Oh, that one."

"You don't have to sound so miffed, Callie. I didn't send you to Nancy to—"

Get me out of the way. "How do I know you didn't?"

Whining again. Lately I'd taken to whining as a way of life. It annoyed me to no end to find myself sulking so often, but what could I do in the face of a man who weaseled his way into my every thought? If Mr. Barnett hadn't wanted me to attend the gala at the Ritz with him then he could have said so instead of sending me on that long and arduous journey to Nowheresville, PA. If he wanted time with Nalia—who seemed to be the City's darling and attending every social function—he only had to say so and I'd have left him alone…Actually, I would probably have trailed him and found a prime opportunity for scavenging dirt for Jules.

Already Nancy and her quaint farmhouse had vanished shimmer-like in the mirage of the city. They were the false ones —they had to be because everything else was so desperately realistic and pressing and commonplace in comparison. Not a single hour back in the office and I was already tense and conniving.

"Don't purse your lips like that, Callie. It isn't becoming."

"I'll purse them if I want to," I said.

Mr. Barnett glanced at me, at his paper, took off his glasses, and leaned back in his chair. "Come here."

I crossed my arms and glared at him, piling a heap of rubbishy grudges as a flimsy barricade against the sudden softening of his manner.

"Come here," he repeated, and this time grabbed my wrist and pulled me gently around the corner of the desk till I leaned against it and was quite near to him. "Now, Callie. Silly, cross little pigeon." Mr. Barnett's voice was soft and lullaby-ish.

He was attempting to appease me and a dozen old vexations sprang up like rows of pea-shoots in a garden.

"Why do you have to talk to me like that, nosebleed?"

"Nosebleed?" His laughter burst through the cool air of the office and drubbed in my chest. "Don't go ape on me, Callie."

Why do you have to be such a looker? Funny I'd once thought him rather commonplace. Now my eyes traced with sweet familiarity that dear dent in his bottom lip, the upward tilt of the left corner of his mouth…the whole simple, rugged man.

And that whole was enough to make me sick to my stomach with feverish anticipation of wondering what he might say or look or think next. If his actions somehow had to do with me, my heart started up on dove's wings. Irritation! I couldn't think poorly of him and I couldn't applaud him. I couldn't forget him, and I certainly couldn't afford to peruse the file marked Wade Barnett any longer—I was already in danger of more leniency on that topic than my position budgeted.

"You say things that make me feel like a kid," I complained at last.

"I'm sorry." And the vexing thing was I knew he meant it. He drew me even closer till my knee touched the leather of his chair and took my hand in his. "I ought to have asked about your trip. How was Oxthwaite?"

"A man demanded a kiss right after I stepped off the train."

Mr. Barnett's eyebrows jerked upward. "You do some quick work, Scheherazade. What sort of philter did you give him?"

"Nothing at all. Don't be a goober." But our eyes met and exchanged smiles. My gaze fell back onto our hands and I realized he still held mine. His thumb made a small circle on the back of my hand.

"Never mind that," Mr. Barnett said, watching the direction of my look. "Your hands feel cold and I'm warming them. Tell me how you like Nancy."

"If you'd read my articles you'd find out for yourself," I answered him with a saucy smile and pulled my hand away, though I would have been happy to let it lie in his palm a moment longer.

"Go on, thing. Slither away and occupy yourself with your witchery while I read your little papers. Shall I need my red marking-pen?"

"Only to mark it 'A+, One-hundred-percent'."

"Vainglorious woman."

"Doubting man."

He took up my papers and considered me with his head to one side, one brow lowered and the other arched in that curious, puppy-like way. His eyes warmed and soothed my nerves so that the last of my prickles were scoured away and the sun shone again.

"It's good to have you back," he said after an interval of a few moments.

My heart thrilled to hear it but my mind rebelled. I wished he'd leave those pulsing words to shimmer on their own in the office air with the pressure of his fingers still warm upon my hand.

But you can't do this, Callie. You can't fall in love with a guy you're supposed to be spying on. Is spying that bad, or isn't it? Who cares? The point is you're not gonna do yourself or him any favors by going dippy.

I nodded emphatically to myself and tried to arrange it all in my head—which was a considerable task when I knew the object of my reflection was somewhere near at hand with those eyes fixed curiously upon me.

One: He is handsome, kind, and tender.

Two: He can be demanding, difficult, and impractical.

Three: He's the best man you've ever met with in your entire life and there is probably not another like him and—Callie! I dropped my head into my hands to stem this tide running in his favor. It was painfully obvious to myself and had been to Nancy that I found Mr. Barnett very...attractive. I would have to remedy this situation because if anything I'd been gathering about the relationship between Nalia and Mr. Barnett was true, I was only blasting holes in the bottom of my own rowboat—and if the roar of water ahead meant what I thought it meant, I'd need a sound vessel to get through those rapids in one piece.

"Oh—Callie."

"Hmm?"

"A week, and then I need you to get packed again."

I wheeled my chair with a squeak to face him. Amusement and mischief were etched in his face.

"What's up now?"

"A trip."

"Look: I'm not going back to Pennsylvania." I shook my head and drummed against the desktop with my fingertips.

"Nor would I have you."

"Then what's the scoop, loony?"

"Only a short, private, yachting trip." He half rose from his desk, seeing me bridle. "Now don't give me that look, Calida Harper—there will be a dozen celebrities coming with me."

"With you?"

He fixed his eyes on his supple fingers and fiddled with his pen. "Of course—it is my yacht."

If he'd suddenly burst in from the street corner with a Smith & Wesson aimed at my chest, I doubt I'd have been more surprised. It had never occurred to me that Mr. Barnett might be that wealthy—rich enough to own a yacht and fill it with guests whose very blood ran heavy with gold-dust. That he even knew enough celebrities to go on a yachting trip with a dozen of them was marvelous enough—that he was to be the proprietor of the event and the master of ceremonies was incomprehensible.

Again, that strange grey-edge gulf widened between me and the rest of the world. I was left gazing upon an image of Mr. Barnett, Nalia, and a dozen greats standing on the White Cliffs of Dover while I tossed—seasick—on the green swells between, without enough energy to look over my shoulder and see if that ever-eager Jerry had accompanied me on this departure of the lower social order. What a depressing idea—why had Mr. Barnett ruined the beautiful morning by announcing the assignment? I suddenly wished I was dead.

"You don't look at all pleased," he said, tipping his head to one side.

"Why would I be?"

His mouth contracted. "Come again?"

"Why on earth would you expect me to jump at the chance to be taken up like a charity-orphan just because I'm a young leech you've somehow attached to your back pocket? You assume you can't leave me in the 'big bad city' all by myself because I'd be offended, or cause trouble, or feel left out. I'll tell you how to feel humiliation: sit by in a world that bestows upon you a patronizing smile and a peppermint, then moves on, careful to modulate its tones and topics so that your naivety won't receive a shock. Oh—I see those glances you exchange with the higher-ups when you believed me to be deep in thought, absorbed in studying....frescoes!" In my rage I'd risen from my desk and now stood before Mr. Barnett's, shaking with passion.

"Callie...will you please sit down and stop staring at me like a specter rising out of a grave?" He brought a chair to me and rather forcefully pushed me into it. "Now start over and I'll try to understand you."

I held my head high—queen that I was—and my cheeks burned hot. I would not stoop to repeat that strange and revealing torrent. I had already said too much—shown my wounds too deep—and all I could hope for was that he had listened to none of it. He stood again and brought me a cup of tepid coffee.

"We have no cream or sugar," he said. "I hope you don't mind."

I stared into the black, oily depths of the cup and thought of the irony—I'd never known a thing so like my own soul.

"Why don't you pause and reflect for a moment?" he said.

"On what?" Bitter, coffee-stained tones.

"On this *hurlement de rage*."

"I don't speak French, remember?"

"The deuce you don't. Please, Cal—quit acting like a hydrophobic raccoon; I'm half frightened at that vicious sparking of your eyes."

"You started it."

"How?"

"By talking about your...your stupid yacht!"

"You don't have to go, Callie. I thought you'd enjoy the chance to relax with some of the people who will be your close friends by and by when you finally reach your giddy heights."

His humble, cautious tone somewhat tamed my umbrage. I stirred the lukewarm coffee with one finger and dropped my head. All the fire dwindled out of me and left only a smoldering coal. "Sorry."

"For what?"

"Splitting."

"Exploding, rather. But all is forgiven and forgotten." How easily he said those words—yet I knew he meant them and it was no flippancy. "Callie—I won't make you be a guest at my yachting party." His gaze was steady and brown—corduroy breeches with a teddy-bear sheen.

What's this? Disappointment? Callie—what is up with you? You practically shrieked at him that you didn't want to go.

"But as your boss I am assigning you to work the party. You'll have all the privileges of a guest, but I expect you to earn your keep. There—does that please the rabid vixen?"

"Does it please her? Gee, Mr. Barnett! You are fabulous!" I actually tipped over my coffee, dashed over to him, and gave him a hug. The lapel of his woolen jacket was rough against my cheek, and his chest solid. So solid and unmoving—secure, like nothing I'd ever known. My arms dropped limp as soon as I realized what I had done, but Mr. Barnett only laughed and his eyes danced like the 'netted sunbeams' in Tennyson's poem.

"Callie Harper—make sure you don't show the public this upsy-down side—they might take you for the charmer you are and then it would be all up with us."

"What is that supposed to me?"

"Nothing and everything in particular."

I bit my lip and my cheeks flamed again—this time with excitement. "Then while we're playing at riddles, may I ask a question?"

"Prying, gentle, direct, or merry-go-round?"

"All of the above?"

"Then shoot."

"Are you any different than everyone else?"

Mr. Barnett sat down on his desk with a hand on each knee. "Jove, she's turning philosophic on me." His quick gaze traveled to my face and lingered there. "I could answer that each of us is created differently. But that would not satisfy you."

"It would not."

"Methinks you are driving at something a bit more insinuating."

"Perhaps."

"You are wondering whether I am like the common rabble... whether I behave like them in every respect. The fact that you ask the question belies a reluctance to believe it...why then, Miss Harper, do you wish it to be untrue?"

I wrapped myself in a hug and turned from him. "And I thought I was the one doing the digging."

"Never try to beat a lobster at his own pinching-game." His voice was blithe. "Will you come a'sailing?"

I looked at him over my shoulder. "As your pet orphan?"

"As my galley-slave." He grinned and I rolled my eyes.

"Not as a slave…but a free-working journeyman…"

"As my employee, then?" he asked.

"Agreed." I stuck out my hand and for the second time that morning Mr. Barnett cupped it in his own and I wondered what it could be that sent a tingle through my entire arm.

I hurried down the sidewalk toward my apartment that evening with firecrackers glowing inside me. There was much to be excited about—despite the shadows of murderous fathers or traitorous coworkers—and the yachting trip was beginning to sound like a downright lark. After all, Mr. Barnett had been right: it would be pleasant to spend several days surrounded by none but the people I meant to become one with someday. And what a peach he was to think of me! As usual in these cases I'd spoken too swift, felt too keen, and made a bloody hash of it all. But Mr. Barnett had behaved just as became him as a gentleman and nothing had been breached beyond repair.

What's more—and the thing that influenced this current warmth of opinion more than anything—he'd paid me my last month's salary in a lump-sum and inside my pocket, I clutched a generous check. I would spend it tomorrow—which Mr. Barnett had consented to give me for a holiday—buying the various little things I'd need for this end-of-summer yachting expedition. I ticked the mental notes off my list. Oh—and I'd have to see if

Jerry could watch Nickleby again as he'd done when I trotted off to Pennsylvania.

I ducked through the door of my apartment-building, successfully avoiding a fellow with a bottle-brush mustache and a paunch who was exiting. "Hey, Jerry!"

"Miss Harper!" He beamed at me and gave his bell an even more vigorous polish than usual.

"How was the day?" I couldn't just pop out with another request for pet-sitting…when I came home from Oxthwaite last night Nickleby had informed me with his claws of the indignity it had been to his Tom-hood to play lobby-mascot for a weekend. I could only imagine how my pet must have behaved for Jerry.

"The day was top-notch," Jerry said. His abstracted smile began again, and I found myself smiling back at him. I'd been so busy lately I hadn't realized the missing hominess of Jerry's blind devotion to me. I hoped he wasn't still in love—even a turtle-dove would freeze when exposed to my temperature of late—and I much doubted that he could be which was comforting. I didn't like to hurt him.

"And how is that fascinating animal of yours?" Jerry asked.

"Nicks? Oh—he's fine. Ah….Jerry?"

"Yes, Miss Harper?"

"I'm going on a yachting trip with Mr. Barnett and some of the gold-dollars. We're leaving Wednesday and staying out through the weekend. Um…I was wondering if maybe you'd be a charmer and…"

"Come with you?"

"With me?"

At my shocked expression Jerry put up a gloved hand and laughed—a short, wheezing, jolly sound. He'd made a joke, evidently. But my mind still chucked and whirred like a derailed model train and I had half a mind to punch him for giving me such a turn. The idea of Jerry Atwood on an extended weekend with Nalia Crosticinni and Ernest Hemingway and who-knows-who-else was flabbergasting.

I drew my head high, vexed that Jerry had got me after all with that ridiculous jest of his. "Actually, Jer, I was hoping you could keep Nickleby for me again."

He saluted. "Anything for you, Miss Harper. He'll be waited on hand and foot—paw and foot, rather." And that expressive wheeze that was meant to be a laugh escaped him again.

"Thanks." I waved my fingers and stalked off toward my room.

Once installed with a crusty loaf and some grapes of a dubious firmness, I felt quite French and adventurous again. I had, too, a letter in my hands written in the elegant script of Nalia Crosticinni. Despite the recent developments between she and Mr. Barnett—despite that fact that something hot and thistle-spurred sprang to life each time I thought of a possible relationship between the two—there still lived in me a fondness toward this first friend I had among the glittering salons of New York City's 'Society.' I had only been assistant to Wade Barnett for a matter of eight or ten weeks—certainly not time enough to make so many friends I could afford to lose one.

I flipped the envelope over and slit it with my fingernail. The cherry-red manicure I'd paid a dollar-fifty for last week was already losing luster—I'd have to get that re-done. I licked my mental-pencil and wrote it down on my list of Things To Do Before Yachting. Get new hat. Starch collars. Buy sailing dress.

Pencil poised, I considered the expense of the next item, then wrote it down. Get a permanent.

All read, it tallied up to the tune of an inheritance. I discarded the mental-pencil and pulled a single sheet of scented paper from the linen envelope. Nalia. Yep—even if the handwriting hadn't given it away, the smell would. What on earth did she wear that smelled like bottled sunset? It wasn't 'Evening in Paris', nor was it 'White Shoulders'. Maybe 'Tigress'. Yes—that would be it. She was so like a tigress herself—tawny and black, elegant and sultry. I unfolded the sheet of paper and settled myself to read with Nickleby looking on:

My Bella *Calida,*

Wade has told me you are coming along with for the yachting party. Meraviglioso! *Since the day I first met you,* mia bella, *I have known you to be an original—a woman of your own stamp and flavor. A charmer with much* zucchero con la spezia—*sugar with the spice.*

I see how you look at Wade Barnett, mia cara, *and it reminds me of myself. How the women of today must work to shake from ourselves that desire to be won. That is not what we want—you of all women know this —but the pathways of a hundred years agone have taught us to become enchanted with the* fascino *of a man who would treat us like his queen. Even I—a woman who is accustomed to attentions—find myself strangely attracted to these rare men.*

Ah, Callie! What a trial it is to be a woman in this modern age! Would that we were men and could dispense with these softer yearnings!

But I ramble—what I took up my pen to tell you is this: it is with great anticipation that I look forward to Wednesday—to seeing you. Wade tells me you would not come as his guest—I think it a wise, alluring choice. A woman cannot be too careful of accepting these favors. Addio!

Yours ever,

Nalia Crosticinni

Well, well, well. I threw the sheet from me and pulled Nickleby into my lap. "What do you say to that?"

His tail was three sizes larger than usual.

"Exactly, Nicks. I am sure this was meant as a warning."

But a warning against what, I could not tell. A warning against me entertaining thoughts of Wade Barnett because Nalia feared for my own happiness? If so, it was an officious concern—I was no mere babe of sixteen—I was this side of thirty with a sensible head on my shoulders. Then if Nalia did not warn me out of fear for my happiness she would be concerned for...her own. She detected the wavering of my heart in Mr. Barnett's case and she—like all those pretty little rich girls at the playground—was tired of sharing the seesaw. She wanted him for herself—hadn't she said it in her own words?

I stood and retrieved the paper, then scored the line with my fingernail: "I see how you look at Wade Barnett, *mia cara*, and it reminds me of myself."

Well this was a handy log of toadstools! I set the letter down like a sensible human this time, crushing it between the potted fern and a copy of *Hard Times* so that I might be able to glare upon it from my seat without bestirring myself. Then I dropped into my chair on top of Nicks—he reminded me of his presence with compound-riposte against my backside. I turned on him with a growl, picked him up by his black-velvet cravat and tossed him from me. "Dratted beast. I hope Jerry....cooks you!"

Cooking reminded me I had not eaten since luncheon—which had been a dull affair of club-soda and club-crackers and shavings of the hardest cheese that Mr. Barnett had produced from some obscure corner of the office. Well...luncheon and that snack of bread and grapes we'd just imbibed. But that didn't count. "We shall have Chinese tonight, Nickleby," I announced. He would not answer me nor look in my direction since my latest affront. "Then you won't get any of the General T'sao's," I warned. At that tone of voice he swiveled about and blinked.

On my way to the other side of the room for the phone, Jerry's familiar pompous knock hacked at my door.

"What's up, Jerry?" I called.

"Letter from a chap says he knows you." Jerry's voice was garbled and fat from coming through the door, but I heard him clear enough. My stomach clenched with anticipation—it could be a letter from Mr. Barnett. It could contain something I would regret to hear—some announcement of his love for Nalia—but I thought I would rather hear it by his own hand then wait to know when I saw them together.

"I'm kinda busy right now. Could you slide it under the door?"

"I can and will and have—you see? Goodnight, Miss Harper."

"Goodnight."

After he was gone—after his faithful tread had long exited the corridor and I could hear the elevator chime as the doors closed behind him—I stayed with my hand resting on the phone. I stared at the slim envelope, willing myself to go and fetch it. The worst it could be was that dread announcement. The best would be some mischievous line or two, or a list of instructions for my further duties leading up to the expedition. I knew Mr. Barnett thought of me as a friend—perhaps even a close friend at this point—so I feared no harsh words or cutting remarks. That consideration lessened the lurid glow surrounding the envelope. Besides, how was I so certain Mr. Barnett felt for Nalia in that way? I'd never seen anything that absolutely indicated such affection. They were friends. Just friends. Like me and him. My heart seized up and scattered in a hundred pieces. He was more than a friend to me. He was a kindred spirit. What then of Nalia?

Don't be a troll, Calida Harper. You know you have to read that letter.

I walked over, tore the paper off without looking at the address, and began to read. My anxiety melted off as I saw the writing in no way belonged to Mr. Barnett. I tensed—it was not Mr. Barnett's, but I think I would rather it had been an invitation to his wedding than the reality:

"Cal—I'm getting impatient. Ten days. I'll give you ten days more and if you don't have something to tell me, New York City will be roiling under the swarm of cats I let outta bags."

No signature, no opening—just that terse, strained line or two that brought the apartment tumbling down around my ears. I was not a free woman any more than Delilah had probably been when she betrayed Sampson. Did someone have a knife at her throat? I chuckled with a bitter, percolating sound, and tore Jules' note to shreds.

Nickleby and I had a regular bonfire that night: we lit one scrap of that hideous note, took a bite of Chinese, and lit another. I gloried in the tawny writhing of the burning things. It was pleasant to be the keeper of the flame for once. I'd had enough writhing.

The Collected Letters of Wade Barnett:

September 10th, 1952

Dear Maralie and Tobias,

I told you I sensed something wrong with Callie, and I have at last found what it is.

Though I've kept tabs on Jules Cameron, I had not been able to discern what he wants from her. I know it is her past he threatens to expose—what stronger bait could he have? But it was not till a week ago—when I sent Cal at last to meet you— that I found the key to this puzzlement. I took a walk down to *The Post* building to visit Mr. Shores and give him an update on production. The second issue of *Ladybird Snippets* is due out next week, and I had promised him the editorial this time—I'm sorry now I did it. He is such a crabbed old creature.

However you wish to describe the thing, I met Jules Cameron in the hall and had much difficulty suppressing the desire to imprint my knuckles in his smooth cheek. You might well say such a violent disposition cannot be a good harbinger of things to come. Perhaps outside of the circumstances it would not be. But I feel no hatred for Mr. Cameron—only a deep pity and disgust and righteous anger that he has been cowardly enough to corner a woman in this way. I know this feeling is not wrong, however you might frown, Maralie.

Jules looked harmless enough—he smiled, asked about Callie's health as if they were old chums, and said he was delighted with the lucky strike *Ladybird Snippets* seems to be. But I caught the scheming smile on his face when he thought I had moved down the hall and could no longer watch him. Thank God for hall mirrors—I saw that look and every suspicion of mine is confirmed double-fold. Jules Cameron has threatened Calida with her ruin unless she exposes some deep, wretched secret of mine.

Thank God she will not be able to find a secret that puts me in the wrong. By Jesus' stripes I've been healed of the wild sins that so consumed my early years. Ah—but they are long ago and I have paid my dues. Nothing my Callie could find would be enough to satisfy that villain.

And there's the rub.

He will not be satisfied, and thus he will expose the poor creature unless I can stop them. Tell me, Tobias, what a man is to do in this situation? Ah—lucky man. You've never been a target of scandal and intrigue, have you?

I have asked my contacts across the city—Annamaria, Badger down at the printers', Gregory at the Stork Club, and many others—to phone immediately if they see Cal and Mr. Cameron together. I only pray I'm by when the call comes, as I have no doubt it will any day now.

This is the first concern in my mind—concern for the precious, wounded woman whom I love. But troubles never come in singles—they're a capricious breed that must have company. Therefore my second trial has appeared in the form of Nalia.

She has not let up.

She has phoned thrice and the Ritz-Carlton gala was a frightful experience. I had a long talk on the phone with Vincent the other night, telling him my suspicions that his wife is aching for more of him, and reaching ever out of their home nest. In short, that she's been pestering me.

Dense, stupid, stubborn Italian! (Both of them!)

I don't know if he has listened, but I invited them on the yachting trip—the both of them—hoping they will find it to be a second honeymoon of sorts. I pray for rejuvenation and on this trip I have the happy task of advising them over what to do with Nalia's odious manager—a fellow who hasn't done a tenth of what she pays him to do for the last year and a half.

He boasts rheumatism as his excuse—he has a problem in his bum, all right. His trouble is that he is one: a lazy bum, not worth the keeping.

I am to meet with Nalia and Vincent one of the afternoons; pity business always will make its way into my pleasure.

But Callie—even mixed with business—is enough for me. To be near her…to watch over her and know that while she is on the ocean and under my wing, Jules cannot dog her every footstep…I wish I could ease this trouble of hers, and kiss away the tears that flood her eyes when she thinks I am occupied with my work.

I would tell her of my love for her.

I would, but with the announcement of love must come the announcement of so much more. Of the truth I've shielded her from, never intending to get my heart entangled. Oh, that my heart would stick to its job of pumping blood and leave my soul be! I would gladly dispense my entire fortune to the task of preserving Callie from the wretched choice she must make.

Am I wrong in feeling curiosity over what she will choose?

If she chooses to preserve her own life, I will not blame her. But I will know she does not love me as I love her, and will crumble my love and hide it away without speaking of it to her. Anything I might have seen to the contrary, that choice will be the telling mark. Could a woman who loves a man betray him? No. I do not think she could.

I will not hold this against Calida Harper.

Her life and choices are her own. But I pray—agonized, deep petition—that she will choose the noble way. All the lessons I have tried to teach her, all the advice I've given, all the hours spent in prayer…will they be for naught?

I will wait and pray and enjoy this love while I can. Calida Harper deserves my faith, if nothing else. I will give her this, and nothing you can say, Maralie—nor you, Tobias—can dissuade me. You don't know her as I do. I think—I hope—she will prove all I think her to be.

Your wretched friend,

Wade Barnett

Chapter 14

"It's far beyond the stars, it's near beyond the moon…" Somewhere in the cluster of men and women gathered at the docks I heard the familiar strains of Bobby Darin's song and knew the voice to be Mr. Barnett's. "Beyond the Sea" had to be his favorite song, because anytime he sang a thing it always started out with a bar or two of that, even if he switched a moment later.

"I know beyond a doubt my heart will lead me there soon…"

This time his voice was close behind me. I whirled around to see him with a new fedora on his head and his eyes squinted against the sun. He spread his arms out, struck a theatrical pose, and finished his song: "We'll meet beyond the shore, we'll kiss just as before. Happy we'll be beyond the sea and never again I'll go sailin'. Ah—you're here at last, Miss Harper."

"As you see." My cheeks burned—I wished he wouldn't be quite so loud about the whole thing. Several of the people about the dock were already staring at us—people whose faces were familiar to me because I'd seen them in the newspapers more than once or twice. "Mr. Barnett—just tell me where to put my things and I'll get out of your way."

"Nonsense—give them to Dirigible."

"Dirigible?"

His lean brown finger pointed at a stout man in blue and brown, before Mr. Barnett whipped off to attend to his guests. I gripped my double-load of travel-cases and squared my shoulders.

"Mr. Dirigible?"

"Ain't m'name," the fellow grunted.

"It…isn't?"

"No, miss. M'name's Dirigible. Ain't no Mistah-Dirigible about it." His voice crackled with a Cockney accent, and his chin jutted like the prow of a boat from under his face.

This reply silenced me for a moment but I could not stand there chatting it up with a coverall-clad sailor. "Well then, Dirigible, would you be a darling and take my things to a cabin?"

"Be you crew or a guest?" His eyes worked me up and down as if he wasn't sure which category to file me in.

No more was I. "Mr. Barnett?" I snagged his sleeve as he passed by and pulled him to a stop. "Am I a crew-member or a guest?"

"Neither, I should think."

"You're laughing at me!"

His eyes twinkled, even under the shadow of his raised hands. "I am laughing. You look like a lost bird with her feathers ruffled because she cannot find her nest. What the deuce do I care if you're crew or guest? You refused one and look cross over the other. Dirigible—find a nice, quiet place for my little bird to lie down for a while." He put a hand out and squeezed my arm in a reassuring manner, then dashed off again to be the ministering spirit of calm to the rest of the party.

When I turned back to Dirigible, I saw laughter in his eyes too.

I shrugged. "Well stow me away somewhere safe and not too close to the engine and I'll love you forever."

I handed the man my bags and followed him to a large, comfortable cabin below-decks. "Room 16," the door plaque read.

"You oughter be comfortable here." Dirigible tugged his hat, nodded at me, and swaggered out the door.

I put my hands on my hips and drew a deep breath of the tarry salt-air that blew in through the open porthole. This was the life. A sunny day glistening outside, a cool white room inside, and a dozen celebrities sandwiched between. I did a little jig on the braided rug and laughed to myself, entirely forgetting my tantrum on Monday when Mr. Barnett suggested I come along on the pleasure outing.

A knock at my open door brought me round. "Yes? Come in."

"Ah—Miss….Harper, I believe?"

I looked at the blond, fair young man with a deal of curiosity. He appeared to be no older that fifteen or sixteen. "I am she," I said.

"Well that's swell. Pleased to know you. Splendid boat, isn't she?" A pair of blue eyes took their time in examining me and the fellow's mouth eased into a lopsided smile.

"Who are you?" I couldn't wait any longer and as he seemed to be quite comfortable—which made me less so—I thought I'd better have it out.

"David Nelson."

I crossed my arms and summoned a more superior tone of voice. "I'm afraid I don't know you."

"Well that's not hard to understand, Miss Harper. But I'm sure everyone will know us pretty soon."

This boy's comfortable, cool manner fascinated me. "What on earth do you mean by that, you provoking thing?" He was such a droll little cockerel.

He laughed and the world seemed pleasanter for it. "Ever heard of Harriet Hilliard? Or Ozzie Nelson? They're my parents and me and my younger brother—all of us—have a television show. It'll be airing on the third of next month."

"I see."

"Mr. B say's you're a reporter—a big-time one."

"Did he now?"

"Sure. Do you want to come up on deck and watch us leave shore? I've wanted to see something like this ever since watching *Captain Kidd*—I've never been around boats much. They make my mother sea-sick. Coming?"

"I'd like that." I grabbed my tablet and a sharp pencil—I might as well cover the story of the television series. Since Mr. Barnett had invited the Nelsons he was doubtless interested in their professional life.

David Nelson and I wandered mid-ships toward the aft of Mr. Barnett's yacht. "*The Calida* is a hundred-ninety-one-footer!" David called over his shoulder as he strode a little way ahead of me through the hall.

I pulled to stop: a tugboat without her power-supply. "*The Calida*?"

"That's her name," he explained. "Mr. Barnett says it means 'beautiful warmth' in Greek and since he only sails her during the warm weather, he figured it fit."

"I see." But it took several minutes of trailing a pace or two behind David Nelson to regulate my heartbeat.

Was it only a coincidence that this yacht and I would someday come together? I'd never before met a person—let alone a boat—with my name. It seemed too strange to be true, yet I dared not assign any more importance to the occurrence than the fact that Mr. Barnett was a talented linguist and probably spoke Greek along with his French and Italian and what-not. Besides—he'd have christened his yacht *Calida* years ago. *Stop torturing yourself, missy.*

We took a narrow flight of stairs, broke through a band of staterooms, and ended up on the second deck at the aft of the yacht. Below were a dozen or so people, and I caught sight of Mr. Barnett's fedora dashing here and there with him as he flashed through his party. We were near to pulling away from the dock and the New York City skyline loomed large before us.

Mr. Barnett gave the signal toward the captain who—as David and I decided—was stationed somewhere on the bridge above our heads. The engines whirred, the anchor lifted, and soon the mood-colored waters of the Hudson were slipping between the city and us like silk through one's fingers.

Those on shore—the motley array of reporters and valets and family members that inevitably accompany a goodbye of any sort—cheered and we replied with a lusty cheer of our own; the pleasure-outing had begun. We stared out on the broadening water for a time. Neither David nor I spoke. What there could be to say, I did not know. My own heart was full to silence with mingled pleasure and anxiety. This was my first luxurious and unnecessary expedition ever, and I was pledged to kill it by finding something horrid about Mr. Barnett and likely ruining my reputation of him. That was the cause of this lousy ache in my chest and the throb behind my eyes—I did not want to think badly of him because I...

I love him.

The moment I let myself think those words, I regretted them. I regretted the sudden joy that leaped in my heart and turned my cheeks to fire. I love him. The words opened a door I had not known was locked and the inward rush of emotion astonished me. I felt the need for fresh air and looked for an exit, not recalling that I was already outdoors and had nowhere to flee.

"See that bird? I think it's an albatross. Do you know, Miss Harper, that they fly thousands of miles without once stopping to rest?"

David's voice seemed to come to me across a great distance as if I had left him on the shore and he called to me—leagues away —to see the seabird. I squinted against the glare of the sun—no more dazzling to my eyes than this new feeling was to my soul— and saw the great bird, pinions flashing and gleaming beneath the sunlight. My heart was like that albatross—wandering, white, alone.

I felt ill.

"David—could you introduce me to your parents and your brother—Ricky, was it? We've been up here so long they'll start organizing a search-party." My tone was anvils lighter than my heart.

David grinned. "Gee—that's right. You don't know anyone here do you?"

I smiled grimly. "I know two people and you make a third. Come—I'm beginning to feel giddy with all this sun and wind."

He led me below, onto the first deck, and I soon found myself speaking with my new friend's parents, and panicking that Ricky Nelson would lean too far over the rail and tumble into the ocean.

Though I kept a weather eye out, Mr. Barnett seemed to have disappeared. Nalia was in the corner, already lounging with that peculiar inane grace she had in one of the deck chairs. Several men in various examples of summer clothing clustered about her.

"For a woman who hates the attentions of men she sure does a good job of collecting them," I muttered to myself.

"Pardon me, Miss Harper—what was that?" Mr. Ozzie Nelson asked, leaning forward to catch my words.

"Oh!" I whipped around. "Just some silliness. I was talking to myself." I smiled at Mr. and Mrs. Nelson. "If you'll just excuse me, I must leave you for now."

I hurried away from their sympathetic glances and from David's curious looks, careless of the fact that I might be questioned later as to my sudden departure. I did not feel like talking to Nalia—not now. Not here.

Somehow I fumbled my way to my stateroom and dropped, exhausted onto the bed. I pulled off my large black hat and cast it into the chair, then got up and hung it properly on the rack—I wasn't rich yet and I couldn't afford a new hat if this one got crushed through carelessness. I wandered to the mirror and stared hard at my reflection in the bright glass. I was pretty—I knew that without the mirror telling me. Tall, slender, elegant…I saw nothing that gave me concern as far as appearances went. I never indulged in false modesty—I was vain enough to know and to make the most of my good points. Any man in his right mind would find me attractive.

Mr. Barnett had often displayed signs of not being 'in his right mind' in one sense of the term. He chose the strangest people as his friends...people varying from the queen-like Nalia Crosticinni to brown, practical Nancy Moffat. Since Nancy turned out to be Maralie Barrymore, one could forgive him that, but he chose people ranging from the Jerry Atwood's to the... me's. I stared deep into that mirror-Callie's eyes and gripped the frame of the mirror on either side, willing my reflection to tell me what was wrong. Why this struggle of soul and heart and flesh with a man against whom I had no power? It would be far, far better for me to leave the entire ordeal—to give Jules what he wanted and to quit my job. Mr. Barnett would be disappointed, but I knew that with Nalia for a sweetheart and his broad acquaintance to entertain him, he'd soon forget me. I could not be worth much to him—why, excepting my rare victory with the pen, I had not even done much as an assistant. Come to think of it...had I done anything?

Self-doubt was bitter, but I could swallow the draught. I had been sickly in that respect all my life and was used to the vile medicines of constant failure. I was no first-class journalist. I wasn't a novelist or a correspondent or anything I had assumed it lay in my talent to be.

"Callie?"

I jumped four feet in the air—I'm certain—and came down hard enough to rattle the mirror in its frame. "Mr. Barnett!"

"I was just looking in to make sure you are settled. All well?"

I swallowed hard, my hand still at my throat, and nodded.

"Good. I saw you with young David Nelson—what do you think of that family? Rather a handsome bunch, aren't they? I'm sure the television series will be a hit. The idea's almost the same as my theory about *Ladybird Snippets*."

He filled the doorway, one hand pressed against either side of the lintel like the pictures of the prophets in the old Bible tales. "I want you to sit close to me at dinner, all right? And no—it isn't because I think you're a baby girl in need of a nurse-maid. It's because you are my particular friend, you are too witty for your own good, you are pretty, you are naive, and I don't want a catamount on my hands because you run off and get offended."

This bluff summing-up of my past behavior instilled enough commonsense into my head to occasion a reply. "This is how you repay me for my slavery?" I asked: "With fawning insults?"

"Would you rather have them administered in vinegar and cayenne?"

"Beast!"

"Beauty." He caught my eyes for a moment and again I was at a loss to look away. "But—" and he broke off the spell of a sudden, "this particular rose has thorns enough to spear a kingdom and she must be handled only by those who know the trick."

"And I suppose you consider yourself an expert?"

"I've been studying horticulture all summer."

I could only smile—pain and satisfaction sharing equal revelry —as Mr. Barnett searched the room with his eyes, his gaze coming to rest at last upon me. "Everything looks right," he said at last, and I was not certain that he spoke of the room. "Be sure you're down for supper."

I was down for supper. Down and dressed to the nine's so I wouldn't look like a slob beside the gorgeous Nalia. She and I flanked Mr. Barnett on either side. I much doubted that the Cold War I sensed was entirely my imagination. It began with a total ignorance of me on her part—that I did not mind so much, but it was the absorbing of Mr. Barnett's every moment that I resented. What right had she to keep him charmed? I could be charming, but there's not a Betty Grable herself who could charm a man away from an equally charming woman without a *bit* of a break in the conversation. I picked at my food in silence for the most part. Now and then, on my left, David roused me from my blue study with a rascally observation of the present company. I kept hoping Mr. Barnett would say something to me, but Nalia had all the trumps tonight.

Maybe he'd escort me to the state-room afterward? But Dirigible rang the supper bell and the company separated.

It continued in such a state for the next two nights. I thought a time or two that Mr. Barnett would have paid me more attention if Nalia would stop speaking for a moment. But she talked everyone into silence—Mr. Barnett, her husband, and the rest of the company besides. I wished there was someone aboard ship who wasn't fascinated by Nalia Crosticinni.

Besides the Nelsons, I had been introduced to an American duchess; a prominent New York banker; the stunning Priscilla Lane and her husband Howard; Nalia's husband, Vincent Crosticinni; several elderly folk of genial appearance who had nothing original to say between them. All and sundry were captivated by Nalia's conversation. So the enforced vow of silence continued, and I felt myself drifting...drifting away from something very dear to me.

During the day there was not much to do but sun oneself on the deck, watching the small islands of the New England coast slip by. David Nelson was my companion during most of my rounds—curious as always, ever at my elbow asking about the journalism business and how I gathered my information.

"How do you know when to ask the questions?"

"How do you know?" I teased, elbowing him.

He grinned that lopsided grin I'd learned to love. "Gee…I always kinda thought there was a formula or something."

I rolled my eyes and re-tied the pale blue bandana that kept my hair from the teasing fingers of the wind. "You and me both, kid."

"Mind if I ask you something?"

"Shoot."

"What do you think about eloping? I mean, if you're already married."

I started to laugh till I saw that David was very much in earnest, his blue eyes clouded over with trouble. "What on earth gives you an idea like that? You aren't thinking of running off with Mrs. Lane, are you? That's a lousy plan." I placed my fists on my hips and stared hard at him—I'd seen those sighs of boyish admiration he bestowed on the blonde goddess every time she entered the room on her husband's arm.

Though David's cheeks turned three shades of red, his mouth was firm. "No ma'am. I'd never do it. I think I'd be more honorable than that."

I placed both my hands on the yacht-rail of the aft-deck and dragged in deep draughts of the salt-flavored air. From behind us came the clink of chess-pieces as Mr. Lane and Mr. Nelson played a game together. Priscilla Lane, Mrs. Nelson, and the old women were deep in discussion at the opposite end of the deck. The others were not to be seen here.

"Why on earth are you thinking of such disagreeable things as elopements on a fine day like this?" I asked.

David bit his lip. "I don't know. It's just…well…these things do happen. And the more people I meet the more often I see it."

"Thus runs the course of life, honey," I said. I put my arm around him and hugged him. Such a fine-grown lad, but such a lad still! "Wait till you're my age. You'll have seen it all by then."

"Callie," –he'd dropped 'Miss Harper' at dinner the first night. "Wanna get some ice-cream?"

"Sounds divine. Catch you in a minute?"

David trotted off in the direction of the galley and I knew Dirigible would give him all the sweeties he could carry off. What was it with sixteen year old boys that proved so irresistible —even to crusty old seamen? I leaned heavily against the chrome rail and sighed. We'd nosed back north and the yacht was, I knew, carrying us every hour closer to New York City. It had been a luscious rest, but I'd not been idling my time away. A story on "Ozzie and Harriet" was quite fat and full of incidentals that I'd garnered out of David who was disposed to be communicative. Another bright on cosmetic tips from Priscilla Lane was also finished and filed in my briefcase next to three short memoirs from the elderly women of their glory days in the Roaring Twenties. Such pieces would—I knew—please Mr. Barnett.

But for all this I still had not gathered the goods for Jules. There had been another telegram waiting for me at Martha's Vineyard. How he knew we would touch there was a mystery to me—though I supposed it a popular place for every pleasure-party, being one of the largest islands around Cape Cod. In the telegram Jules assured me in the sharpest terms that he would not wait longer than three days more for the information he desired.

The breeze attempted to muss my hair again and brought me back to the moment. Ice-cream sounded like a fabulous idea, now that I came to consider it seriously. Perhaps a bowl or two would bring me some idea of where I might find a chink in Mr. Barnett's impervious armor.

Well into my second bowl of strawberry ice cream, I still had not come to any definite conclusion of how I'd blow the man's cover. David had long-since vacated the kitchen to raid the storeroom with his younger brother, Ricky.

I licked my spoon and moped to myself. Why couldn't Mr. Barnett be guilty of embezzlement? That was scandalous while much less detrimental to my feelings—much anyone cared about those. I scooped another bowl of ice-cream and doused it with chocolate-syrup, then sighed.

I needed Nickleby.

I stirred my ice-cream into a malt-like, grey mixture—I never ate my ice-cream from a bowl in any other fashion. Licking the spoon, I reflected on the unfairness of life: Because my father had been a man, he'd killed another man. Because my brother had been a man, he'd signed up for the war and got himself killed. Because Jules was a man he'd discovered my past and blackmailed me, and because Mr. Barnett was a man I'd fallen in love with him and now had to discover something shameful about him that I'd rather not know. The only person in this whole business who wasn't a man was me—much good that did me now! I'd far rather have been born a fellow, now that it came down to it. That would at least have eliminated this horrid churning in my stomach when I thought of the task I'd accepted.

I looked at my ice-cream and decided I didn't want it after all. A bowl and a half was quite enough when piled on top of what might amount to stomach-ulcers. Dirigible was nowhere to be seen and the rest of the staff and taken themselves to their cabins for their brief hour or two of rest at this time of day when few guests were stirring.

I slid off the galley-stool and sighed. Since when had I added sighing to the list of weak things I was in the habit of doing? Sighing…whining…what next? I peered at the round-faced clock. Two hours till dinner. This would be the last dinner we'd have together, for the next morning we were scheduled to dock in New York harbor and the holiday would be over. There was dancing planned, and Nalia was to sing for us. I'd even heard rumors of Ozzie Nelson leading the band for a portion of the evening. I'd want to look especially nice for this last shot at glamour. As planned, when I returned to the City and defected to Jules, I would resign my position. This evening would be my last as a "successful" journalist.

I hung a left out of the galley and headed aft—my cabin was somewhere relatively midships. I braced myself lightly with one hand on the wall against the faint pitching of the boat—something I'd grown used to, unlike Mrs. Nelson who had remained below-deck much of the trip, bedridden with seasickness.

I'd wear the daffodil silk again—the one Mr. Barnett had liked so well. Yes, I wanted to please him. I wanted him to look at me one last time and to feel his satisfaction. He would never look at me in such a way again after tomorrow. I knew for a fact—even if I didn't find any dirt on him directly—that Jules would expose my past and the result would be the same.

Yes—the yellow silk and the set of pearls; they would spin their magic one last night.

I had been moving silently down the hall, careful not to make a noise that might wake one of the old ladies—I had a dread of encountering one of them if she'd been interrupted in her napping. The soft hush of my fingertips running against the wall was the only sound in the corridor. But I heard voices—a man and a woman's—coming from one of the rooms. My fingers found the door to be ajar, and the silence of the hall was such that I heard the conversation clear as if I was a part of it.

I had always been curious and not over-cautious in what I chose to hear. I was not disposed to mend my ways now, and when the voices rose a degree and I could discern them as Mr. Barnett's and Nalia's, my heart froze, thundered, and generally made a rodeo of itself.

"He needn't know, Wade,"

Needn't know what?

"It would only cause him...unnecessary concern." Nalia's voice was rich and chocolate-flavored as usual—soothing while alluring.

What a teasing cat! Spit it out, floozy.

"Nalia....you know how much I want this for you." That was Mr. Barnett in his corduroy tones.

"For *us*,"

"Well, yes. That's right. But we must be careful—we can't let the news get out too quickly—it might cause a scandal." There was that well-known smile-sound in his voice and the recognition of it—my favorite of all his tones—sliced into my heart. He was smiling at Nalia. *For* Nalia.

Heart full of spite, eyes flashing daggers, teeth clamped onto my bottom lip, I pulled my tablet from my pocket with its accompanying pencil, and wrote down what I'd heard. This was the break Jules was waiting for. This was what I was waiting for. The news jarred me, but hadn't I expected it all along?

"What will we do with Miss Harper?" At hearing Nalia speak my name, my hand froze. My breath came so fast and trembling I was much concerned the two would hear it.

"With Callie?"

Yes, Mr. Barnett. What did you plan to do with me? Not that you'll have a chance—I'll save you that trouble by getting rid of you first.

"I'd rather not tell her outright. She'll find out soon enough. There's enough old-world innocence about her to make me wish to be careful with her feelings.

Old-world innocence?! It was all my outraged will-power could do to hold my arms back from thrusting open the door and decrying him to his face. Old-world innocence! As if it wasn't bad enough that he was taking Nalia away from her husband, he wouldn't give me the satisfaction of hearing about it? I could take many things before I could swallow this treatment.

The occupants of the room had been quiet for a moment—I could only imagine the soft sheen of Nalia's eyes….she was likely toying with Mr. Barnett's cuff with those slender, shapely fingers.

"When will we tell him?" she asked.

"No later than Tuesday."

"Gives us three days." Nalia sighed heavily—that silken, purring sigh that was her trademark. "Hardly time enough to arrange everything to our satisfaction."

"But then—happiness forever."

I could listen to no more. Already my paper tablet was splattered with teardrops and any more threatened to blot out my writing—I'd taken the whole conversation down in short-hand and was prepared to hand it to Jules on a silver platter.

Hateful man! And I was not certain the epithet didn't belong to Mr. Barnett as much as it did to Jules.

I knew now how the Christian martyrs felt when they watched the tribal hoards sharpening their knives before a kill. Dinner on the deck was a gay affair made horrid for myself by the knowledge that it was all a lie. A sham, masquerade, fib, act. Nothing was real—not the warm brown glow in Mr. Barnett's eyes when he looked me over... not the hearty, "By Jove, Cal—you're magnificent!", nor the soft pressure of his hand on mine as he pulled out my chair for me to sit down. Now that I knew all, I hated him for making me love him.

I watched Mr. Barnett and Nalia, and Nalia and her husband in turn. My, what a pair of actors, this Mr. Barnett and his paramour! All congeniality to everyone present...charming, easy, relaxed. If I had not heard every word of that conversation—if I had not read it ten times over, typed it up, and stored it in my briefcase alongside the rest of my work—I could not have believed the afternoon's events to be anything but a nightmare.

The whole party—the Lanes, the Nelsons, the old women and their hoary-headed escorts—were in the finest of spirits. It seemed that I was alone in feeling the palpable expectation which seemed to invade the very air I breathed.

Nalia sang for us, and only in that moment did I have the slightest relief....wishing the high notes would rend her throat in two. My hand tapped a restless rhythm against the tablecloth and my thoughts so far removed themselves from the present moment that I was genuinely startled by David Nelson at my elbow.

"Callie—will you be my partner? I mean, when the dancing starts?"

I opened my mouth to reply when Mr. Barnett leaned in, his voice close to my ear and his eye bent mischievously on David. "Don't you know, Mr. Nelson, my Lady Disdain never consents to dance if she has pledged her word to do so? The way to catch her is by sweeping her into the crowd when she least expects it."

I bridled at this taunt. "Do you speak from experience?"

"Of course. You surely haven't forgotten our wager."

"Never."

"Fine. Then you'll dance with me for the very first dance— only don't swear it; I wouldn't risk losing you."

Mr. Barnett waved young David off and I returned my attention to Nalia's song which was drawing to a close. But I knew I was blushing, and it brought back the roiling anger.

"Stop staring at me!" I hissed, turning round to find Mr. Barnett—just as I had felt—with his eyes warm upon me.

"I can't help it—you look especially...furious tonight. Ah—I see I've hit upon it. You are furious—and why? What brings this flame-color into your cheek and this dark glitter sparking in your eyes?" He brushed his knuckle against my cheek and I felt my defenses tumbling under that clumsy, tender touch. "You remind me of Shakespeare: '*I understand a fury in your words but not the words.*'"

I gathered the shreds of my dignity about me—a threadbare enough covering—and preserved an infuriated silence. But I could not flee his glowing, warm presence—not in front of all these people who would demand to know the cause for my flight. Besides that, I had the frozen journeyer's longing for a hearthside...I could pay later for warming my hands at this blaze.

"I will *not* pledge to dance with you." And by saying so I knew —and he knew—that I'd surrendered to his will.

Nalia's performance was soon over, the proper applause granted, and Ozzie Nelson jogged to the front of the group with a wide, boyish smile, so like David's. "Folks, I'd like to propose we have some dancing now. Pair up and off and—to use the young peoples' vernacular—'come on snake—let's rattle.'"

A ripple of laughter ran through our group and out to join the ripples on the water, creamed by lances of moonlight.

"Well…shall we do as he says, Cal?" Mr. Barnett stood and offered me his hand. A sudden overwhelming desire for something familiar—even if it would fall to pieces the next day —overcame my better judgment. I put my hand in his and felt his strong fingers close over mine in utter rightness. He pulled me to my feet and led me to the small cluster of couples—Mr. and Mrs. Lane, Mrs. Nelson and David, Nalia and her husband. But I shut out every thought of the others. What business did they have here in this Cinderella-esque moment? I'd wake to find it all pumpkins and moonlight, but the Here was glorious and comforting after my recent heartbreak.

Ozzie Nelson directed the band—comprised of the yacht's crew with Dirigible on an upright bass—to commence playing, and the first strains of music wrapped us in our own rainbow shred of glory. Mr. Barnett slipped his arm around my waist and guided me through a slow waltz. My cheek was close to his shoulder—so close. I knew my head would fit perfectly in that hollow under his chin if—but I would not tempt myself with such happiness.

I conducted my thoughts down a different channel: Mr. Barnett was right—he was a good dancer. A darned good one… which meant I had lost our bet.

But somehow I could admit it without feeling anything but deadness where I ought to be enraged. What did any of it matter now? I was never to have permission to love him…how then could I enjoy virulent anger when there was no lurking passion to fuel my temper?

The music continued to weave its witchery over the deck of the ship and us in the center—a spider or two in a web of vividry.

"Callie?"

"Hmm?" I dared not look at him for fear of doing something irrational…crying—or worse.

"Did I ever tell you that when you wear that dress you remind me of something?"

I couldn't respond—my heart was over-full with barbed pleasure in these pretty lies of his.

"You remind me of the first jonquils of spring…of a lovely, nid-noddy daffodil—all slender honey and cream."

"So you can make pretty speeches as well as shoot poison darts? Talented man." I had broken the spell—however much I hated doing it—and Mr. Barnett's arm loosened a little from its grip around me. He spun me slowly out, then in again.

"Haven't you learned yet that I always have a surprise up my sleeve?" His voice was natural and jocular again—nothing in it of the strange tenderness I thought I detected a moment before.

You bet I've learned. I wondered what Mr. Barnett would think if he knew that I knew. Again the tears rose against the sad spinning of events. Mr. Barnett would be gone in three days— gone with Nalia on the high road to Hell. Bitterness filled my mouth.

"What a contortionist you are. You look positively warped at the moment, where you were all shimmering beauty an instant since. What is wrong with you, Callie?" The beginning was said in that light, taunting tone, but at the end he paused with me at the rail of the yacht and put one hand on either of my shoulders, pulling me round so that I had no choice but to look him in the eyes. "Is there something troubling you?"

"Did David ask you about his writing for *Ladybird Snippets?*"

"Heaven help me, Cal—you are enough to drive a man out of his mind with your red herrings."

"You are the red-herring."

"Then *you're* a sardine—tight as an oyster with all your bewitching insults and elusive hints."

"Deplorable creature."

"Hostile enchantress."

But these old-time railleries clung to me with talons tonight. I felt sick and cold all at once and willed the shoreline to come closer. Perhaps if I went to bed the morning would come sooner —Dirigible had assured me that we'd be in New York harbor at daylight tomorrow. Then all that remained to be done was to meet with Jules and wash my hands of Wade Barnett.

"You're pulling away as if you didn't care to dance any longer."

"I don't care to." I finished the job of pulling away and started for the stateroom door, hating the loss of warmth and joy the farther I moved from his presence.

"Where do you think you're going?" he asked.

"To bed."

Nothing he could say—he, nor David or Priscilla Lane and especially not Nalia—could induce me to stay on board. I hoped they'd chalk it up to seasickness and leave me alone—I planned to indulge in a deep, heart-rending cry once I had barricaded my cabin door.

At three o'clock—six hours later—my weeping finally pulled to a dripping, sniffling stop. Not that I felt any sense of relief or peace after the storm, but the tears made my eyes gritty and my pillow was hot and damp with mascara-inked drops. Besides—there was nothing left in me to cry even if these things had not been true. I poured myself a cup of water from the pink enamel pitcher and wished it was coffee. Fourth of July was being celebrated with great éclat inside my head by a dozen cannon pounding, pounding, pounding in a succession of explosions.

I smirked at my reflection in the mirror—I had a certain vengeful satisfaction in realizing I'd performed a feat like crying for six hours for a man who had betrayed me in the way Mr. Barnett had. It almost amounted to heroism.

But the smirk was followed by a shuddering sigh—I was still only a shattered, weak woman who had let her heart wander and found it broken and bruised beneath the heels of yet another man...first my father, then Tristan, then the few dates I'd ever involved myself with...There was nothing heroic about my weeping fit; weeping is any woman's response to betrayal, any day, the world over.

Oh, God, that I had never been born! Not sure whether it was a curse or a prayer, I paused. *Oh God...dear God. I am miserable. Utterly, incomparably miserable. Help me? I mean, if you can.*

I had given up religion as archaic the day Tristan told me about Dad. Under Mr. Barnett's sandpaper-persistence I had almost begun to believe something again. Many was the time I had watched him—patronizing at first, then with curiosity—as he bowed his head before each meal…even before a snack, on occasion. But that wasn't what had struck me most, of course. The thing that I hadn't been able to fathom was his persistent optimism and the way he seemed to find something of interest in every person he crossed paths with. *Lord, I do believe you can help me. I can't think why I believe it, but I think I do believe it all the same. If Mr. Barnett is the way he is—was—because of You, I can only imagine You must be the Truth.*

I smiled, mist-dim, over the memory of our fight over poor Jerry Atwood, and the conclusion that had come of it: I hated people and he loved them. I recalled the day I'd confronted him about the waste of religion. And somehow through the dim hall of memory his words came winging back to me: "It comes with a peace the wealthiest of us can't buy." That peace, born of the uncanny love Mr. Barnett spoke of. Born of the grace of a God I had rejected…how I was beginning to long for it!

But all that, too, was in the background. Mr. Barnett's faith— if indeed, it had ever existed—must have grown cold and dust-covered over the past few months. I beat a fist in my pillow as if with it I could beat away the wretched turn Mr. Barnett's world had taken.

This plot to steal another man's wife must be the byproduct of the death of an ideal—an ideal that I'd always known was too old-fashioned to exist nowadays. And the sudden disappointment—for I had unknowingly clung stubborn to a shadow-hope—was all I needed to assure myself of my wisdom in refraining from any sort of belief. Well, any sort beyond that comfortable doctrine that all people were good, except the bad ones, and sooner or later we'd all die. I almost wished I could take back my prayer, but something pressed through the folly of it, and dared me to try the thing and see how impossible it was.

I rolled out of my bunk and took my hairbrush from the nightstand. The effects of crying for six hours straight might show on my face at breakfast, and the last thing I wanted was to give Mr. Barnett any sense of triumph in having vanquished me and made me cry. I brushed my hair till the last of the knots were gone, tied it with a pink satin ribbon, and dressed myself— hose first, petticoat next, pink sailor-dress third. Sure, it wasn't even four o'clock yet, but there was no way I could sleep tonight.

I perched on the stool and let the swaying of the yacht rock me to and fro, my back against the wall-paper. I commenced the task of composing myself and rehearsing the conversation required of me tomorrow morning. I would have to pretend nothing was wrong—Nalia would likely hook that shapely arm of hers through mine and want to parade the deck, sharing some sugar-coated hints about the scandal to come. Hints that she'd not understand I could and had fathomed already.

You've always liked acting, Callie. Now's your chance.

Funny how a person's dreams will rise up and taunt them when they most need support. I squelched every mocking voice and sat stiff and cold on my stool till the first dye of coming day purpled the water under the eastern sky.

Chapter 15

Rule Number Eight: Never share a look with a man who has brown eyes.

I scrawled the last direction in the book and nodded my head. My sense of humor had somewhat returned with daylight and I set myself the task of recording a list of dos-and-don'ts for young women in the professional work field. So far I'd come up with eight very good reasons never to work with a famous journalist—brown eyes not the least of the risks.

"Miss Harper!"

I stowed the guilty notebook in my pocket and turned with a flicker of a smile to David Nelson. "David! Goodbye fella—it was one long bash with you on board."

His ruddy cheeks grew even redder and he smiled. "I had a swell time too."

Mr. and Mrs. Nelson and Ricky stood nearby next to the heap of luggage piled helter-skelter on the pier beside the yacht. I waved at them then returned my roving gaze to David. "Well, I wish you all the luck in the world with your TV series, and I'll be sure to send you a clipping of the article when it's published. Got it?"

"Gee—that's fabulous Callie, thanks a million."

With a wave, David melted away in the crowd around the docks and once more I was left to myself. Why I hung around when the very sight of Nalia wrapped in her furs made me sick, the sight of her husband at her elbow turned my blood cold, and the sight of Mr. Barnett changed my stomach to a lump of cold iron, I could not say. But somehow I could not leave without saying "farewell" to the one man I'd ever loved.

Strange, the workings of a heart! Until I set foot on The Calida, I had never admitted the fact that I might love Mr. Barnett. Like him? Undoubtedly. But I'd never assigned it a particular name, and now that I knew the truth, I was not certain I could handle it. Love? What did I—a failure in every respect but my looks—know about love? Gee—I could never even draw a proper heart, let alone examine my own thumping, erratic organ.

Dirigible limped over with my suitcase. "Be you needin' a taxi, ma'am?"

"You don't suppose I'd like to carry my things all the way home…" My reply was tart as a granny-smith-apple and I felt sorry for it. I bit my lip, then smiled in apology: "Thanks, Dirigible—you were a darling."

Dirigible tugged his dark blue cap and winked. "Not sure which one on' us was the darlin', but I thankee."

Well then—Dirigible had hailed a taxi, I had my belongings, and there was nothing left to do but leave the pier-side and with it, this fleeting, happy, hurly-burly summer of the *Ladybird Snippets*. I sighed, fluttered my fingertips at Nalia—who wasn't looking in my direction anyway—and slipped into the taxi-cab. Half of me wished Mr. Barnett had come to bid me *adieu*, part was glad he hadn't noticed my departure. The cabby peered around the back of his dirty seat and flicked an eyebrow.

"Where to, lady?"

"Tarleton Apartments—West Twenty-third Street." The cab lurched from the curb and we jerked into the stop-and-go traffic exiting the area near the piers. I threw an arm over the seat behind me and peered through the dusty window at the receding pier with the buxom *Calida* at her moorings. And somewhere in the confusion of pleasure-boaters, shoremen, and sailors, I thought I could see brown-clad arm...shiny at the elbows... waving goodbye.

Chapter 16

In a short time the cab pulled up at home and deposited me on the curb—two dollars poorer, and on the verge of tears once more.

I collected Nickleby in a sort of haze, administered trite, conventional replies to all of Jerry's questions, and escaped upstairs. I barricaded the door with the much-abused Boston fern as if memories and regrets were howling at my lock like so many creditors. I jerked the curtains open, wanting the well-known touch of sunshine, and turned on the radio. A stream of static poured into the room, gradually knitting into a gentle tune:

"Somewhere beyond the sea, somewhere waitin' for me…"

"STOP it!" I screeched at the radio and Nickleby's fur sparked. He bared his teeth, huddling into a corner of the couch.

"My lover stands on golden sands and watches the ships that go sailin'…" I thought about throwing my high-heel at the radio to kill that poignant reminder of all I'd just left behind, but such a paroxysm of anguish and rage tumbled through my slight frame, I had no energy to remove my shoes and make the effort.

"Somewhere beyond the sea she's there watchin' for me…"

I clamped a hand over my mouth and pinched myself with the other hand to keep from crying, but it was little use. With Bobby Darin's easy, smooth voice singing in the background like a soundtrack of all I'd lost, my thoughts swung back to Mr. Barnett and the events of the past few days. Could he be guilty of something so horrid as….adultery?

I didn't want to believe it, but I could do nothing but believe when I had heard so clearly the entire conversation. The fault was Nalia's—of that I was entirely certain. Nalia Crosticinni…I knew if she had never chosen him, he would never have chosen her. And the thought gave me enough strength to get up and flick the switch on the radio. Bobby Darin drowned mid-song and I stood with my hands on my hips, breathing deep and attempting to order my thoughts.

Call Jules and set up a time to meet him and spill the news. Horrible, vulgar, cheap news that it was.

Someone rapped on my door. "Miss Harper?"

Saints preserve us, it's Jerry. What was he doing here? Now?

"Miss Harper, are you there? I brought up your luggage—the cabbie came back and said you'd left it in the trunk…I had to pay an extra dime."

"I'll…pay you back later."

"No rush, Miss Harper. But listen—won't you open the door? This stuff is heavy."

Of course—silly me to forget about the luggage. Somehow I glimmered with indignation at the cabby for charging Jerry a dime as if the mistake was his fault. I had to have someone to heap my wrath upon; it might as well be an entirely unconnected cabby, for I could not make myself angry with Mr. Barnett. Sorrowful and beaten-down, undoubtedly. But not angry.

I pulled the Boston fern from sentinel duty at the door and unfastened the lock. Jerry staggered in under the load of my suitcase, satchel, and hatbox. He set them down near the register, smiled, and dusted off his hands. "It is good to have you back, Miss Harper. But see here—what's wrong with old Nickleby?"

I glanced back over my shoulder to see Nicks, fur still spiked as a hedgehog's over my recent temper tantrum. "Oh—he saw a banshee."

"A banshee?"

"Oh yes—I've a resident one always lurking about somewhere."

"Have you now?" Jerry's hazel eyes flickered about the room as if half fearing to see the banshee I spoke of. It rose in my throat and I might have yelled at Jerry to get out if he hadn't been so absurd the next moment:

"Well, I tell you what, Miss Harper. Next time you see it give me a ring and we'll see if we can't set a trap for it."

I was generous and stifled the laugh that stuffed the banshee down and welled up in my eyes. "Thanks, Jer. You're a dear."

"No problem." Jerry rocked on his toes for a moment, winked sadly at Nickleby, and sighed. I could read his thoughts like a headline in seventy-two point type: Banshee Infestation at Tartleton Apartments. Residents Evacuated. What a crazy.

I crossed my arms and shrugged. "Well...thanks a million for carrying up my things but I have a lot to do so..."

"Ah! Right-o, Miss Harper. I won't take up anymore of your time. And cheerio to you, Nickleby."

Jerry tugged his cap, saluted me, and exited the room, taking with him any semblance of cheerfulness his presence conjured up. I had never thought I'd be sorry to see him go, but with the recent departure of so many many friends, I clung to anything—anyone—that reminded me of happier days. But those days were over and gone and wishing them back was spun-sugar. There was a betrayal at hand and I could not delay it any longer. If I did not act quickly then Mr. Barnett would have the satisfaction of knowing he'd cut me to mince-meat.

No—I had to play my part first. Then I could take the rest in stride. I dropped, exhausted, into the easy chair then reached for the phone and dialed Jules' number.

One ring, two rings, three rings…I wrapped the cord through my fingers and bit my lip…four rings…five…six…*rats in the Louvre! Will he never answer?* Seven rings….eight….

"Hello?"

"Jules!" I heard a grunt of surprise and a scuffle as if Jules had moved something to the side in his astonishment at hearing my voice.

"I've got it Jules."

"Got what?"

"Don't be scum."

"How good is it? Worth me keeping the secret?"

Triumph over getting Jules on the phone faded as I remembered my reason for the call. "Worth ten."

"Ten? Hmmmm…." I heard him draw on his cigarette; the slow inhale, the puffing exhale, and the acrid smell of the smoke seemed to seep through the receiver into my apartment. "Well that's good because you were taking so long, baby-doll, I thought I might raise the price."

I held my breath. Raise the price? Whatever could he want now? I could barely afford this humiliation, let alone guilt of some deeper shade.

"But seeing as you've got something worth ten secrets— something real big, you say—I'll be generous."

"Thanks, Jules."

"You are welcome, Miss Sarcasm. Where you wanna meet?"

"Annamaria's." It was befitting, somehow, that the ill-fated story should end where it had begun. It was at Annamaria's that I'd first come to love Mr. Barnett. I saw that now: sitting at the little table with my resident banshee howling at him over something that was in no way his fault. My smile twitched through the sadness.

No...no smiling. That was all over and done with.

Jules pushed through my memories with a yawn. "When will you meet me there?"

"An hour?"

"You sure?"

"I'm sure."

"Cuz this is big stuff, sugar-cake. You disappoint me you'll find yourself out of a reputation."

"Yeah, I know." Silence and static on the other end...then drawing on the cigarette. "Well....an hour?"

Jules blew smoke out and sighed. "Yeah. An hour."

Sixty minutes. Sixty minutes to thwart someone's destiny, or else my own. What a hash. I dressed myself with special care as if I was laying a body out for a funeral. White jacquard sprinkled with red flowers and belted with a crimson velvet band. A hat to match. Sling-back heels to match the hat. Red lipstick to finish it all.

I went through the motions of dressing but took no pleasure in it, and when I surveyed myself in the mirror I saw nothing. Nothing but Mr. Barnett's eyes searching my face last night as we danced. Nothing but that beautiful, painful, horrible moment on deck with the moonlight about us.

I had no tears left to cry, and already my heart was building up a crust—a scab of sorts—over the wound. The best healing came slowly, but I'd always been the slap-happy sort: pour the scathing, stinging antiseptic of derision on a wound, wrap it tight in a grudge, change the dressing occasionally with an insult or two and voila! A first-rate scar in a month at worst. Sure it ached when the rain came round, but from the outside all looked well.

I picked up Nickleby and sighed as he rubbed his cheek against mine and purred. His tail wrapped around my neck, thrashing with that impatient gesture peculiar to all cats. Whip... whip...whip...

"Nicks? G'bye. This is the last you'll see of the Callie you know. Come this evening I'll feel like moving to the Antipodes. Maybe we will! You and me...traveling the world on the lam." I shook my head, kissed my capricious pussy, and tossed him in the corner.

Then I went downstairs and hailed a cab, taking with me one of Jerry's supportive smiles—why had I ever despised them?

I asked the driver to stop a few blocks away from Annamaria's; I needed time to collect myself for this interview. I paid the cab fare, bit my lip, and stalked past our office toward the little café, head pounding to the pace of my feet. The situation was deplorable. The news was deplorable. Jules was deplorable. Men were deplorable...I was deplorable! But my mind—contrary to everything expected of the human brain in a crisis—was in no mood to function as a mind ought. Finding that every thought whirled back to Mr. Barnett and tried to defend him, I plugged my ears against it and hurried on toward Annamaria's to finish the deal.

The bell jangled as I entered, and Annamaria smiled. "Miss Harper! So glad to see you...but where Meestah Barnett?"

A wave of sickness bowled me over and I searched, feverish, for Jules. There he was—at our table. I hurried to his side and pulled on his sleeve. "Jules—not here. I can't do it."

"Devil take you, Cal. What's wrong with here? I just ordered a sandwich."

I glanced at Annamaria, frustrated tears pooling in my eyes. "Well come back and get it later, doofus. I can't do it. I swear!"

With great reluctance Jules followed the general pull of my body toward the street and we moved with the current of the crowd further down the avenue. I knew there was a Parisian bakery somewhere in the vicinity. We could talk inside. "That French place," I said. "We'll go there."

"Sure." Jules grabbed the sleeve of my blouse and slowed me.

"What are you doing?" I hissed.

He slipped his arm through mine. "We can't have it looking like I've blackmailed you."

"Well at least you acknowledge the fact."

Jules inclined his head and flashed me that poisonous smile. At the threshold of the French café I was able to extricate myself from Jules' grip. My companion slung himself against the wall and lit a cigarette.

"Aren't we going in?" I asked.

"What's the point? I've got a sandwich waiting for me at Annamaria's. And you won't have a stomach for food after I'm done with you."

I froze, dread seeping into my marrow.

"Where you wanna start, sugar?"

I sat in one of the tiny wrought-iron chairs pressed against the café's front. Where could I start? That evening at the Stork Club when I first met Nalia? When Mr. Barnett and I forged the Flint and Steel pact? The evening at the Opera House when Nalia shared with me her heart? The countless moments between when Mr. Barnett had made me love him in spite of my best and firmest intentions?

Jules' cold, possessive eyes swept me up and down. He doubted I'd do it. He doubted I had the gall to betray the man I loved. I'd show him the iron I was made of. The way I could take care of myself and cling to the life I'd built. Glamor and Glitz? I was well on my way already. Why did I need Wade Barnett? His reputation could go to the devil for all I cared.

For all I cared.

A broken shard of love pierced my soul and killed the arrogance. How much I did care! Memory upon memory swept over my heart in a crushing avalanche. That laughing-color in his eyes, his half-smile, that interminable coat with the shiny elbows...the verbal sparring and the battles of wit, his clumsy fashion sense, his dear *dear* simplicity....

My stomach clamped and see-sawed as I tottered on the edge of the abyss; it had come to this, and Jules prowled like a cougar on the side, his dark eyes sweeping me top to bottom again and again as he waited for my report.

Oh how I loved Wade Barnett.

Not a single doubt in my mind that despite what I had heard, he was the best man I'd ever known. How could he be guilty? How could he have done this to me? How could he—the only friend I'd ever known—give over that friendship for a whim of elegant Society?

With sudden clarity I saw Society for what it was: a shaky ladder of maddened cats clawing one another off the top rung. Jules hovered there, one rung below the top, and reached for Wade Barnett. That wasn't surprising. What took me aback was the sight of myself right behind him, claws unsheathed and teeth bared. Me: prepared to bat Wade Barnett off his pedestal to usurp his place myself—to save my own hide. *There is no greater love than this: that a man layeth down his life for his friend.*

The words crashed with all the conviction of a thunderclap on my senses; a dart of gentle pain spread through my heart; I was never to be allowed to love him in the one manner.

So be it.

But I could love him in this.

I glanced at Jules. He glared at me through a gray cloud of cigarette smoke, waiting.

I was in possession of something.

I held Mr. Barnett's reputation in my palm, and I had a free choice as a women: sacrifice my hopes and dreams for his sake, or continue climbing that wretched ladder. I saw that self-salvation was no salvation at all—just a temporary lull in the rabid race for pettiness. To become a scandal myself so that I could remain momentarily "unscathed"…was that something I could stoop to? *Lord help me. There is none righteous. No, not one.*

"I can't do it, Jules." The words clashed with the cacophony of my mind and startled me into a surge of triumph.

He dropped his arms and leaned forward. "What?"

I drew back a bit. "I'm sorry, Jules, but I can't do it."

"Devil take you, Callie—what do you mean? You have got something, haven't you? You aren't playing with me?"

I drew myself proud and tall. "I have."

"Then what do you mean you 'can't do it'?" His eyes glittered like black ice and his smile was dangerous.

"Fine—let me try it another way. I won't do it. I will not stoop to a tit-for-tat. It's stupid."

"You're stupid."

"Fair enough."

He tried another tack: "Callie, come on now. It's not like you're betraying anyone's trust. If you found something on Barnett it's his fault—he ought to have been more careful."

"*More* careful? Is that what you think?" My sudden display of temper seemed to surprise Jules. His eyebrows drew high on his forehead and his head jerked like a pigeon's.

"More *careful*?" I shouted. "So it's 'who cares what you do as long as you don't get found out'? Is that your philosophy?"

"Keep your fur down, Callie-co. What's wrong with that philosophy?"

"Everything. It isn't *right*, Jules."

"Oh, now don't start preaching to me."

"I'm not preaching. But some of us still have values."

"Like who?"

"Me and…"

"And Mr. Barnett? Too late for that. See how well morals worked out for him?"

Tears nipped at my eyes, but I swallowed and shook my head. *Greater love hath no man than this…Oh God. God, give me strength.* "I don't care. I don't care. I won't do it, Jules. I've got a little dignity, a little respect left, and I will not sacrifice it."

"Fine." Jules stood. "Keep your dignity. But I'll tell all of New York City about your guilt. Then where will your dignity be? Your reputation will be ruined."

"Hang my reputation."

"Thanks—I plan to."

My gaze flickered up—all fire and lava—and rested on Jules. I would not cast my pearls to swine and tell him of the other reason—that I loved Mr. Barnett. "There's more to it than keeping my dignity. Wade Barnett has hurt me—there's no sense in denying it; you already know. But I've done with hurting people in return and expecting that to help me somehow."

"Vengeance is sweet, Cal—sure you won't fold?"

I wasn't certain my speech had worked any effect on Jules— truth is I wished he would hit me hard enough to knock me cold. I tucked my chin and squeezed my eyes shut then opened them and shook my head.

"You're sure." And Jules' tone was less question, more answer. He stood and followed it up with a five-letter name I hadn't heard since my Wexford days; the lines around his mouth were white and his hands shook. I shrank inside, recognizing pure hatred and rage when I saw it. In that moment Jules looked nothing like himself; it seemed some demon had taken up residence in his frame.

"I never told you I'd do it, Jules. I said I'd think about it." I hoped he'd see sense and quit looking at me that way.

"You damned liar!" he shouted.

I stood, matching my height with his. "I will thank you not to speak to me in that way."

"Oh believe me: I'll speak to you any way I want. I'll toss your precious reputation in the sewers and spread the muck over the whole City. I'll smear it on billboards and tell the world you're nothing but a back-country mare whose daddy killed a man over a glass of moonshine." Following this torrent of threats with several foul names, Jules took a step forward and raised his arm to strike me.

I stood there to take it, bracing my slender frame. One heavy-handed blow from this enraged man and I'd slip mercifully into unconsciousness. He froze. Why didn't he strike? What was he waiting for?

I raised my head, intent on meeting his mockery with courage. But what was wrong? What had happened? Jules' face was frozen in that horrific expression, and his eyes fixed on someplace behind me. I stared at him a moment, then shifted in my seat and came as close to having a heart attack as I ever hope to: Mr. Barnett jogged toward us, concern etched in his features.

"Stop right there," he shouted, pulling up. His usually smooth hair fell in a boyish shock over his forehead and his cosmopolitan face had a handsome red flush to it. "Thank God I got home in time to catch Annamaria's call." His right eyebrow bent at a furious angle, and he thrust his shoulders backward. "Mr. Cameron, *what* is going on?"

My stomach turned eight somersaults and flung into my throat. Jules would tell him. I had no doubt. Tell him in my presence that my father was a murderer and I was a fake.

Jules had regained his composure. His smile was still dark, deadly, and he drew near and wrapped his arm around my waist. "We were having a lover's tiff," he explained.

"Jerk!" I hauled off and slapped him as hard as I could. It hurt me as much as it hurt him—probably more--but I smiled to see the red streaks form against Jules' five o'clock shadow. I cradled that hand in my other palm then donkey-kicked him in the shins for good measure. Jules' leg buckled under the blow from my high-heel. Good. I glared at Mr. Barnett.

"What are you doing here?" My voice was hollow and threaded with tears like an overturned canoe taking on water.

Mr. Barnett's glare flickered from Jules' face to mine. "I was under the impression I was rescuing you."

"Her?" Mr. Barnett and I both snapped back at the sound of Jules' voice. "The slut doesn't need any rescuing. She's the one in the wrong."

I felt the world whirl around me and wondered for a second if this was what drowning felt like. Jules was going to tell him. My life was over. "Jules, please," I whispered, but I knew it was useless.

"If you don't talk right now, Mr. Cameron, I'll call the police and you'll have to explain why you were assaulting a defenseless woman," Mr. Barnett said. He seemed so calm and composed— the opposite of me.

"I am not defenseless!" I countered, coming alive only to defend that point then sinking into mist again.

"Callie, please. Let me do the talking." Mr. Barnett's brown, bluff voice held me in reality like a tow-line. "Mr. Cameron. Now."

Jules shifted, and the white lines around his mouth faded. He'd do the slander justice, I was certain of that. "The truth is, Mr. Barnett, Calida Harper is…well, it pains me to say it…"

I bet it does.

"She is a fake."

"In what way?" Mr. Barnett asked.

I held my breath as Jules drew one in, then let it out. He puffed on the burnt-out cigarette then lit another. "How about a cocktail of murder, intrigue, romance, and lies? Your precious Miss Harper is nothing but a—"

"That's enough, Mr. Cameron," Mr. Barnett said.

Yep. I had been served the ball and let it drop. My day was over. I felt the tears spilling down my cheeks, and I swayed on my feet. An arm slid around my waist and it was a moment before I realized it belonged to Mr. Barnett, not Jules. I leaned against the solid mass of his chest and felt like crud.

"Cal won't try to tell you it isn't true—she knows she's stuck." Jules leaned forward as if to take possession of me again, but Mr. Barnett set his broad hand against Jules' chest and held him at arm's length. Jules relaxed, and the white lines again appeared at the corners of his mouth. "Answer me this, Cal. Is it true? Is what I'm about to tell Mr. Barnett the truth or a lie? You gonna continue the wretched Harper line and keep the lies going?"

"I won't," I murmured. I pulled away from Mr. Barnett, and stood on my own, glad for the taxi that whizzed by and gave me a moment to collect myself. If the story was going to be told, I would not give Jules the satisfaction of the telling. "It's true, Mr. Barnett. Everything he was going to say. My father—"

Mr. Barnett put a finger against my lips, and confused me by smiling. "No need, Callie."

Jules growled. "Are you both nuts? Mr. Barnett, Calida Harper is a conniving vixen."

Here it comes. Goodbye, world.

He pointed an accusing finger at me like a judge's gavel. "Her father—"

"Killed mine. I know."

If the world had stopped spinning on its axis, if the sun had been snuffed out like a candle-end, I could not have been more shaken. I think I would have fainted then and there if it wasn't for the fact that Mr. Barnett somehow steered me to the wall and forced me to lean against it for support.

"What?" Jules' voice croaked as if from a great and foggy distance. He sounded like I felt.

I struggled to stand, and pinched the bridge of my nose. My vision cleared. "Who are you?"

Mr. Barnett moved close to me and wrapped me in his arms.

"What is going on?" I asked it in a very polite manner as if asking for the time or the day of the week. There was no need to expend energy—if I had any—on elaborate phrasings. I just needed to know the answers to several very simple questions as soon as possible.

Mr. Barnett brushed my hair away from my forehead, and as much as I wanted to look into his eyes, I couldn't help a glance past him. Jules was standing just there, gape-mouthed and white as his starched collar.

"You are right to ask who I am," Mr. Barnett said.

"I know it." Dense. Stupid, like saltwater taffy weighed down with sand. "Please explain. I'm feeling faint."

"If you do that, Sleeping Beauty, I'll have to kiss you," he said with a smile.

Kiss me? The world was getting stranger. I hung in his arms like a Raggedy Ann doll, and tried to make a coherent thought out of the shrapnel in my brain.

"I have not been quite honest with you in regards to my identity," Mr. Barnett said gently, as if to explain a matter to a small child. I mentally shook hands with him for his good sense in that regard. It seemed to me a child in grammar-school would be more level-headed than I.

"You aren't Wade Barnett?" Jules asked. He pulled Mr. Barnett's shoulder so his grip on me eased, and stared from Mr. Barnett to myself, and back again. "He's not Wade Barnett?"

I shrugged.

Mr. Barnett laughed—a dangerous, fire-streaked laugh. "Sorry to disappoint you, Mr. Cameron, but I'm afraid not—not quite."

"Then...who is?" My thoughts reeled like a merry-go-round with a busted spring.

"I am Wade Barnett as the world knows him, but I'm afraid that isn't my true name."

"Who are you?" I repeated in a dull, detached tone.

"Callie, I need you to listen to me—you too, Mr. Cameron, because if you misunderstand my directions in any way, I'll have you sued and locked up for libel."

Glorious man! I gloated over Jules' pasty complexion then turned my attention back to Mr. Barnett.

"I was born James Fleetwood," he said.

I was going to be sick. I *knew* I was going to be sick. James Fleetwood—the son of the man my father had killed? The boy who beat Tristan to a pulp that awful day…was it possible? I drew back, afraid of him all at once. What would this man do to me? After all, Jules had said it…vengeance is sweet.

"Don't look like that, Cal—please don't." He silenced the words that might have come with a hard, determined kiss. My heart crumpled beneath the heavy, warm embrace. It lasted only a few seconds before he pushed away and shook me softly, adding weight to his next words: "Don't torture me with that look, Callie-girl. It's what I've feared since I first met you. That you'd…recoil like that and stare at me like I was a viper." He crushed me to himself again, and some bitter hatred inside me died.

Jules stood rough and ready, arms loose and powerful-looking. "Listen, Mr. Barnett. I don't have all day to stand here looking like a fool." His tones were dead, but threatening all the same.

Mr. Barnett let me go—gentle but firm—and spread his arms wide in an exaggerated apology. "Forgive me, Mr. Cameron, for failing to notice you were only *looking* like a fool. Did you really think you could blackmail my assistant and I would fail to detect it? That alone—apart from the attempted assault and libel—is enough to send you to cool your heels in a jail-cell for at least six months. Don't make me add to the brawl by punching you in the face."

This was certainly a new side to Mr. Barnett. It shook me awake enough to kick-start my brain into proper function. What Jules had tried to do wasn't only malicious—it was illegal. I felt better immediately. The police could handle this if we couldn't.

Jules winced as if dodging Mr. Barnett's proffered blow, then attempted a smile. "She refused to do it anyway," he whined.

"Does that matter, Mr. Cameron? Your intention was to ruin her. The information you say you have is all known to me. You need not repeat it. I want you to go now and leave Miss Harper alone from this day till the day you start to rot in the ground. If I so much as see you within twenty feet of her, I will personally escort you to the police station and give you good reason to wish you'd kept away."

Jules' face went a shade whiter—if possible—and he backed off, staring at Mr. Barnett with unblinking terror. At the far end of the block, he hailed a taxi, climbed in and slammed the door.

"Good riddance," Mr. Barnett remarked, waving cheerfully. "The coward almost threw me into a temper-fit. And as for you, Calida Harper…"

He kissed me again, and this time my mind was awake enough to know what it meant to me. What of the information I'd found about him? I could not let him hold me this way if…I pushed against his chest and the tears welled up again.

"Don't touch me—I can't bear it!" I started to weep—deep, wracking sobs that welled from some scalded, frightened place. "Nalia." I managed to gulp out the single name and drop into the wrought iron chair. I mastered myself with difficulty. "What about Nalia?"

"What about her?" Mr. Barnett asked. He covered the few steps I'd put between us, and knelt at my side.

Had he no idea the wretchedness of my heart? "You— eloping. With her."

"Eloping?" It was Mr. Barnett's turn to draw back. "What the blazes do you mean?"

I sniffed tried to speak once…twice… a third time. "You were discussing letting some scandal out slowly…not telling him beforehand…"

"Of all the—" Mr. Barnett looked as if he wanted to kiss me again, but refrained, for which I was very glad. I needed every bit of fortitude I possessed. "Callie, listen to me. I was advising Nalia—*and* her husband, who was sitting next to me in that very room—as to the best way to get rid of her agent. He's a selfish, dishonest fellow who needed to get the pink-slip, though they have been together for fifteen years. It isn't my business to confirm what designs Nalia might have upon me, but I certainly have none upon *her*."

"Oh." It was a small word to state the Grand Canyon of relief that cracked into my very soul. Torrents of questions with a single answer flooded my body from my eyebrows to my toes. There could only be one answer; one solution to this puzzle. "You aren't in love with Nalia?"

"Her?" It was enough and more than enough when accompanied by the joyous flashing of his eyes.

I was a child again, rendered helpless by his love. Innocent! Innocent as I could ever have been. He was not Nalia's. He was mine. My own. That precious moment on deck full of dancing…moonlight…my cheeks flamed and I buried my head on the familiar brown shoulder. His arms enclosed me—shiny at the elbows, rustic and simple and so strong.

"Mr. Barnett—Mr. Fleetwood—" I hiccuped and laughed simultaneously and scrubbed at my eyes with my glove. It was too beautiful and horrible and magnificent all at once.

He shook his head. "Not Fleetwood—please. I'd rather let the other tale mold."

"How could you stand me when you found out who I was? My father…*killed*…your father." I choked over the black-hearted word and compassion for Mr. Barnett—this good, good man whose father mine murdered—swept over me. I buried my face again and sobbed once.

His voice was infinitely gentle and so so tender. "I knew the whole time. I…I searched for you."

"For me?"

"For any child of your father's that might be living that I could…apologize to."

"Apologize?" I felt stupid, sitting here crushed against my employer repeating everything he said like a kid at Sunday-school; I extracted one arm from his embrace and traced the path of a single tear on his patient face. "What could you possibly have to apologize about?"

"For my bitterness. My hatred.'

His words gleamed in the noisy air of the City. I realized for the first time the irony of the setting for this heart-to-heart. The precious words wrapped around me and through me and brought my spirit humbled and broken to this man's side. He—the victim of the circumstance—asking my forgiveness for a sin my father had committed. A passing car veered away from a taxi and laid on the horn. Someone shouted, and a delivery truck revved its engine in passing.

"How?" I finally choked out. "How could you forgive me?"

Mr. Barnett tipped my chin till his gaze poured into mine. His soul shone so bright it hurt my eyes to see it. Burning but beautiful. It awoke a kindred light within me, and I felt a strange thawing under his look. "I have been forgiven the sum of all my sins for a lifetime…how could I accept that gift, knowing I held an innocent person in contempt for one sin her father had committed?"

"An evil sin," I whispered, dropping my eyes.

"All sin is evil." The lightness of his tone begged me to look upward, and when I did, I could not tear my eyes away from the compassion and…*love*…gleaming there. "So I hunted for you—an education in research and obscure tips is worth something—and found you under the guise of chasing another of my dreams. I attached you to me with the paltry excuse of being in need of an assistant."

I gasped and pushed away from him, gladdened and vexed at once by the strength of his encircling arms. "*Ladybird Snippets.*"

"Yes; however, there was an error in my calculations." He took possession of my hands again and held them—his thumbs rubbing my fingers in that methodical, eager way in which he conducted everything. "I had not counted on my heart running past forgiveness the very first time we met. I had not intended to love her," he said, as if discussing the matter with the stream of traffic bustling through the streets.

"But how did you know Jules was blackmailing me?" I asked. This was a point I had to get settled before my head cracked beneath the strain.

"The poets speak of the fury of a woman scorned, do they not?"

"Umm…"

"A man in love is quite as susceptible, I'm afraid. At first I watched Jules out of a vague sense of jealousy. Then, when I noticed how he cornered you every time you met in public, I did a bit of research of my own and discovered the truth. That black-hearted scoundrel had my pet between an enormous rock and very hard place."

"That is the understatement of the millennia. Why didn't you stop him earlier?" I asked. "This has been going on for weeks—months."

Mr. Barnett sighed. "I didn't know how to help you, if you'd want my help, or if you even needed it. I didn't *know* you, Cal."

"What is that supposed to mean?" We'd spent the entire summer together and unless he was blind and deaf, I didn't see how he could sit there and tell me he didn't know me.

He shrugged. "Every time I looked, you ducked behind a false front. Masks are for parties, love, not life."

My heart thundered at his accusations. Like the mask was my fault. "You know why I couldn't be myself."

He spread his hands in a surrendering gesture. "I was in love with you."

When he put it *that* way…

"But you have to understand my side of things," he pressed.

"Do I?" I arched my eyebrows and crossed my arms, wondering if his statement warranted my throwing a punch at him.

"Well you have to try."

I pressed my temples. "Fair enough."

He settled himself back on his heels and made a tent of his fingers. "I was in love with a shadow-girl. I never saw her but for a second or two when you forgot to play the game, and I couldn't be sure if the shadow-girl was you or not. How was I to tell your character if you never let me get close?" He sighed. "I sent you to Maralie, hoping she'd be able to see more than I and in the meantime I waited. I admit it was stupid.

"I'll say."

He nodded. "Yes. It was stupid. But love is stupid—or behaves so on occasion—and I had a very good reason for watching how you'd react. I wanted to see if I could let the little gypsy carry my heart away or if I'd have to tear it from her."

I felt sober now. "You very nearly lost both." A curious, fearful look sprang up in his eyes and I rejoiced to see it. He did love me; maybe even more than he knew. "I was close to telling Jules and hating you," I said. "You could easily have lost me."

"I know that. I admit my journalistic side got the better of my judgment, and God knows I realized it today." The roguish tilt to his smile and the way his eyes flickered over me again and again made me weak. "I should have told you who I was beforehand and kept you from this awful mess with Jules Cameron. I'm sorry, Callie. It was wrong of me."

"Wicked man!"

"Artful child."

"Dashing racketeer."

"Mysterious female." He laughed. "You were so darned alluring, Cal. I wanted to see if the shadow-girl would flare into something real and tangible. Someone to whom I could give my heart freely." He smiled an apology. "I never meant to let Jules press you this far. Perhaps it was vanity, but I was reasonably sure you'd not be able to find a blot on my character. I hadn't calculated the effects of eavesdropping." He winked.

I blushed and pressed my fingers to my temples. "I can't decide if you're the stupidest fool I've ever met, or a darling."

"Both?...The former?"

"The former."

"Ah. Well, I…I am sorry." He was sorry—he looked like a rejected puppy with its tail swinging low and a whine in its throat.

I stood. "Was I really mysterious?"

He stood as well and slipped his arms around me. "A perfect case for Scotland Yard."

"And you care for me…a little?"

"God knows I do." He dropped a kiss on my hair.

I tipped my head so I could see into his dark eyes. "Do you love me?"

"Yes, Mother Confessor. I love you." He sealed that announcement with a kiss on the tip of my nose.

"And you think I'm a silly goose and an innocent little girl?"

"Perfectly innocent. And therefore innocently perfect."

That last bit lingered in the air—sweet solace to my spirit. I was a novice. A child. I knew very little, but that I knew well. I loved him…he loved me…and Christ—Christ!—loved us both. I saw it now and my heart folded and blossomed like a frost-blighted rose in the warmth of a June sun. *No greater love than this…*

I twined my fingers through Mr. Barnett's and smiled into his eyes—brown as chestnuts, warm as a bonfire. "Well…what shall we do now?"

Mr. Barnett winked at me, and the world had never felt so right. "What does anyone do in this sort of situation—I'm an amateur!"

"So am I."

Our eyes met and the soul-light danced between. "Well…" he said, "…how about coffee?"

And I smiled—smiled for me and for him and for the mad, confused world flying by on the street. I could think of nothing I wanted more in this world than to sit with my teacher, my friend, my love, basking in this new-found warmth. I sighed and nestled closer in that perfect hollow beneath his chin.

After a lapse of some moments he sighed, and my head rose and fell with his breath. I laughed.

"What are you thinking?" he asked.

"Your coat is scratchy."

He chuckled, held me the closer. "Funny puss."

"Knight-errant."

"Beautiful warmth."

"Silly old darling." And I traced the edge of his jaw with my fingertip, wondering what Nickleby would say.

Acknowledgements:

I have so many people to thank when I contemplate the friends—old and new—who helped me bring *Fly Away Home* to its concrete form.

Thanks to my mother, Lynne Heffington, for teaching me to love the written word; without her, there would be no novel. A million ounces of gratitude go to the rest of my family for your patience and support in not disowning me when I act like a writer.

I also owe thanks to my fellow writers who have aided me, many of whom I have never met in person but are treasures nonetheless: Rachelle, Meghan, Jenny, Abigail, Mirriam, Katelyn...you girls are priceless.

To my cover designer, "St. Rachel" Rossano, goes much love and deep thankfulness for her creativity and advice. She was a saving grace.

I am thankful for the technical assistance of my "Riley Pool", Daniel Tate, in creating the Ruby Elixir Press emblem and to Wyatt Fairlead who argued philosophy with me and told me I was quotable.

To Bree Holloway for the mock-up, Jessica and Sarah for formatting help, and Bertie and Gussie for bolstering my courage with caps-lock and good cheer, many thanks.

I suppose I may also thank Gregory Peck for being so darn wonderful in *Roman Holiday* as to inspire a certain character.

Without the love and assistance of so many, *Fly Away Home* would not be half the book it is. Thank you all, and thanks be to Jesus Christ my Lord for giving me the opportunity to represent His Name and to hold His standard high for all the world to see.

If I have managed in any small way to reflect a miniscule part of His story, I have succeeded.

Soli deo gloria

About the Author:

Rachel Heffington is a Christian, a novelist, and a people-lover. Encouraged by her mother to treasure books, Rachel's favorite pastime was (and still is) reading. Outside of the realm of words, Rachel enjoys the Arts, traveling, mucking about in the kitchen, listening for accents, and making people laugh. She dwells in rural Virginia with her boisterous family and her black cat, Cricket.

You may find Rachel on:

Her blog: www.inkpenauthoress.blogspot.com

Facebook: https://www.facebook.com/rachelheffingtonwrites

Twitter: https://twitter.com/Rachelswhimsy

Instagram: http://instagram.com/heirloomrosebud

If you wish, you may write to her at:

Rachel Heffington

C/O Ruby Elixir Press

20305 Garrison Dr.

Windsor, VA 23487

www.ingramcontent.com/pod-product-compliance
Lightning Source LLC
Chambersburg PA
CBHW020307200626
46814CB00006BA/2130